LEGION
BOOK
ONE

# Blood
# & Bones

A.D. STARRLING

# COPYRIGHT

# PROLOGUE

*I AM LIGHT. I AM DARKNESS.*
    *I am salvation. I am wrath.*
    *I am rebirth. I am destruction.*
    *I am savior. I am oppressor.*
    *I belong to Heaven. I belong to Hell.*
    *P.S. I like bunnies.*

# CHAPTER ONE

ARTEMUS STEELE WALKED INTO THE SHOP, TOSSED HIS windbreaker on a coat stand, and headed briskly toward the rear of the old brick building. He opened the door to his office and had one foot over the threshold when he froze.

A package sat on his well-worn antique desk. He stared at it for several seconds before carefully releasing the doorknob and backing out of the room.

"Hey, Otis! Did you take a delivery this morning?" he shouted down the gloomy passage to his right, his gaze still on the object taking up a considerable amount of space on his one-of-a-kind bureau.

Artemus grimaced when the sound of his own voice reverberated painfully around his skull; it felt like someone was swinging a hammer inside the damn thing.

Footsteps sounded on the rickety staircase that connected the first floor of the shop to the apartment above it. A figure in a worn housecoat and fluffy slippers shuffled into view at the end of the passageway.

Otis Boone yawned, blinked blearily behind his glasses, and scratched the expanse of pale chest visible above the sagging neckline of his flannel shirt. "What delivery?"

Artemus studied his assistant's sleepy expression and slowly counted to five.

*Don't bite his head off. It's not his fault you've got the mother of all hangovers and lost five grand last night.*

He indicated his office with a cocked thumb. "*That* delivery."

Otis joined him and peered inside the room. His eyes widened.

"Shit! Is that blood?"

"So, you didn't see who brought it?" Artemus demanded sharply.

He regretted his tone instantly when an invisible force drove a chisel straight through his left temple.

Otis shook his head. "Nah-huh. I was out like a light. Got me some new cocoa. Stuff's magic."

Artemus sniffed the air and caught a familiar smell above the faint odor of stale human sweat emanating from his assistant.

The hot cocoa had evidently been supplemented with weed.

They stood and stared at the package. It was two feet by one foot and wrapped in heavy-duty, brown packing paper. Someone had tied the whole thing up with string and finished it off with a deceptively cheerful bow on top.

Artemus narrowed his eyes.

It would have looked like one of those quaint parcels delivered by a smiling postman on a bike to a picture-perfect housewife in the classic fifties movies he and his mom used to watch on TV when he was a kid, were it not for the bloody handprint on the side and the congealing crimson puddle beneath it. It didn't help that he was getting bad juju vibes from it. Like, uber bad.

The package rustled.

Otis let out a strangled scream and clutched Artemus's arm. "Oh my God, did that thing just move? Is it—is it *alive?!*"

Artemus swallowed the bile rising in his throat, peeled his assistant's fingers from his flesh, and reached for the knife tucked in his left boot. The weapon looked like any switchblade you could buy from a military surplus store. He flicked it open and started across the room, pulse hammering away in his veins in tandem with the vicious pounding in his head. Floorboards creaked softly beneath his feet as he approached the desk.

The package rustled again. A sudden stillness came over it. Artemus hesitated.

He couldn't shake the feeling that he was being watched.

He glanced at the bottle of bourbon standing on top of the filing cabinet to his left.

*Another drink is not going to make this shitty situation any better.*

He sighed. *Let's just get whatever the hell this is over and done with.*

The dark red blemish staining the inlayed, brown leather surface of his beloved Victorian oak pedestal desk caught his attention once more. Artemus frowned, ire rising and overcoming the thread of apprehension thrumming down his spine.

*And some asshole is going to pay for that.*

He reached out and slipped the knife under the bow. It sliced effortlessly through the string.

For a moment, nothing happened. Then paper swished

and crinkled, the package slowly unraveling before him like some kind of gory Christmas gift.

Limpid brown eyes locked onto him from behind the bars of a steel cage.

Artemus stopped breathing. The room faded around him.

For one wild, dizzying moment, he was back there again, in that field behind his house. The night he turned six. The night he saw strange lights in the sky. The night he witnessed the birth of a monster.

Artemus's fingers clenched around the blade in his hand as the world came sharply back into focus. The handle grew hot and the metal trembled under his touch. *Why the hell has* he *turned up again?*

Gazing at him steadily from inside the metal cage sitting in a pool of blood on his priceless antique desk was the ghastly beast he'd seen that ungodly night when his life had changed forever. Except it didn't look like a beast. Instead, it had assumed the shape of something so mundane Artemus would have laughed had he not known what lay beneath the innocent facade.

"Is that a—*a bunny?*" Otis stammered in a horrified voice.

There, looking like an exact replica of the first and only pet Artemus had ever owned, was a tan and chocolate Rex rabbit. Considering Artemus's love of all things fluffy and floppy-eared, he should have been in a fit of rapture right about now.

Except this particular Rex rabbit had glowing red pupils and was gnawing on the remains of a dead rat, the unfortunate creature's blood staining the velvety fur around his cute rabbit muzzle in gruesome wet streaks.

"That ain't no bunny," Artemus stated coldly.

The animal's lips peeled back to expose two rows of deadly fangs.

# CHAPTER TWO

"No, Elton, I can't come to the auction house right now!" Artemus snapped into his cell phone.

He stormed inside the workshop at the rear of the building and dumped the metal cage unceremoniously on a table. A low growl emanated from the rabbit inside.

Bells jingled faintly in the distance; Otis was putting the "Open" sign on the shop's front door. Not that the place was likely to see much traffic today. Even though Chicago's North Side was usually a bevy of tourist activity, it would be a brave soul indeed who would venture out into the icy depths of a winter's day to check out an antique dealer in Old Town.

"Why? Because I have an emergency that I need to deal with, that's why!" Artemus barked. He put the cell on speaker, stripped to his waist, and donned an old work shirt. "And, FYI, you owe me five grand. That tipoff was useless. All I have to show for it is a damn headache and a hole in my pocket. Those bastards ripped me off big time."

Artemus ended the call, slid his smithy's apron on, and

grabbed a bar of iron from a pile of metal in the corner of the workshop. He looked at the rabbit.

The creature was cleaning the gory evidence around his muzzle with his pink tongue and fluffy paws. He paused and blinked at him innocently.

Artemus scowled and swapped the iron for a steel alloy bar. He headed for the old stone forge and anvil in the center of the room.

They had been there since long before the shop existed. In fact, from the historical photographs he'd seen in the Chicago Public Library, the forge and the anvil were as old as the city itself.

He dumped anthracite coal and kindling in the hearth, ignited the lot with a propane torch, and started working the footpedal of the old-style bellows connected to the forge. The coals soon glowed red, then yellow and white. He placed the steel bar in the hearth, selected his tools, and got to work.

Artemus's headache faded as he fell into the rhythm of working the metal, flattening, bending, and twisting it into the shape he could see in his mind's eye. Smithing was a skill he seemed to have been born with, which was strange considering his background.

His gift had not been lost on the man he'd inherited the antique shop from. Nor had his other, more unusual talents.

Artemus's arms ached pleasantly while he hammered and fashioned the steel. He added other metals into the mix, carefully blending and folding them into the original alloy. Sweat soon beaded his forehead and ran in rivulets down his face. He crossed the room and opened the back door.

Cold air swooshed inside the workshop, bringing with it a flurry of snow.

The sky darkened outside as he continued molding the composite he had made. The snowstorm intensified. Otis came into the room to ask if he wanted lunch and got a grunt in response. A bacon cheeseburger and a soda appeared on a table next to him and were promptly devoured. The rabbit got a carrot. He ignored the offering and sat quietly watching Artemus, as he had the entire morning.

Artemus had just dunked the object he had made in the slack tub next to the forge and was laying it on the anvil to add the final ingredients it required when a burly figure appeared at the back door and blocked out what remained of the daylight.

"So, what the heck is this emergency?" Elton LeBlanc grumbled as he strode inside the workshop, snowflakes melting in his gray-speckled hair and beard. He grimaced at the heat blasting from the forge, shrugged out of his expensive cashmere coat, and laid it over the back of a Queen Anne chair.

Artemus pointed at the rabbit in the cage. "*That* is the emergency."

Elton's rugged face turned stony. "You got a pet rabbit? That's the piss-ass reason you're giving me for not turning up for this job? The client's been waiting for you for three hours! I told you he was coming all the way from New York."

"He's not just any rabbit," Artemus said. "He's THE rabbit."

Elton looked at him blankly. Realization slowly dawned in his dark gaze.

He frowned. "Not that story again. Look, we've been through this before, kid. Monsters like that don't exist."

"Really?" Artemus said sharply. "After everything you've witnessed since you met me, you're gonna stick with that story?"

An uncomfortable expression replaced Elton's frown. "That's different."

Artemus stiffened. "You mean *I'm* different, right?"

He nearly kicked himself when he saw the hurt that flashed in Elton's eyes. He knew he was being an asshole and had no one to blame for it but himself. And his stupid hangover.

Artemus blew out a sigh, took the switchblade out of his boot, and headed for the table where the cage sat.

"Hey, Freakshow, why don't you show us your teeth again?"

He rattled the steel bars with the knife.

Redness filled the rabbit's pupils from edge to edge. The creature growled and peeled his lips back.

Elton startled. "What the hell?"

Artemus put the knife away. "I think I've made my point."

He returned to the anvil, laid his hands on the intricate chain upon it, and concentrated. A warm feeling sparked inside his chest. It blossomed and expanded until it filled his entire body, flowing down his arms and legs all the way to the tips of his fingers and toes, radiant threads of energy that pulsed gold and red with his every heartbeat. He focused them into the metal.

For a moment, nothing happened. Then, the chain trembled and glowed beneath his touch. White light danced through it as he moved his fingers expertly along its length. The composite blurred, molecules stretching and contracting at incredible speeds, lending them an elasticity and tensile strength that no metal on Earth should possess.

By the time Artemus finished working on the chain, it was a shiny, thin, pliable metal leash. He lifted it to the light from the forge and examined it with a critical eye. Though it looked dainty, he knew it would be damn near unbreakable.

"That trick never gets old," Elton murmured. He was leaning against the wall and studying the rabbit with a faint frown. "Still freaks me out when you do it though." He glanced at Artemus. "So, what happened last night?"

"I don't know where your informant got his story from, but the guy I met up with knew jack shit about the Ming vase. And he cheated at poker."

Artemus strode over to the floor-to-ceiling shelves that lined half of the workshop's east wall, climbed onto a rolling library stepladder, and took down a wooden crate.

"Whoever stole it from your place is long gone from the city," he said, rifling through the box. "I'd be checking the black markets in New York and Paris if I were you. And Moscow. Those nouveau-riche Russian oligarchs never tire of old trash from the Orient."

"I would be grateful if you could stop referring to my two-million-dollar vase as 'old trash,'" Elton said coldly. "And *everyone* knows those guys cheat at poker. It's like their trademark move."

Artemus found the objects he was looking for and took them over to the anvil.

"You still owe me, Elton," he said in a hard voice. "You're the one who said it would be a walk in the park. You never told me I was meeting with the freaking Triad.

It's a miracle I walked out of that club with my balls intact!"

"I knew you'd be okay. You can handle yourself in any situation," Elton said gruffly. "Besides, the leader of that particular group has a penchant for pretty, blue-eyed blonds."

Artemus froze in the act of folding a strip of leather over one end of the leash. "Wait. You mean *that's* why that asshole got me drunk and pawed at me? *He wanted to get in my pants?*" He closed his eyes briefly and shuddered at the memory of the Triad group leader's hand on his thigh. "You bastard!"

Elton shrugged. "Judging from the way you're walking, it doesn't look like you were violated, so no harm done."

Artemus scowled and shoved a middle finger in Elton's direction before removing a thick sewing needle and a spool of sturdy black thread from a metal tin. He stitched the ends of the leather together and secured the other item he'd found in the crate to the center of the strip. It jingled faintly.

"Is that a bell?" Elton asked woodenly.

# CHAPTER THREE

O<small>TIS WALKED INTO THE ROOM WEARING A DOWNCAST</small> expression. "I've closed up shop, boss. No biters today, I'm afraid." His face brightened slightly when he saw what Artemus was holding in his hands. "Oh. You made Mr. Bunny a collar?"

Elton raised an eyebrow. "His name is Mr. Bunny?"

Artemus took a small steel padlock from a chest of drawers and tucked the key in the back pocket of his jeans. "No, it isn't."

"Why are you giving him a collar?" Elton said. "Are you planning on taking him for walks?"

"Heck no." Artemus crossed the floor and stopped in front of the rabbit. "It's just...I have a feeling this cage is for show."

The creature's eyes were limpid pools of brown once more. They followed Artemus as he reached for the bolts holding the cage together.

Elton stiffened. "Hey, you sure that's safe now?"

He straightened, stepped away from the wall, and reached toward the small of his back.

Artemus knew the older man was going for the Sig Sauer pistol tucked in his rear waistband.

"Trust me, bullets won't work on this thing," he muttered.

Now that the moment of truth had arrived, he found himself feeling strangely nervous. He placed his switch-blade within easy reach on the table. The rabbit's gaze flickered to the weapon.

Artemus held the leash in one hand and undid the bolts. The cage walls stayed put for one gravity-defying moment before slowly falling down.

Otis jumped at the clatter of steel against wood.

Artemus's heart pounded in his chest as he studied the creature crouched less than a foot from him. Twenty-two years after their first meeting, there was nothing separating them once more but layers of air. Memories of that day rushed through him.

Since his mom had had to work the graveyard shift at the diner that night, they'd had a small birthday party and a picnic in the afternoon with some of the neighborhood kids, most of whom Artemus knew from school. She'd kissed him goodbye after dinner and left for work just as his father had come home from his day shift at the garage.

Artemus had taken one look at his old man's bad-tempered expression and known that he'd totally forgotten it was his own son's birthday. He'd dashed off to his room under the eaves of their modest house and played with his new pet rabbit until he fell asleep, the animal snuggled up in his arms while the TV blared noisily downstairs.

He'd loved bunnies since his mom first read him *The Tale of Peter Rabbit* when he was four. After two years of his pleas falling on deaf ears, she'd finally relented and bought him one for his sixth birthday. Though Artemus had only had the animal for a few hours, he had already lost his heart to it. He and his mom were going to buy a hutch the next day, after school.

Except they never got to.

That night, Artemus had awoken from his first and only sleepwalking spell to find himself standing in the field behind his house. The first thing he'd noticed was the strange lights in the sky. There was no missing them. For a moment, an excited laugh had burst forth from his lips as he stared at the eerie flickerings and throbbing pulsations lighting up the Heavens.

It had felt as though they might burst at the seams at any second and flood the world with dazzling brilliance.

His excitement had lasted but that. A moment.

For he'd realized then that he wasn't alone in the field. His new pet was with him. And so was something else. Something that did not belong in this world, but in a place where man's worst nightmares dwelled. That night, as the world flickered and the clouds glowed above him, Artemus had stood in knee-high grass and seen the monster in all its unholy glory before its garish transformation.

Over the years, Artemus had convinced himself that it had all been a bad dream. That the demon he had seen crouched on the earth before him under that uncanny sky had been a figment of his imagination. That the voices and screams he'd heard inside his head in those fractured moments of reality had all been of his own making.

Except no one could explain the switchblade his father had found him clutching in his small, grimy hands when they'd discovered him in the field the next morning. Nor could anyone elucidate the mystery of the marks that had appeared on Artemus's body.

At first, the authorities had suspected his father of having inflicted the injuries. Almost everyone in the small, Midwest town where Artemus had grown up knew of his old man's drinking habits and his tendency to speak with his hands; the bruises Artemus's mother turned up with at her waitressing job had been the subject of much neighborhood gossip over the years. It wasn't until the purple contusions on Artemus's back had transformed into permanent marks that his father's vehement denial was finally believed. By then, it was already too late; his old man had lost his job at the local garage.

What had followed was an unraveling of the simple life Artemus had known.

He blinked. The rabbit was staring at him intently. All it would take was one leap and the creature would be at his throat.

For a crazy moment, Artemus thought he read an apology in the chocolate depths. He rid himself of that insane notion, took a deep breath, and brought the leash and collar up. The creature tensed.

Artemus frowned. "I *will* cut you if you bite me."

The rabbit glanced at the switchblade. He rubbed his nose with his paws and let out a disgruntled huff. The silver bell with its cute, red satin bow jingled as Artemus slowly looped the collar around the creature's neck.

His fingers made contact with soft, warm fur.

For the second time that day, the world stilled around Artemus. His eyes widened as he registered the savage energy pulsing under his touch. Because what he was sensing wasn't what he'd been expecting at all. His gaze clashed with the rabbit's.

In that moment, nothing existed but the two of them. He, a man who was more than a man. And the rabbit, a beast disguised as a creature he had once loved with all the heart and childish passion of a six-year-old.

*Shit, you're strong. Really strong.* Artemus clenched his jaw. *I don't think this chain will hold you.*

Something passed between them then. Something that felt like a reluctant agreement.

*I will allow you this despicable infringement for now, boy.*

Artemus blinked and wondered whether he'd really just heard those sibilant words inside his head. He snapped the padlock closed.

# CHAPTER FOUR

SNOW AND ICE CRUNCHED BENEATH ARTEMUS'S BOOTS.

He shivered and pulled his muffler up over his ears. "Christ, it's cold enough to freeze Satan's balls. Why didn't you bring the car?"

Elton matched his pace as they walked rapidly along the pavement. "'Cause I like the fresh air. And did you really have to bring that...*thing?*"

The rabbit hopped between them, button nose twitching and bell jingling while snowflakes melted on his dark fur. The end of the leash was looped around Artemus's left fist, which he'd tucked inside the pocket of his windbreaker.

"I still have no idea how he ended up at my place. He's staying where I can see him until I figure out what the hell is going on."

The rabbit glanced at him with innocent eyes. Artemus reflected that it was a miracle the creature hadn't taken his fingers off back at the workshop when he'd put the leash on him. He was also still trying to come to terms with what he'd felt when he'd touched the animal.

The creature had remained strangely docile since inheriting the collar and chain. Artemus wasn't fooled. He was dealing with a bad-ass bunny and they both knew it.

Elton's auction house was located in a leafy street in Lincoln Park, one mile north of Old Town. They were on their way there to meet the client who had come all the way from New York to have his collection valued. The task was something Elton would usually have asked one of his regular appraisers to do. There were certain circumstances however, or more specifically certain *items*, that necessitated Artemus's unparalleled skills when it came to antiques and rare objects.

They drew some curious looks when they entered the affluent neighborhood. Most people hurried along the dark streets though, their shoulders hunched and their eyes cast down after the briefest of stares. There were much stranger things around these days than two men out walking a rabbit. Things that were whispered rather than talked about. Things that most averted their eyes from and erased from their memory, for no ordinary man or woman could believe that such wretched beings existed or such dreadful deeds had been allowed to pass.

A bittersweet smile twisted Artemus's lips at the thought.

And so the world rotated on its axis and society and governments continued to spin lies. Over two decades' worth of lies, to be precise. He'd done some digging over the years. Most of the evidence he'd uncovered pointed to a specific time as the point of origin when freaky things started to happen on pretty much every continent on the globe. That this period coincided with when his own life had taken a dramatic turn for the worse was not lost on him. Nor was the fact that the fabrications concocted by those in power were a dire necessity. They could hardly do anything else.

What could humans hope to do in the face of the arcane?

One side effect of the uncanny events of the last twenty odd years was religion being at an all-time high. Following decades of passionately embracing all the material comforts of modern capitalism, many had turned to faith in these dark days. They still indulged in the party life and their luxury consumer goods, but church benches were packed and donation boxes were full to the brim for the first time in ages. It had, in fact, never been a better time to be a priest.

Artemus was pondering whether he should change careers and become a man of the cloth when he felt a tug on the leash. He stopped and turned.

They'd just passed a fire hydrant on the corner of an intersection. The rabbit had cocked a hind leg against it and was expelling a horrid, yellow discharge.

Elton pulled a face and brought a gloved fist under his nose. "Christ, what *is* that stench?"

Artemus scowled. The beast's urine smelled like a decomposing corpse dunked in a septic tank.

The rabbit finished his business, rubbed his butt in the snow, and hopped up to Artemus's side, bell jingling with macabre cheerfulness and a butter-wouldn't-melt expression on his furry face.

There was a creak and clunk of metal behind him. Artemus and Elton stared at the hydrant.

The metal corroded and disintegrated before their eyes, the pump tilting precariously sideways as the section of the base stained by the foul emission vanished into the ether. A small jet of high-pressured water escaped the gaping hole and fountained into the air.

They watched it for a moment.

"Well, that's somebody else's problem," Artemus said flatly.

He turned and carried on walking.

"Hey!" Elton jogged up to him. He pointed back the way they'd come. "Can we talk about the fact that your pet rabbit just pissed out acid?!"

"No," Artemus replied. "And he's not my pet anything."

The rabbit huffed as if to confirm this.

Elton's left wrist buzzed. He peeled back his coat sleeve distractedly and checked the display of the paper-thin device wrapped around his forearm. He tapped it and took the call.

A hulking, black man appeared on the screen. He had the face of a former boxer and was wearing a smart aqua-marine business suit, a checkered blue tie, and tinted glasses.

"What is it, Shamus?" Elton said.

"Mr. Gato is getting impatient," the suited guy rumbled.

"We're around the corner," Elton said. "Has our other guest arrived yet?"

"Yes. She just got here," Shamus replied. "She has quite the entourage."

"Make sure they have plenty of champagne and caviar on hand," Elton instructed.

Shamus hesitated. "Are we talking Dom Perignon or Krug?"

"Dom," Elton said wryly. "We wouldn't want to insult her."

"Okay, boss."

"Nice smartband," Artemus murmured when Elton ended the call. "Isn't that the fancy one that's still out on pre-order? I thought it wasn't meant to be released for another two months."

"It wasn't. I know a guy who knows a guy who knows a guy." Elton glanced at Artemus. "I'd get you one for Christmas if you weren't so stubborn about sticking with that ridiculous antique of yours."

Artemus pulled his cell out of his pocket and waved it at Elton. "Excuse me, there's nothing wrong with this!"

Elton snorted. "It's over ten years old. I'm surprised you can still charge the damn thing."

"Well, I've never been comfortable with all this newfangled biometric tech," Artemus said grouchily. "I'd rather stick to something that doesn't know when I'm taking a dump and wants to give me advice on my digestive cycle."

"There are days when I wonder if you're really twenty-eight," Elton said dully.

They reached another intersection and turned the corner into a cul-de-sac. The auction house came into view.

Artemus slowed. "Are you having an event tonight?"

He stared at the queue of sleek limousines pulling through the gates of the sprawling brownstone mansion at the end of the street.

"Yes." Elton overtook him and led the way toward the building. "A special item just came in. I want you to take a look at it before it goes to bidding tonight."

"Special how?" Artemus narrowed his eyes. "It's not something from the goddamn Orient again, is it?"

"No, smartass," Elton muttered. "It's part of the private collection of a very rich and very dead billionaire from Philadelphia. His young and vivacious widow has decided to part with the items since they remind her too much of her recently deceased husband. Did I mention the dirt is still fresh on his grave?"

"She the guest you were just referring to?" Artemus asked.

"Indeed. The collection is being auctioned privately at various locations around the country tonight. A clever move by the mourning widow, if I say so myself." Elton grimaced. "Means she'll be bypassing tax laws in several states."

They entered the mansion through a side door in the north wing and headed up a flight of stairs to the second floor. Artemus glanced through the tall, leaded windows overlooking the mansion's courtyard as they navigated a carpeted corridor. Guests in smart eveningwear were stepping out of the limos and heading for the steps leading to the main entrance.

A wry smile curved Artemus's lips. Elton's evening functions were always well attended by the rich and famous, some travelling from as far as the west coast for the privilege of taking part in these private events. The objects that went up on auction during these closed-doors affairs were always one-of-a-kind. He of all people should know; he'd valued most of them.

His gaze swept over the men and women in dark suits who stood discreetly observing the new arrivals from around the quadrangle. They were but a fraction of the security team Elton had guarding the auction house at any given time. Artemus knew the lenses of their tinted glasses would be streaming the registration plates and biometric data of Elton's guests to the security room in the basement of the building, where the visitors' IDs were being processed.

Elton veered away from the main foyer and led Artemus toward the rear of the mansion. It hosted a range of private suites where clients could have their goods appraised at leisure, and where sales and purchases were negotiated.

Shamus was standing guard outside one of the doors, his hands crossed before him and his gaze seemingly lost in space. Artemus wasn't fooled.

Shamus Carmichael was the head of Elton's security team and a man not to be taken lightly. A three-time world heavyweight boxing champion, he could bench press eight hundred pounds on an average day. Artemus had gone in the ring with Shamus only once and borne the bruises for two weeks.

"Hey, Art," Shamus murmured.

"Hey, Shamus."

The black man's gaze dropped to the rabbit. "You got a pet?"

Artemus rolled his eyes.

# CHAPTER FIVE

"How's Gato holding?" Elton asked his security head.

"I had Chef prepare him his favorite meal," Shamus replied. "That seems to have shut him up for now." He paused. "I'm afraid we had to open one of the Château Lafites."

"Christ," Elton muttered. "This is gonna be an expensive evening."

He glared at Artemus.

"What?" Artemus said defensively.

Elton let out a disgruntled sigh and led the way into the suite.

Two bodyguards stood to attention next to a small, round dining table up ahead, where an Asian man with a headful of pepper hair sat polishing off a steak-frites.

Artemus's mouth watered at the delicious aroma of cooked meat. It'd been a long time since that bacon cheeseburger. A low rumble sounded next to him. He looked down. The rabbit was drooling.

Artemus's lips twitched in an involuntary smile. He

masked it with a frown in the next instant and looked at the display table to the left, where Gato's collection was laid out ready for his inspection. He knew instantly that a third of the items were fakes.

"Ah. You have finally graced us with your presence, Mr. Steele."

Gato put down his knife and fork, wiped his lips with a napkin, and rose from the table. His cheeks were flushed from the wine and his tone only mildly belligerent.

"Mr. Gato," Artemus murmured with a dip of his chin.

"Again, my deepest apologies for my associate's tardiness," Elton said smoothly. "He had an emergency he had to attend to." He smiled. "I hope the meal was to your liking?"

The "emergency" hopped beside Artemus's feet as they headed for the display table.

"It was most agreeable, thank you." Gato stared at the rabbit. "I didn't know you had a pet, Mr. Steele."

"I don't," Artemus muttered as he started examining the eclectic collection.

Gato's face fell when Artemus spelled out the truth about the items.

The Asian man never doubted his word and neither did Elton. Artemus's reputation as a rare goods valuer was the worst kept secrets in the world of antique collectors. The fact that he chose to work exclusively for Elton was one of the principal reasons the Chicago auction house was so highly regarded internationally.

Many were curious as to why Artemus repeatedly refused the generous offers he received from other famous auction houses and fine art brokers from around the world. Some wondered whether Elton had some kind of invisible hold over him, or even if the older man was Artemus's sugar daddy, a rumor that had sent chills down Artemus's spine when he'd first heard it and had Elton howling with laughter.

Only one other person in the world besides Artemus and Elton knew the truth of the bond that linked them. He was currently six feet under, in a mausoleum in the private cemetery adjoining Artemus's house.

"A million dollars?" Gato said, his face pale. "Are you certain? I was told this collection was worth three times that."

"I am and it's not." Artemus indicated a jade brooch and an imitation Ottoman letter opener. "And I would get rid of those two if I were you. They're tainted."

Elton stiffened, his gaze focusing on the objects.

Gato frowned. "Tainted? What do you mean? Tainted how?"

Artemus looked steadily at Gato. "Tainted as in cursed." He sighed at the Asian's man incredulous expression. "Have you had any bad luck lately? Anyone in your family suffered from any serious illnesses or been in an accident?" He glanced at the items. "I'm talking specifically in the last six months. That's how long those have been in your possession, right?"

Gato's face grew haggard. "How could you possibly—?" He stopped and swallowed convulsively. "My son was in an accident four months ago and my daughter-in-law was just diagnosed with cancer."

Artemus felt a sudden wave of pity for the man. He gestured toward the two antiques. "Burn them. And bury the remains in your place of worship. As for the person who gave them to you, break all contact with them. Do not retaliate." He frowned. "I cannot emphasize this enough. This man or woman is aligned with forces beyond your understanding."

"Are you talking about — about *black magic?*" Gato said in a shaky voice.

Artemus shrugged. "Call it what you want. Magic, witchcraft, sorcery, voodoo. It's all the same thing."

"And what is that?" Gato quavered.

"Evil," Artemus said flatly.

A knock came at the door.

It opened to reveal Shamus. "Auction's about to start, boss."

"Thanks, Shamus." Elton looked at Gato. "I would invite you to stay but something tells me you're in a rush to get back to New York."

Gato nodded, his eyes those of a man suddenly plagued by invisible ghosts.

"May I request that you leave the brooch and the letter opener with us for a couple of days?" Elton added. "I would like to examine them more closely, if I may."

"You can keep them," Gato said hoarsely. "I don't want them back."

Elton frowned. "Are you sure?"

Gato looked at Artemus. "I trust Mr. Steele's judgment on this."

Elton dipped his chin at the Asian man. "Then I shall dispose of them as Artemus instructed."

They bade Gato goodbye and left the suite, the rabbit in tow.

"I really want to know what you do with all these cursed objects I find for you," Artemus said lightly.

Elton's gaze grew hooded. "I think it would be best if you didn't."

Irritation darted through Artemus, as it always did when they had this conversation. Which was often. "I'm not a child anymore, Elton. And considering what you know about me, I doubt I'd be shocked by whatever you tell me."

"Trust me, you would," Elton said gruffly.

"Did Karl know?" Artemus said suddenly.

Elton stopped dead in his tracks. He stared at Artemus. "You've never asked me that before."

Artemus studied him curiously. He could see the answer in his friend's eyes. "So, he didn't know?"

Elton hesitated. "No. But he's one of the reasons why I do it."

There was another unspoken admission there. What it was about, Artemus didn't know. He was aware of the rabbit glancing at them discreetly.

"Maybe we don't need to burn the brooch and the letter opener," he mused out loud. "Maybe he can pee on them."

Elton looked from the creature to Artemus. "What, and burn a hole right through my floor in the process?" He scowled. "No, thank you." He paused. "It doesn't look like I'm gonna have time to introduce you to the widow and show you what she brought for the auction. You wanna stay anyway? I can drop you home after."

Artemus shrugged. "Sure. Might as well get some entertainment out of this."

The foyer loomed ahead of them, its pale marble walls and elegant furnishings highlighted by an enormous crystal chandelier suspended from a beautiful, inlaid, mosaic ceiling. They descended the steps and headed into the south wing. A pair of large double doors appeared at the intersection at the end of the hall. They were manned by two security guards.

"Hi, Art," the pretty blonde on the right said with a smile. "We heard about the bunny." Her grin widened as she studied the rabbit. "He suits you."

Artemus narrowed his eyes. A low hubbub of conversation reached his ears from behind the closed doors.

"Stop flirting, Isabelle," Elton said briskly. "How's the crowd, Mark?"

"Buzzing and ready to spend some serious dough, boss," the male security guard said, an amused expression lighting up his face as he gazed from the rabbit to Artemus.

"Good," Elton said. "Let's get this show on the road."

He grabbed the doorknobs and twisted them.

"By the way, you never told me what special item the widow brought," Artemus said.

"It's a silver-and-gold-plated ivory cane dating back to the sixteenth century," Elton said as he pushed the doors open. The hubbub grew to a muted roar. "It was valued by Sotheby's at ten million dollars last year."

Beyond a set of shallow steps was a ballroom that served as the venue's main auction chamber. The rows of chairs that normally filled the tiled floor had been cleared to make way for Elton's private guests where they sipped champagne and nibbled on canapés under the dazzling glow of half a dozen chandeliers.

Artemus was about to follow the older man down into the crowded room when the hairs rose on the back of his neck. He froze and looked straight ahead.

His gaze locked onto the object inside the display cabinet on the raised stage on the other side of the floor.

# CHAPTER SIX

T<small>HE</small> <small>LEASH</small> <small>TREMBLED</small> <small>AROUND</small> A<small>RTEMUS'S</small> <small>LEFT</small> <small>FIST</small> where he held it inside his jacket pocket, distracting him for an instant. He glanced down and realized the rabbit's attention was similarly riveted to the item on the stage.

It wasn't years of study or professional accreditations that had rendered Artemus the skills to be able to assess the authenticity of any period or collector's piece that had ever crossed his hands. Though he had passed the required exams and held the necessary certifications, he'd done so without opening a single academic book or spending time in the backrooms of museums pouring over thousands of rare goods.

It was, rather, yet another mysterious gift he appeared to have been born with. Or that had awakened inside him.

And it wasn't just the authenticity and age of an object Artemus could see with his eyes, smell with his nose, and feel with his touch. He could do more than that.

If the object was one of power, Artemus could discern its innate nature as accurately as a Geiger counter could detect ionizing radiation.

Right now, all his senses were screaming at him that the ivory cane in the display cabinet, the one about to go on auction in the next few minutes to the highest bidder in the room, was an immensely powerful object. As powerful as the switchblade in his boot and the monster at his side.

What stunned him more than anything else though, was the fact that the invisible energy the ivory cane was projecting was unlike what he was used to detecting in the objects that occasionally crossed his path at the auction house.

This thing was not evil. In fact, it was the exact opposite. Like the blade he had inherited the night he turned six and, more shockingly, the monster who now crouched next to him, it emitted pure goodness and righteousness.

Something else drifted on the edge of Artemus's consciousness. He stiffened, his gaze sweeping the floor and scanning the sea of faces around him. There were other energies circulating the ballroom. Strange, ominous forces that raised goosebumps on his skin. He took a shallow breath and focused his mind's eye.

Wisps of darkness materialized above the milling crowd, invisible to everyone but him. Thin and ethereal, they coiled and danced through the air like trails of black smoke. They were concentrated above seven men and four women.

Artemus knew the rabbit had sensed them too; the creature's attention had shifted to the people he'd just identified.

There was something else in the room with them. Something different. Something Artemus couldn't see but knew was there in the marrow of his bones. Something that felt alien and yet achingly familiar at the same time.

Artemus descended the steps rapidly and went in search of Elton. He found the older man at the far end of the ballroom, in deep conversation with a beautiful, willowy blonde with pale green eyes.

"There you are," Elton said when Artemus appeared at his side. "Let me introduce you. Mrs. Stone, this is Artemus Steele. Artemus, this is Callista Stone, the owner of the antique we're auctioning tonight."

"Mrs. Stone," Artemus said distractedly, flashing the woman a half-smile. He turned to Elton. "Look, there's something I need to tell you—"

A cloud of expensive perfume engulfed him as the newly widowed Mrs. Stone stepped up to him and kissed his cheek. Surprise jolted through Artemus.

"Your reputation precedes you, Mr. Steele," Callista Stone murmured, her crimson-tipped fingers lingering on his chest for a moment before falling demurely to her side. "And please, call me Callie."

Artemus froze and stared at the woman in the midnight-blue dress.

*What the hell?*

He didn't think he'd mistaken the interest in her eyes. Artemus was objective enough to know his looks were striking. He had long become resigned to garnering the attention of both men and women wherever he went. Not that he ever responded to the invitations that came his way.

His heart already belonged to someone else.

But it wasn't the blatant sexual invitation Callie Stone had just issued that had given him an 'oh fuck' moment. He'd sensed something inside her when she'd touched him. A power that was unlike any other he'd ever—

*Wait a minute. I know this energy signature.*

Artemus looked at the rabbit. The creature was studying Callista Stone unblinkingly. The blonde became aware of the bunny's engrossed stare. Her mouth rounded.

Artemus blinked. *They're similar! Their powers share a common—*

Callie Stone stooped and scooped the rabbit up in her arms, her face melting in a gooey look of pure adoration.

Artemus and Elton took a hasty step back.

"*What a cute bunny!*" the widow cooed as she petted and kissed the creature. She paused when she registered their expressions and gazed at them curiously. "What's wrong? You two look like you've seen a ghost."

Artemus and Elton shared a glance. They'd both expected the rabbit to go feral on the woman and rip her to shreds. Artemus met the bunny's gaze.

The *'what-the-hell-just-happened-and-why-are-you-standing-there-not-doing-anything-about-it'* expression on his furry face was so comical Artemus would have burst out laughing had he not remembered why he'd come to find Elton in the first place.

"Excuse us for a second," he murmured to the widow.

He gave her the end of the leash and pulled Elton to the side. Callie nodded distractedly and continued stroking the rabbit.

*Traitor.*

Artemus glanced over his shoulder into the creature's faintly accusing eyes and knew this time for certain that it was the rabbit's voice he'd just heard in his head.

"What is it?" Elton said.

A bell sounded across the ballroom. It was the cue that the auction was about to begin. The crowd shifted and started to move toward the stage.

"The cane," Artemus said urgently. "You can't sell it."

His skin prickled. He could feel the forces in the chamber moving around him.

Elton frowned at the tension in his voice. "Why?" He looked at the object in the display cabinet. "Can you feel something from it?"

"Yes," Artemus replied. "It's incredibly powerful. There's more." He hesitated. "I know you're gonna find this hard to believe, but there are people in this room right now who are not what they seem either. They share the same energy signature as those cursed objects you like to study so much."

A change came over Elton then. He grew still, his face and body so motionless Artemus thought he'd turned to stone. He unfroze into someone Artemus hardly recognized in the next instant, his rugged face gaining a hardness and zealous focus that made his eyes gleam with an almost unholy light.

Elton tapped the smartband on his wrist. Shamus's face appeared on the screen.

"We're a go," Elton said. "It's a Code Black."

A muscle jumped in Shamus's jawline. "We got an estimate?"

Elton narrowed his eyes at Artemus. "How many people?"

Artemus glanced from his oldest friend to the smartband. "Eleven. Seven men and four women. What the hell is going on Elton?"

That was when the shit went south.

# CHAPTER SEVEN

THE SOUND OF BREAKING GLASS SHATTERED THE MURMUR of conversation around them. Artemus's head snapped around.

One of Elton's security guards stood frozen to his right, eyes wide and a shocked expression on his pale face. His hands were wrapped around the handle of the knife buried to the hilt in his belly. Standing opposite him was one of the women Artemus had identified earlier.

The crown of darkness above her head had intensified and spread to engulf her entire body. A sadistic look distorted her once pretty face. It was her eyes, however, that sent a shudder of pre-recognition through Artemus and made his pulse jump. They had turned an unearthly obsidian from edge to edge, the pupils glowing with a yellow light in the center.

A scream rendered the air. Artemus startled when the sound of a gunshot followed from his left.

Smoke curled from the end of the gun in Elton's hand. Artemus blinked. It wasn't the Sig Sauer he was holding but a weapon Artemus had never seen before. The older

man's features were locked in an enraged scowl. He
gripped what looked like a modified, stainless steel Beretta
pistol and glared at the creature who had just stabbed one
of his men.

The woman wreathed in shadows raised a hand to her
flank and looked curiously at the thin stream of black fluid
staining her fingertips. She lifted her chin and flashed an
inhuman smile at Elton.

A frozen moment of stillness followed while the world
held its breath. Then, chaos descended on the ballroom.

Artemus glimpsed the other men and women he'd
picked out moving through the crowd of screaming, terrified guests rushing for the doors. His heart thumped
against his ribs as he foresaw their intent. His gaze shifted
to the stage and the display cabinet.

*They're going for the cane!*

There was no more time left to think. The woman
Elton had shot was upon them, her movements so fast her
body practically blurred as she crossed the fifty feet separating them in leaps and bounds.

Artemus stooped and snatched the switchblade from
his boot just as she launched herself into the air, the nails
of her hands and feet extending into wicked dark claws
while a high-pitched shriek erupted from her throat.

Elton's eyes widened as gravity brought her plum-
meting toward him. He blocked her attack with his forearms and grunted when the impact sent him skidding back
two feet. He cursed, ducked beneath her next blow, and
brought his gun up. A gasp left his lips when the weapon
was knocked violently out of his hand. The woman snarled
where she crouched on all fours before him. She sprung
and went in for the kill.

A choked sound escaped her when Artemus grabbed the back of her dress.

"I don't think so, lady!" he growled.

He jerked her close and buried the knife in her neck, at the very base of her spine. It was like turning the lights off.

The woman went limp in his hold. Artemus yanked the blade out of her flesh and let go. She crumpled at his feet and came to rest on her side, her stunned gaze meeting his for a moment. The eerie light faded from her eyes. She regained her human appearance once more as she exhaled her last breath.

"How did you know—?" Elton started in a stunned voice.

"You and I need to have a serious conversation about trust after this," Artemus said grimly as he started for the stage. "Tell your people to aim for their heads! And whatever the hell happens, that cane *cannot* leave these premises, understood?!"

Some two dozen men and women from Elton's security team had entered the auction room and were engaging the remaining creatures in a deadly fight. Shamus lifted a man whose body swarmed with blackness off Isabelle and backhanded him across the face.

The creature staggered backward and crashed into a marble column. He slid down into a crouch and shook his head slightly. His inhuman eyes locked on the former boxer. He let out an animal roar and bolted for the black man, the seams of his evening suit ripping as his shape grew, the muscles of his shoulders, arms, and thighs swelling and bulging to twice their size.

Shamus raised the Beretta in his hand and started firing, Isabelle joining him. Their gleaming bullets slammed into the man and slowed him down a fraction. He shrieked in pain and charged toward the two guards.

Artemus scowled. *Shit!*

He stumbled to a stop and glanced at the stage fifteen feet ahead of him. Surprise jolted him when he saw Callie Stone and the rabbit in front of the display cabinet. He'd forgotten all about them.

The widow looked lost and confused, as if she couldn't quite comprehend what she was doing there. Next to her, the beast's pupils were red and his fangs exposed once more. His gaze met Artemus's.

*We have this. It is time to do your thing.*

Artemus blinked at the gravelly words bouncing around inside his skull.

Darkness coiled through the air in thickening waves as the other creatures mutated into their true forms. The skin on Artemus's back itched and trembled. He clenched his teeth and felt power flow through him from the marks he'd inherited the night he turned six.

The switchblade shivered in his grip as he started to run. Its shape shifted, growing longer. Thicker. Stronger.

By the time Artemus reached Shamus and Isabelle where they stood engaged in brutal hand-to-hand combat with the monster, the knife had transformed into a double-edged sword with a wing-shaped cross guard and a grip that flared out slightly into a flat, round pommel. It was the seventh time in his life the switchblade had manifested its true nature.

Artemus swung the blade. It carved through the neck of the creature like a hot knife through butter.

Shamus and Isabelle stared at the black liquid spurting from the decapitated trunk before them. Their gazes moved in unison to the head rolling across the floor in the direction of the doors, its face locked in a frozen expression of shock.

"I think I'm gonna hurl," Isabelle said dully.

The dead man's body thudded to the floor, a monster no more.

Artemus glanced at the gunshot wounds peppering the corpse. "Were those silver-coated bullets?"

"Silver-leaded. They're impregnated with Holy Water." Shamus stared at the sword. "Where did that come from?"

Two more of the creatures homed in on them. A third of Elton's security team was already down for the count.

"You people realize werewolves and vampires don't exist, right?" Artemus said, his fingers tightening on the hilt of his blade as he studied the man and woman observing them with cold, obsidian eyes from a few feet away.

"Yes, smartass," Isabelle replied, some of the color returning to her cheeks. "It's the only thing that seems to work against these...things."

"Demons, Isabelle," Shamus muttered. They shifted until they were standing back to back. "They are demons."

Artemus pondered this for a moment. *It's as good a word as any.*

# CHAPTER EIGHT

CALLIE STONE WAS FEELING STRANGE. SHE COULD SEE her secretary and bodyguards lying wounded and unconscious around the ballroom. In the middle of the chamber, a battle was unfolding, one unlike any she had ever witnessed. She stared at Elton LeBlanc and his security team with a surreal feeling of detachment while they faced off against a group of odd-looking men and women.

A faint frown marred her brow.

*Come to think of it, the last time I was in a fight was when that little harlot Pamela Solomon put a turd inside my school locker in seventh grade.*

By all accounts, Callie should have been shocked and terrified by what she was seeing. Yet, she felt oddly...calm. Which was staggering in itself, considering the sheltered life she'd led growing up in California and the privileged one that had followed her marriage to one of the wealthiest men in the country.

Callie knew most people thought of her as a clever little gold-digger who'd ensnared her much older billionaire husband with her charms. This included her own family, who incidentally didn't seem to mind so much once they started benefiting from her generosity. They were right, to an extent. Her marriage to Ronald Stone had not started out as a relationship founded on love and affection. Having met her at the yacht club where she'd been wait-ressing for six months, he'd been very clear from the start that he wanted a pretty companion, a trophy wife, and would offer her a lavish life in return. He'd also stated from the get go that he would be unable to satisfy her in the bedroom and that, if she chose, she could have affairs, so long as she be discreet about them.

They'd been married for three years, ten months, and twenty-eight days when Ronald had died of a heart attack while playing golf. To her surprise, Callie discovered that the tears she shed at his funeral were utterly genuine. For Ronald had been a good husband to her. Her feelings for him had changed over the time they had been together from benevolent tolerance to fondness and what felt a little like love.

She had come to Chicago to fulfill the promise she had made to him four months ago. It had been a hot summer day and they'd been sitting out by the pool at their villa in Baja when Ronald had turned to her and said, "Callie, when I die, I want you to sell the private collection of antiques in the basement of our home in Philadelphia."

And he'd gone on to say more. Specifically, he'd asked her to bring the most prized piece of that collection to Chicago and to Elton LeBlanc's auction house.

When Callie had asked him why, Ronald had smiled and said, "An angel told me to."

At the time, she'd thought he meant it as a joke. It

wasn't until his will was read by his estate attorney that a shiver of alarm had danced down Callie's spine. For written in the legal document was a note to Callie to remind her of the promise she had made that summer day.

Callie glanced at the silver-and-gold-plated ivory cane propped up inside the glass cabinet behind her. She'd never thought much of it before. Sure, it was pretty if you were into that kind of thing and it was ridiculously expensive, but she didn't harbor any strong feelings about it.

Yet, tonight, as the reality she had known all her life came crashing down around her and the world revealed itself to be full of things straight out of her worst nightmares, a singular truth resonated through Callie.

The cane was important. And she had to defend it with her life.

She knew she wasn't alone in believing this. She could see the same conviction in the cold, blue eyes of Artemus Steele and the red gaze of the weird rabbit next to her.

*And speaking of weird, my marks are tingling.*

Though most people assumed they were tattoos, the designs etched in dark pigment at the base of her neck and the bottom of her spine were not adornments she had had deliberately engraved into her skin. They would have been called birthmarks had she be born with them. But she hadn't.

They had appeared one night, when she was three.

Although plenty of doctors had examined them over the years and her mother had even paid to have them removed by laser when she was old enough to have the procedure, they had remained as stubbornly evident as the day she'd woken up with them.

And right now, they were prickling with an alarming heat that was slowly spreading through her body. In fact, her entire being felt like it was on fire. Something was also happening to her hair and her head. She could feel her blonde locks thickening and expanding to frame her face and neck, while two spots itched near the front of her scalp. Her tailbone was tingling too.

Two of the figures crawling with darkness leapt onto the stage. They headed for the display cabinet holding the cane.

ARTEMUS DUCKED BENEATH A CLAWED HAND AND DROVE the sword into the chest of his attacker. The demon stiffened and sagged to his knees, the light fading from his eyes. Artemus jerked the blade out, twisted on his heels, and kicked a female demon off Elton. The older man brought his gun around and shot her in the head.

They had regrouped in the middle of the room and were fighting the last of the creatures. Only four remained of the original eleven. Two of them moved toward the stage.

Artemus gritted his teeth. *Damn it!*

Though he and Elton's security detail had almost defeated the demons, the fight had taken a heavy toll on Elton's team. There were only five of them still standing, including Artemus and Elton.

He was debating whether to head for the display cabinet when he felt a shift in the forces swirling around the chamber. Something was happening on the stage.

As the remaining two demons charged toward it, Artemus caught a glimpse of Callie and the rabbit. His eyes widened.

*What the—?*

Callie Stone looked different. For one thing, her hair now resembled a luxurious mane wrapped around her face. And her features had transmuted, rendering her an almost leonine appearance.

As for the rabbit, he'd trebled in size and, by the looks of how he was attacking the demon closest to him, viciousness.

Artemus and Elton struck down the man before them just as Shamus, Isabelle, and Mark finished off the female demon.

Up on the stage, the creature opposite Callie leapt.

The widow's eyes glittered green. She inhaled deeply, her chest expanding to gargantuan proportions, before letting out a deafening roar.

The sound echoed to the ceiling and made the chandeliers tremble.

The demon froze mid-air, as if caught in an invisible vortex of energy. Callie swung her arm around and backhanded him across the face. He sailed off the stage and across the ballroom before smashing violently into a marble pillar thirty feet to Artemus's left.

Elton gaped, his gun swinging down limply to his side. "What the—?"

Two gunshots shattered the stillness of the room. The glass cabinet exploded behind Callie and the rabbit.

Before anyone could move, a man dressed all in black dropped down from the rafters on a winch line, grabbed the cane from the shattered remains of the box, and zoomed back up into the air with a grin on his face.

Artemus's gaze collided with the dark eyes of the thief who was literally stealing the antique from under their noses. That was when he felt it once more. The power he had detected earlier. The force that was different and yet seemed like something he was already acquainted with. Like something he'd known all his life.

The feeling swept over Artemus like a warm breeze.

Resonance.

# CHAPTER NINE

DRAKE HUNTER LEANED OVER THE FLEXIBLE FRAME OF his BMW superbike and gently depressed the slim throttle control under his right hand. The machine hummed between his thighs as it accelerated, the dynamic tires gripping the slush-covered blacktop firmly. The data display on his tinted visor told him he'd hit 110 mph.

Sitting inside the storage compartment under his left leg was a padded, metal roller tube containing the ivory cane he'd just stolen from Elton LeBlanc's auction house.

To say that the robbery had gone beyond Drake's wildest dreams would be an understatement. Having crafted an elaborate plan to steal the auction piece after it had gone through the sale that night, he'd been able to grab the antique much sooner than he'd anticipated. And all because of a fortuitous distraction.

Though he'd not paid much attention to the other guests when he'd arrived at the auction house, Drake had been aware that some of them were not quite human. The dark energy swirling around the men and women he'd identified when he'd entered the ballroom had put his teeth on edge and made the marks on his back tremble. Not because it frightened or disgusted him. On the contrary.

When the fight broke out minutes before the auction was due to start, he'd left the ballroom with the other guests as they streamed toward the mansion's exits, before slipping through the crowd and darting up the stairs without detection.

As he'd crouched in the rafters and readied his gear, Drake had finally gotten his first full view of the battle raging between Elton LeBlanc's security team and the monsters who'd invaded the mansion. And he'd frozen for a moment.

For the first time in a long time, the hairs had risen on the back of his neck and the cold, dark place where his heart dwelled had jolted with a flash of heat, as if he'd received an electric shock. Because scattered across the chamber beneath him were three others. Three beings that were neither human nor monster.

One of them was Artemus Steele, a man whose reputation in the antique world was unmatched by any other and who now stood wielding a sword as if it were an extension of his body and killing demons like it was something he did every Friday night.

The second was Callista Stone, the widow of the billionaire whose cane was the prized auction piece on show tonight. She was standing directly on the stage below him facing one of the monsters when she should rightly have fled the ballroom in hysterics or been dead by now.

The third was a huge brown rabbit with red eyes and fangs who was attacking a demon with savage ferocity.

Their energies were unlike those of the creatures they

fought. In fact, despite their fierceness, they were the very opposite of darkness.

When he'd sensed the battle drawing to a close, Drake had fired armor-piercing rounds into the bulletproof display cabinet beneath him and dropped down on a winch line to snatch the cane from the glittering debris. As he'd zipped back up to the rafters with his prize and a satisfied smile on his face, his eyes had met a pair of startled blue ones.

For the second time that night, Drake had frozen while the world vanished around him and his heart contracted in pure astonishment. Because in the instant he'd locked gazes with Artemus Steele, Drake had felt something he'd never experienced in his long and cursed life.

A connection. A bond. One that was as old and as familiar as his own existence. One that his every instinct told him he had known before his life had taken a turn into darkness.

Drake had just passed the Lincoln Park Conservatory on West Fullerton when headlights flashed in the metallic reflectors of the BMW's right handlebar. He brought up the rearview mirror display on the visor. Surprise darted through him.

*That was quick.*

He glanced over his shoulder and eyed the sleek, green Kawasaki seventy feet behind him. A black-clad rider in a helmet was crouched low atop it. Drake frowned.

Something told him his pursuer wasn't part of Elton LeBlanc's security team.

He crossed a lagoon with the bright lights of a marina to his left, flashed under a highway, and took the ramp leading onto North Lake Shore Drive with hardly any deceleration, the superbike's gyroscopic self-balancing system correcting smoothly for the abrupt change in direction.

The Kawasaki stayed on him as he hit the expressway.

Drake clenched his jaw, tapped a button on the left handlebar, and studied the digital map that opened up at the bottom of his visor. He'd originally been planning to detour around to Midway Airport and the private plane his client had waiting for him.

*Ah, well. Looks like I'm going to have to lose this asshole first.*

Snow fell from the overcast skies as he took the exit after Cricket Hill, two miles up the road. It turned to sleet while he headed into the stretch of greenbelt lining Montrose Beach.

His intention was to evade the Kawasaki in the maze of trails that wound through the one-mile-long parkland between Uptown and Lake Michigan.

Drake killed the BMW's lights, put the visor in night mode, and hunched low over the body of the superbike as he swerved onto a narrow path and darted between rows of trees.

The Kawasaki roared behind him as his pursuer gave chase.

Drake checked the layout ahead. He cut through some bushes and hit another dirt trail to the west. An embankment appeared on his left. He veered down the incline and touched the front brakes slightly when the superbike reached the path at the bottom. The tire locked and the back end of the machine rose as he spun it around through a ninety-degree turn. He pushed the throttle and charged into a dark culvert.

The headlights shadowing him disappeared. Drake dashed out of the tunnel seconds later and climbed a slope. The lights of the expressway appeared some hundred feet on his left when he emerged into the main park. He zoomed through a copse of trees, came out on a blacktop road, and was congratulating himself on having successfully escaped his pursuer when an SUV barreled into his path out of nowhere.

The superbike's safety system locked the brakes and sent the machine twisting sideways. Drake's stomach lurched as the world spun violently around him. He came to a screeching stop with the flexi-frame tilted at a forty-five degree angle to the ground and his head about an inch from the vehicle's left rear door. The superbike rebalanced itself with a low hum.

That was when a giant opened the driver's door of the SUV, ripped Drake's visor off his head, and punched him in the face.

# CHAPTER TEN

"A few of the guests we interviewed reported seeing some of the thieves...change appearance. Can you comment on this, Mr. LeBlanc?"

Elton gazed steadily at the young detective sitting opposite him. "I'm not sure what they thought they saw. You've inspected the bodies yourself."

"Still, we would like to examine your security recordings," someone said gruffly.

Artemus swallowed the last of his bourbon and studied the man who'd just spoken.

Jeremiah Chase stood by the window of Elton's study, a faint frown on his hardened face. He was the lead detective assigned the case of the multiple homicide and burglary at the auction house. From the vibes Artemus was getting, the man didn't tolerate fools lightly. And he appeared to be the kind of cop who would stick to a case like a dog with a bone until it was done with.

*Which is not necessarily a good thing under present circumstances.*

"I'm sure that can be arranged for the morning, Detective Chase," Elton said in a tone that indicated he'd also deduced the mettle of the man. "You'll understand if my staff are a bit shaken up tonight."

Chase hesitated before dipping his chin. "We'll be in touch first thing."

Someone knocked at the door. Shamus came in, his expression somber. A murmur of voices rose behind the former boxer from the direction of the foyer.

Despite the late hour, the auction house was still a bevy of activity as crime scene worked the ballroom and the last of the bodies were carted away by the medical examiner's officers. There had been twenty-five fatalities and almost as many wounded during the incident.

"Have the remaining guests left safely?" Elton asked his security head.

"Yes," Shamus replied. "Mrs. Stone just returned from the hospital. Her bodyguards and her secretary are in a stable condition. She would like a word in private." He glanced at the detectives. "After these gentlemen finish questioning you."

"We're done," Chase said briskly. "Let's go, Goodman."

The younger detective rose from the Chesterfield sofa and accompanied the older man to the door. Chase paused on the threshold.

"I don't need to tell you that you shouldn't leave town for a while," he said coolly to Elton and Artemus.

"Of course," Elton murmured.

The door thudded closed behind the cops and Shamus. Silence descended inside the room. Artemus stood up, went over to the mini bar in the corner, and poured himself another glass of bourbon. He leaned back against the counter and eyed Elton as he sipped the drink.

"I think you have something to tell me, don't you?"

Elton sighed. "Before we get to that, what do you make of Callie Stone?"

Artemus hesitated.

"She's not completely human," he said finally. "She shares the same...powers as the rabbit."

Lines furrowed Elton's brow. "So, she's a monster too?"

Artemus sighed. "Not quite." He walked to one of the Queen Anne chairs opposite the sofa and plopped down onto it. "It's my turn. What do you know about the people who attacked us tonight?" He frowned slightly. "Shamus called them demons. It seems to me this isn't the first time you and your security team have encountered their kind."

Elton looked steadily at Artemus. "You're right. It isn't." His gaze grew hooded. "The first time I personally came face to face with those creatures was the day Karl died." He paused, his voice hardening. "They were the ones who killed him."

Artemus's eyes widened. A buzzing sound filled his ears.

"What?" he said hoarsely once he could speak, his pulse racing wildly in his veins. "But—but you said he died of a heart attack!"

The memories of the day Karl LeBlanc had passed from this world flashed through Artemus. With them came an age-old heartache and a wave of regret.

It was Elton's older brother who'd saved Artemus the night he'd been cornered by members of a rival gang in Old Town. Karl LeBlanc had just locked up his antique shop and was making his way to his car when he'd heard the sound of a fight coming from a back alley close by.

Artemus had been sixteen at the time and a brand new member of the North Side's Phoenix Club. He'd been picked up by the gang leader shortly after getting off the

Greyhound from Kansas City, a teenage runaway for less than twenty-four hours.

The decision to flee his home was not one Artemus had taken lightly. He'd even planned for it, taking any jobs he could find over the summer holidays and after school to save money for the big day.

As far as Artemus had been concerned, anything was better than the rundown Kansas City apartment where he'd been living with his mother and her new beau, a man twice as vicious as Artemus's old man and who seemed to delight in tormenting him. Her mother's latest boyfriend was but one of many in a line of men she had attached herself to ever since they left Artemus's father and their hometown when he was in seventh grade.

The night he'd ended up in Chicago with a rucksack on his back and threadbare trainers on his feet, Artemus had had seven hundred dollars in his pocket.

It was only afterward that he'd realized the Phoenix Club's gang leader had had plans to make him the fall boy for one of their schemes all along. Ten days after arriving in Chicago, Artemus had found himself tasked with taking a package to an address in Old Town. He'd not given it a second thought, so grateful had he been to have a place to sleep in the dilapidated apartment building where most of the gang members lived.

The address he'd travelled to had turned out to be a deserted parking lot in the home turf of the Phoenix Club's main rivals, the Chicago Trolls. Unbeknown to him, his belongings and the money he'd worked so hard to save had already been pilfered back at the apartment building.

That day, Artemus was supposed to become the hapless victim serving as a distraction while the Phoenix Club ambushed one of the Trolls' main officers a couple of miles away. The guy had apparently been sleeping with the Phoenix Club leader's girlfriend, an unforgivable sin in the world of street gangs.

Except it hadn't quite worked out like that.

As he stood in the middle of the dead-end alley he'd run into and stared at the six older boys with knives and baseball bats facing him, Artemus's heart had filled with fear and despair. He'd known then that he would die here, in this cold city where the winds always blew. If not tonight, then another night. And he would be alone and unloved when it happened.

That was when he'd heard it. A voice he normally only perceived in his dreams. The same recurring dream he'd had since the night he'd awakened in the field and his life had changed forever. The dream of the girl with the blue eyes and the chocolate hair.

In all the years since he'd first started having the dream, Artemus had never seen her face. Her features always remained blurred, as if someone had painted over them with a water brush. He'd only ever seen her startling eyes and her lustrous locks.

She'd been a child like him when he'd first dreamed of her and had aged alongside him as the years went by, her eyes gaining in maturity and strength. Artemus wasn't sure when he realized he'd fallen in love with her. The feeling was just there one day, as real as the blood flowing through his veins and the sun shining on his face. And it had only grown stronger with time.

Seconds before the first gang member had swung a bat at him that night, Artemus had heard her. For a moment, he'd thought he'd already been struck in the head. But as a drizzle of autumn rain started to fall over the city and soaked into his hair and clothes, he'd realized he was very much awake.

To this day, Artemus didn't remember what had happened in that alley in the seconds that followed. It was Karl LeBlanc who'd told him the details afterward. The man had witnessed it all. He was the one who had taken a shocked and shaken Artemus away from that place, past the unconscious and beaten bodies of the Chicago Trolls' gang members.

All Artemus recalled was the feeling that had swirled inside him in that forgotten time. A feeling unlike anything he'd experienced before or since.

Power. A power so pure, so bright, so frightening in its righteousness, that he was unable to recollect what it had made him do.

It had taken him a while to fathom what the girl from his dreams had said to him that night. When he'd finally grasped its meaning, he'd understood that it had been that word that had saved him, in more ways than one. And deep in the marrow of his mysterious soul, Artemus realized it had been more than just a simple declaration. It had been a key that had unlocked something inside him.

*Rise.*

All this he'd told Karl LeBlanc and eventually Elton when he'd met him a few days later. The younger LeBlanc had initially been highly suspicious of the boy his brother had taken under his wing; Karl had hired Artemus as his assistant and apprentice at the antique shop that had been in their family for almost two centuries. But when Artemus's inherent and unusual talents as a metalsmith had become apparent, Elton had also grown intrigued.

It had been the younger LeBlanc who'd persuaded Karl to allow Artemus to learn how to fight, not just with his bare hands but with all kinds of weapons. And it had been at the end of one of those training sessions, which normally took place in Karl's backyard, that Artemus had made the switchblade transform into a sword. He'd been angry with Elton at the time and frustrated at losing yet another fight against the older man. Before he knew it, he'd dropped the practice sword in the grass, snatched his knife from his boot, and charged at Elton.

They'd both frozen in the next instant and stared at the weapon that had appeared in Artemus's hand. It was exactly as Karl had described seeing it, that night in the alley. In the years that had followed, Artemus had grown more adept at controlling the power that flowed from his body to the switchblade and all the other objects he made in Karl's workshop.

As for the other thing Karl said he'd seen Artemus do that night, he'd been unable to recreate it, however much he'd tried.

Artemus stared at Elton. "Tell me." His voice hardened. "Tell me what really happened to Karl. Tell me everything."

# CHAPTER ELEVEN

ELTON'S HEART TWISTED AT ARTEMUS'S REQUEST AND the agony he could see reflected in the younger man's eyes. The same agony coursing through Elton.

He'd made a promise to his brother six years ago, on the day of his death. He'd promised he wouldn't reveal the truth to his young apprentice. Not unless it became absolutely necessary.

In the time they'd gotten to know Artemus, both brothers had come to cherish the boy. Karl like the son he'd never had, Elton like a recalcitrant nephew whose ears he sometimes wanted to box.

Both men had realized early on in their relationships with the young man that he was meant for something extraordinary. Something beyond their understanding. Something sacred.

And it seemed others had sensed this too.

The world had changed a lot in the last twenty years. Elton no longer recognized it as the one he'd grown up in. This new world was stranger. Darker. Full of mystifying things. Of forces and beings that seemed to originate from both the brightest of man's visions and his most wicked nightmares.

No government or religious official could openly admit that evil existed and walked among ordinary men. That witchcraft and sorcery and black magic were all faces of a single power and entity, one hellbent on mankind's very destruction. Just as they couldn't admit that other forces also prevailed in these strange days. Beings who had awakened at the same time as the darkness now pervading the world. Beings who represented the opposite of evil.

It was sheer coincidence that had brought Elton to the antique shop on the day Karl was killed. He'd been in the area on business and had decided to invite his brother out for an early dinner. He'd entered the building through the front door like he always did and gone through to the workshop at the back, where he knew he would find Karl and Artemus working at the forge. Except Artemus wasn't there that day. Karl had sent him on an errand on the other side of town. Which was fortuitous in many ways.

∼

"WHEN I WENT INTO THE WORKSHOP THAT DAY, THE back door was open," Elton started. "I didn't think anything of it. Karl kept wood and coal stored in the shed in the alley, so I presumed he was out getting some. After a while, I went out to see what was keeping him. That's when I saw them."

Artemus's heart pounded violently in his chest as he watched the older man's mournful expression.

"There were two of them. A man and a woman. They'd cornered Karl against the wall at the end of the alleyway. They were talking to him. Asking him things. By the time

I got to them, the man and the woman had gone. They just leapt onto the wall and...vanished." A shudder ran through Elton. "I saw them up close just for a couple of seconds. Their faces were not human. And they moved as if they were made of shadows."

Artemus's mouth went dry. He swallowed convulsively. "What did they do? What did they do to Karl?"

Elton's eyes darkened. "Nothing that I could see, at first. It wasn't until I loosened his clothes that I saw the mark on his chest. It was a black handprint. It looked like it'd been burned into his skin. But it wasn't there for long. By the time the paramedics got there, it had disappeared." He rubbed a hand over his face. "The official verdict given by the medical examiner was that Karl had suffered a heart attack. But I knew." The older man's voice grew stony. "I knew they'd killed him."

Artemus watched him for a stunned moment as the reality of what had really happened that day sank in.

"Why didn't you tell me?" he said shakily. "Why did you hide the truth from me for all these years?"

Something shifted in Elton's face.

Artemus suddenly didn't want to hear what he would say next. Because in that moment, he grasped the unspoken answer in Elton's gaze.

"It was me, wasn't it?" he said after a moment's silence. "They were looking for me."

A muscle jumped in Elton's cheek. He clenched his jaw and nodded once. A wave of dizziness swept over Artemus. He stared numbly at the drink in his hands.

The man who had been the closest thing to a father he'd ever known had died because of him. A hot feeling filled his chest, making it hard to breathe.

Artemus jumped to his feet and hurled the glass into the fireplace, an animal sound leaving his throat.

Elton stiffened. "Look, I didn't tell you this to make you feel guilty. Hell, neither of us blamed you for what happened that day. Especially not Karl."

Artemus's vision blurred as he looked at his old friend. "You have every right to hold me responsible. I'm the reason they came to the shop. The reason Karl had to die. I'm the *monster* they were after!"

Elton scowled and rose to his feet. "If you ever say those words again, I will slap you to kingdom come! You are *not* a monster. The reason Karl didn't want me to tell you was exactly this. He knew how you'd react. That you'd blame yourself."

He closed the distance between them and pressed his hands down on Artemus's shoulders.

"There are strange forces at work behind everything that has happened," he said after a moment, his voice softening. "Karl always believed that. He was convinced it was Fate that put you in our path. That we were meant to meet. That's why he taught you everything he knew about metalwork. Of the two of us, he'd inherited the talents of our forefathers the most." Elton smiled gently. "I also believe that's why I was compelled to teach you how to fight. I think we both knew you would need those skills one day." A determined expression dawned on his face. "Do you remember what Karl was working on in the months before his death?"

Artemus swallowed the lump in his throat. "You mean his secret project? The one he wouldn't show me?"

Elton nodded. "It's time I gave it to you."

Artemus watched, puzzled, as the older man turned and walked over to one of the bookcases lining the walls of the study. He reached for a late nineteenth century copy of the Bible, tilted the spine toward him, and stepped back.

Artemus gaped when the bookcase moved inward three feet before pivoting on its axis. A room appeared beyond it. Elton headed inside.

Artemus followed and stopped dead in his tracks in the middle of the hidden chamber. "What the—?"

Weapons crowded the stone walls and display cabinets around him. There were revolvers, semi-automatic pistols, machine guns, knives, swords, shields, maces, hammers, axes, even bows and arrows. Beneath them were recessed drawers labeled with different types of ammunition.

Elton ignored the deadly arsenal and made for a safe in the back wall. He stared into the retinal scanner, pressed his right hand against the biometric panel, and keyed a code into the digital screen that emerged from the metal door. The vault opened with a pneumatic hiss.

Elton removed a polished walnut box from inside, closed the safe, and took it over to a table. He flicked the latches holding the lid closed and lifted it.

Artemus joined him and stared at the weapon sitting inside the black, velvet-lined, French-fitted interior. It was a stainless-steel gun, unlike any he'd seen before.

The slide was long, with the barrel protruding slightly beyond it to accommodate a suppressor. He could tell without touching the weapon that Karl had blended other metals and alloys into the steel. Mounted on the frame were textured ebony grips. Words had been engraved into them. They were written in a language Artemus had never seen before but instinctively felt he knew.

"Take it," Elton said. "It's yours."

Artemus reluctantly dragged his gaze from the gun. "Why did Karl make this?"

"He told me you would need it one day," Elton replied.

Artemus hesitated before reaching for the weapon. Goosebumps broke out across his skin when his fingers made contact with the metal. With it came a wave of sadness.

He could feel Karl's touch in the gun.

Artemus lifted the weapon lovingly from the case and smoothed his hand over it. It was well balanced and fitted his grip as if it belonged there.

"I had the runes looked at by paleography and linguistic experts some time after Karl's death," Elton said. "Their best guess was that it was written in a tongue similar to Enochian."

Artemus raised an eyebrow as he ran his index finger over the inscriptions. "The heavily disputed holy language named after Enoch, Noah's great grandfather?"

"The very one," Elton murmured.

Artemus's flesh tingled at the power he could feel thrumming through the engravings. "They aren't wrong. It's a blessing. A prayer, you might say." He grimaced. "Or a curse, in another context."

Elton stared at him for a moment before heaving a sigh. "I'm not even gonna ask how you know that."

Artemus frowned slightly. "There's something I don't understand. If those creatures were looking for me on the day Karl died, why haven't I seen them since?"

Elton rubbed his chin. "I'm afraid I don't know the answer to that."

Artemus ejected the gun's magazine from the expanded well and inspected the cartridges. "These the same silver-leaded ones you used in your gun tonight?"

"Yes," Elton said. "We modeled ours on the cartridges Karl made for your weapon."

Artemus pulled a face. "And they're really impregnated with Holy Water?"

"Yes." Elton hesitated. "It comes all the way from the Vatican."

Artemus froze. "What?!"

# CHAPTER TWELVE

DRAKE WOKE UP WITH A JOLT. HE BLINKED AND SHOOK his head. Ice-cold water sprayed out from his hair and face and dripped onto his sodden clothes.

He was sitting with his arms and legs strapped to a metal chair inside a gloomy warehouse. He scanned the space before studying the figure standing opposite him.

The woman put the empty pail down, placed her hands on her hips, and cocked her head to the side. "Evening, asshole."

She was beautiful, in a cold, clinical way. Like a pretty snake. Drake's eyes drifted over her feminine curves and athletic build.

*Or a deadly praying mantis.*

"Do I know you?" he said.

Fury flashed in the brunette's pale eyes. She regained her composure and smiled at him grimly.

"Don't worry," she said in a steely voice. "By the time morning comes, you'll know our names intimately."

Shadows shifted to Drake's right. The giant who'd hit him at the park came into view. The man was tall and built like a tank. He had the same eyes as the woman. Cold. Detached. Lifeless.

Drake grimaced. "I don't want to rain on whatever parade you've got going on here, but I'm not into threesomes."

A bark of derisive laughter escaped the woman. "You think you're funny, don't you?"

Drake shrugged and subtly tested the ropes holding him prisoner. "My friends tell me I'm a regular riot."

They'd taken his knife and his custom-designed Kimber Aegis. He could see the weapons on a table twenty feet to his left. But they hadn't taken his watch.

Drake suppressed a bleak smile. *Big mistake.*

He looked past his captors to the faint outline of the SUV at the other end of the building. The Kawasaki and his BMW were parked in the shadows next to it. His gaze shifted to the metal roller tube in the giant's left hand.

"Since you have the cane, I'm not quite sure what you want with me," Drake said in a light tone.

"Oh, there's plenty I want with you," the woman said, "but our client wished to take a look at you first. It's the only reason you're still alive right now."

Drake's pulse jumped at her words. He didn't like the sound of that.

"Not that I wouldn't fancy a little roll in the hay right now, but I'm afraid you're not my type," he said.

The punch came out of nowhere.

Drake's ears rang as his head snapped violently sideways. For a moment, he thought the giant had hit him again. He blinked and realized the man was still where he'd last seen him.

The woman stood before Drake, her chest heaving and

her pale eyes blazing with hate. She slowly lowered her fist to her side.

That was when he remembered.

"Sarajevo," he whispered. "The mercenaries."

The heist was meant to have been a straightforward job. Drake had taken on the contract knowing that stealing the precious artworks of the former Bosnian banker his client had targeted would be an uncomplicated operation. All he had to do was scope out one of the removal men who'd been vetted by the banker's insurance company, temporarily incapacitate the guy on the day the target was moving house, and take his place. Except he hadn't accounted for the soldiers of fortune the banker had hired as his security two days before the planned robbery.

He didn't know to this day what had given him away. He'd managed to grab the goods and escape from the grounds with minor flesh wounds. Things had gone downhill rapidly when he was making his getaway into the city. In the chaotic chase that followed, one of his pursuers had crashed into a gas tanker. The resulting explosion had wiped out three vehicles and damaged the facade of several houses and shops.

There had been two casualties in that accident. The driver of the tanker and the man behind the wheel of the SUV that had crashed into it.

A muscle twitched in the woman's cheek. "So, you do remember."

Drake carefully wriggled his jaw from side to side. The coppery taste of blood struck his tongue from his split lip.

*She packs quite a punch.*

He appraised his opponents with fresh eyes. "What are you?"

The pair exchanged a glance. Though they tried to mask it, Drake read surprise in their eyes.

*I was right.*

He knew they weren't human. He'd sensed something odd when the giant had hit him in the park. He was certain of it now that the woman had touched him too.

There was also the fact they were incredibly strong and fast.

A frown wrinkled Drake's brow. *But I don't know what they are.*

He watched them for a silent moment. "So, is this retaliation for what happened two years ago?" He arched an eyebrow. "Are you avenging your fallen comrade?"

The woman's hand shot out so fast Drake nearly missed it. She grabbed the front of his shirt and hauled him toward her. His eyes widened as he found himself lifted into the air, the chair tilting forward on its front legs until it barely touched the floor.

"He was more than a comrade, you bastard!" she hissed inches from his face. "He was our brother!"

Drake's heart sank. *Ah, shit. I hate it when things get personal.*

He glanced down at the woman's fisted knuckles where she gripped his shirt, half choking him. "I've changed my mind. I like a dominant partner in the bedroom." He grinned when she blinked at him. "Also, I gotta admit, that lace bra is a turn on."

She glanced down at the gap in her cleavage, swore, and let go of him. The chair clattered back onto the ground. Drake braced himself when she drew back her arm to strike him again.

"That's enough, Serena."

Drake stared.

The giant had crossed the distance to the woman in a heartbeat and stood holding her wrist in an iron grip.

"Let me go, Nate," she said between gritted teeth.

Her biceps bunched as she struggled in the giant's hold.

"Hitting him won't bring Ben back," the giant said in a passionless voice.

The woman glared at her companion. She resisted him for another couple of seconds.

Drake knew the move was futile. Though they were both inhumanly powerful, the giant was the stronger of the two. The woman's shoulders sagged a moment later. The giant slowly released her arm.

A low rumble of engines sounded outside. Drake tensed.

A humorless smile curved the woman's lips. "Sounds like our client has finally arrived."

The engines died. The faint sounds of car doors opening and closing followed. Hinges creaked and metal rattled as someone slid the warehouse door open. Footsteps drew close.

Drake's skin prickled. The hairs rose on the back of his neck.

His suspicions had been correct. He'd have had to be dead to miss the energy he'd sensed in the last couple of minutes.

*Fuck.*

Figures appeared in the gloom. Drake slowly fisted his hands and watched the group of demons cross the floor toward them.

# CHAPTER THIRTEEN

"AGENTS OF THE VATICAN?" ARTEMUS REPEATED DULLY.

"Yes." Elton said, watching the younger man's incredulous expression.

He sighed and glanced at Shamus and Isabelle. The two security guards had joined them in the study.

Artemus leaned a hip against Elton's desk. "All of you?"

"Uh-huh," Isabelle said with a nod, her expression serious.

Artemus stared at them incredulously. "So, what, you're saying you're all— *priests?*" He pointed at Isabelle. "She's sleeping with Mark." He indicated Shamus. "He gambles every Friday night." He narrowed his eyes at Elton. "And I know you've got a thing going with the widow who lives down the road."

"Hey, how'd you know about me and Mark?" Isabelle said with an indignant scowl.

"You doing the widow?" Shamus asked Elton bluntly.

Elton muttered something rude under his breath. "No, I am not 'doing' the widow. Christ, at least give me some credit for being a gentleman."

Artemus gasped. "You just took Jesus's name in vain!" He pointed an accusing finger at Elton. "That's blasphemy!"

The beginning of a headache throbbed between Elton's temples. "We are not priests." He frowned at his head of security. "And really, Shamus? Gambling?"

The former boxer shrugged. "It's for work. I've got contacts in that place."

Elton ran a hand down his face. It was gone two a.m. and he could feel fatigue seeping into his bones. He masked a grimace.

*Well, it's not as if I'm getting any younger.*

He turned to Artemus. "After Karl's death, I started looking into anything I could find about the people I'd seen in the alley that day. Not the man and the woman specifically, but their...kind. My investigations led me all over the country and across the Atlantic to Europe. It seemed I wasn't the only one who'd uncovered the monsters living among us and witnessed what they could do." He looked at Shamus and Isabelle and saw the old hurt reflected in their eyes. "All of us have lost someone to those people."

Artemus blinked. "You mean—?"

Elton nodded. "Yes. My entire security team has encountered these creatures at one time or another. We were all looking for answers. And we found them. In Rome."

He still recalled the shock that had resonated through him when he was first told about the secret task force set up by the Church over a decade ago by the archbishop he'd arranged to meet in Vatican City. And it wasn't just the Catholic Church involved in the global organization now spanning over one hundred countries. Other religious bodies, governments, and private enterprises were too.

Their mission was simple: to identify the nature and objectives of the inhuman creatures who now dwelled amongst mankind and to fight them.

"The auction house is a front," Elton said presently. "It allows us to raise funds for the organization as well as uncover clues as to these monsters' whereabouts and motives."

Artemus watched Elton for a moment. "Like the cursed objects?"

"We have the Vatican's scientists studying those, as well as private labs invested in our cause. We hope they'll help us figure out how to detect them."

"The demons?" Artemus said.

Elton nodded tiredly. "Yes."

Artemus pursed his lips and studied them thoughtfully. He finally sighed and ran a hand through his hair. "Well, it looks like today is your lucky day."

Elton stared. "What do you mean?"

"I can sense them," Artemus said. He grimaced. "Your demons."

Elton stiffened. "What?"

"They have an aura." Artemus waved a hand vaguely above his head. "Like a black cloud crowning their bodies."

Elton glanced at Shamus and Isabelle and saw his shock reflected in their eyes.

"You can see their dark powers?" Shamus said in a quiet voice.

"Yeah," Artemus admitted ruefully. "I've been able to detect, well, people's energies, I guess, since I was a child. I didn't know what it was at first. Once I realized what I was seeing, all I had to do was concentrate and I could tell if someone was evil or good."

Elton gazed blindly at Artemus. *Did Karl know?*

"Is that how you're able to tell the true age and origin of the antiques and objects you examine? And—make the things that you make?"

Isabelle glanced from Elton to Artemus, puzzled. "What things?"

Artemus ignored her question and looked steadily at Elton. "I think it's all linked, yes."

The staggering revelation was still echoing through Elton when the study door burst open.

Callie Stone marched in, the rabbit at her side. She'd changed into black jeans, a cream blouse, and red heels. She stopped in the middle of the room and glared at them.

"It's rude to make a lady wait!" she snapped.

"I'm sorry. There were some urgent matters we had to attend to—" Elton started.

"Yeah, yeah," Callie interrupted with a dismissive wave. "Magical gun. Agents of the Vatican. International organization. Demons and shit." She looked at Artemus. "We gotta go, Blue Eyes. It's close."

Elton opened and closed his mouth soundlessly. "How the devil—?"

"The rabbit told her." Artemus was staring at the bunny. "You little spy." He narrowed his eyes. "And by the way, I thought I distinctly heard you say you 'had this' earlier, in the ballroom. You had diddly squat, is what you had."

The rabbit rubbed his muzzle with his paws and assumed an innocent air.

"What the hell is going on?" Isabelle said. "Why is he talking to the fluffball? And how does *she* know this stuff?"

She glared at Callie before looking around the study suspiciously. "Hey, Elton, maybe we should check the place for bugs—"

"You won't find any," Artemus said briskly. He pulled his new gun from where he'd tucked it against the small of his back and checked the magazine again. "You got more ammo for this?"

Elton nodded numbly. "Yeah. There are drawers full in the chamber as well as crates of the stuff in the basement."

"Good. Get as much as you can carry," Artemus said in a hard voice. He looked at Callie. "How far?"

"About five miles, I think. I'll get a better idea when we're on the move."

Elton stared between the two of them. "What are you talking about?"

"The cane, Elton," Artemus replied. "Callie can feel it. We need to get it back."

Elton rose to his feet as Artemus followed Callie and the rabbit to the door.

Callie slowed before they reached the threshold. "By the way, he needs a name."

She glanced from Artemus to the rabbit crouched between them.

Artemus stopped and frowned. "He told you that?"

Callie nodded.

Artemus hesitated and scratched his cheek. "Well, I guess Smokey is as good a name as any."

"Oh." Callie raised her eyebrows. "Because of his color?"

"Nope." Artemus sighed. "It's the name of the pet rabbit I got for my sixth birthday." He cocked a thumb at the bunny. "The one *he* ate the night I met him."

Callie sucked air between her teeth. "Well, if it's any consolation, he didn't mean to. It was instinct."

Artemus scowled. "I know that now. And why the hell is he spilling his guts to you? He's barely said two words to me."

Callie's brow furrowed. "Because we're kinda the same, I guess? Although I get the feeling he's not telling me everything." She shrugged. "By the way, he says the rabbit still lives inside him."

They exited the room and headed down the corridor.

"Oh yeah?" Artemus said, his voice growing fainter.

"As do the souls of everyone and everything he's ever, well, eaten," Callie said.

"That's gross," Artemus said. "So, does the original Smokey, you know, think about me?"

"Nope," Callie reported after a pause. "All it does is dream about humping, apparently."

"Uber gross. By the way, where's the leash I made for him?"

"He ate it."

"Why, that little—"

"What do we do, boss?" Shamus said as silence descended inside the study.

Elton looked at the two security guards. He didn't understand how or why Callie Stone knew the things that she knew or, indeed, why Artemus seemed to trust her. And he didn't know what bond it was that linked them to the creature disguised as Artemus's dead pet, or even why they were all convinced that the cane was important enough an object to be retrieved at any cost. But one thing he was confident of. The three of them could detect their enemy in ways he and his agents couldn't.

"We go with them," he replied.

# CHAPTER FOURTEEN

"MISS BLAKE, MR. CONWAY. IT'S A PLEASURE TO SEE YOU again. And so soon too," Erik Park said suavely, strolling toward Serena and Nate. "I wasn't expecting your call until later tonight." His gaze shifted to the man bound to the chair beside them. "Is this the thief?"

Serena narrowed her eyes slightly as she studied the Asian man's entourage. There were fifteen of them, men and women dressed in dark suits. A few she recognized as the bodyguards she'd seen with the businessman two days ago, when they'd met him at a hotel in New York to take on the job to steal the cane. The rest she'd never seen.

*Why so many? It's only one guy.*

Serena glanced at Drake Hunter before sharing a guarded look with Nate. She could tell he also found the size of their client's escort puzzling.

"Is that the cane?" Park asked.

He indicated the roller tube in Nate's hand.

"It is," Serena replied coolly.

One of Park's men took the receptacle from Nate.

Park smiled and headed over to Drake. He stopped a

foot in front of him and cocked his head to the side. "And what do we have here?"

Sweat beaded Drake's forehead and upper lip. He was gritting his teeth, as if he were in pain. Serena frowned.

*What the hell is wrong with him?*

A thoughtful look came over Park's face. He placed a crooked finger under Drake's chin and tilted his head up.

"You are...interesting," he murmured, staring into the bound man's dark eyes. "I would love to study you in more detail but, alas, time is not on our side." A chuckle left his lips. "You know how it is. Places to go. People to kill." He let go of Drake. "Speaking of killing."

The hairs lifted on Serena's arms and the back of her neck. A strange undercurrent was filling the air inside the warehouse. She stiffened.

Something was happening to Park's companions. Shudders started racing through them from head to toe, as if they were convulsing.

Serena stared.

The men and women's limbs twitched and lengthened, their fingers and toes extending until they resembled talons. Their faces changed next, features morphing into hideous masks that seemed to float just above their skin.

But it was their eyes that sent a shiver of unease bolting down Serena's spine. They had gone midnight black from edge to edge, with amber pupils glowing in the center.

*What the hell?*

"I am truly grateful to the two of you for doing such a great job securing the cane, but I'm afraid we can't leave any witnesses," Park said, wearing a jovial expression. "No hard feelings."

Serena scowled. *Backstabbing bastard!*

Drake grunted next to her. He was scowling and biting his lip hard enough to draw blood.

DRAKE COULD FEEL IT RISING. THE DARKNESS THAT dwelled inside him. The darkness that mirrored the sickening energy he could feel emanating from the demons in the warehouse.

It was an evil that he'd spent most of his life suppressing.

His skin quivered and his knuckles whitened where he'd fisted his hands on the armrests of the chair.

The feeling was stronger than back at the auction house. Now that they were close to him, the demons' foul auras seemed to be resonating with his own power and dragging it out from the depths of his soul.

He felt it flood his blood, a potent, decadent, wicked force. A force that had awakened inside him the night he turned into a monster. One he loathed with every fiber of his being.

That was when he heard the voice of the demon.

The marks on Drake's back trembled as heat suffused his body. He clenched his jaw and crunched his eyes closed.

*No. I won't. I will NOT give in to you!*

He threw his head back, opened his eyes, and glared at the distant ceiling. *"Get out of my head!"*

THE ROPES BINDING DRAKE SNAPPED AS HIS SHOUT echoed to the rafters. He bolted out of the chair, his pupils flashing with an unholy red light for a second.

Serena's pulse jumped. She took a step toward him. Motion flashed at the edge of her vision.

She twisted, raised her right hand, and blocked the fist sailing toward her head. The blow sent her skidding a foot backward across the floor before she dug her heels in and held her position.

Park's bodyguard halted in his tracks, a curious expression on his grotesque face. Serena could tell he was puzzled by the fact she'd deflected his inhumanly powerful strike. He swung his other hand at her, the movement so fast his fist practically blurred.

Serena stopped his attack an inch from her face. She stared at the black claws grazing the back of her left hand, looked into her attacker's ghastly eyes, and kneed him viciously in the groin. He grunted and sagged.

*Well, at least that part is still human.*

She punched him in the throat and reached for her guns while he dropped to his knees, a choked sound gurgling past his lips. Her bullets slammed into the chests of two other creatures lunging toward her at superhuman speed. To her right, Nate fired at the monsters springing at him.

Surprise jolted through Serena. Their shots barely slowed the monsters down.

"Aim for their heads!" she shouted at Nate as she backed away toward the rear of the warehouse.

A flash of light drew her attention to the left, where Drake stood fighting the rest of the creatures. She blinked.

The watch on his wrist glittered as he weaved and bobbed amidst a flurry of talons, his fists connecting with faces and bodies, his movements matching the attackers' speed. The shape of the timepiece changed, extending and widening until it formed a shield that protected his entire arm. He brought it up in time to repel two powerful blows.

Metal clattered ten feet to Drake's left. The knife Serena had stripped him of trembled and rose from the surface of the table before hurtling through the air toward him. His right hand closed around the handle just as the blade transformed, lengthening and broadening into a sword in the blink of an eye.

Though the whole thing lasted only a handful of seconds, the distraction cost Serena her weapons. A gasp left her lips when a fist connected powerfully with her solar plexus. Her guns were knocked violently out of her grip.

Something sharp sliced across the back of her left hand. Blood bloomed on Serena's skin where one of her attackers had torn through her flesh with a wicked talon.

The woman's lips peeled back in a hideous smile. She brought the claw to her mouth and licked the scarlet drops coating the dull, black surface with a forked tongue. A guttural purr left her throat.

Serena twisted on one heel and roundhouse-kicked her in the gut. The woman grunted and went flying into a concrete pillar fifteen feet away.

Serena saw more claws heading for her face. She dropped to the floor and swept her attacker's feet out from under him with a spinning sweep-kick. He thudded onto his back and would have risen again had she not grabbed his throat in an iron grip. He hissed when she climbed to her feet and lifted him bodily into the air with one hand, his legs kicking and thrashing as he fought her hold. Crimson lines formed on Serena's skin where he clawed at her arm.

His gaze dropped to the wounds on her limb. His eerie eyes widened.

Serena smiled grimly as her flesh healed, tissues knitting together seamlessly.

*You're not the only monsters in the room.*

# CHAPTER FIFTEEN

DRAKE SWUNG HIS BLADE AND SLASHED ONE OF THE demons through the gut. He deflected a lethal blow to his neck with his shield, drove his knee into his attacker's thigh, and thrust the sword into the man's heart as he sagged.

Wicked claws raked Drake's right flank. He cursed, elbowed the female demon in the face, and dropped into a crouch with the shield above his head a second before a storm of fists rained down upon him.

Something went flying through the air to his right. He caught a glimpse of a female demon smashing into a concrete post and glanced at Serena Blake where she fought the creature attacking her. His eyes widened when he saw the jagged lacerations on her arm mend themselves seconds after the man she'd hoisted into the air sliced into her flesh.

*That's interesting.*

Fifteen feet to Serena's right, Nate Conway sucker-punched three demons in rapid succession, his fists connecting with their bodies with so much force his knuckles left imprints in their flesh.

Drake clenched his teeth as he watched the creatures they had brought down get back to their feet. The shield vibrated against his arm, the demons surrounding him pummeling the metal with supernatural force and driving him closer to the ground.

*It's not enough. We need more power.* He closed his eyes. *Damn it!*

Even though he hated the idea, he knew what he had to do. He took a deep breath and was about to lift the lid on the darkness churning and straining against the barriers he'd erected to contain his unnatural soul when the warehouse door opened and all hell broke loose.

ARTEMUS STORMED INSIDE THE SHADOWY DEPOT AT THE head of Elton's agents, saw the demon leap toward them, and raised his gun. The bullet sang out of the muzzle.

It caught the creature in the chest and punched a four-inch hole into its flesh.

The demon jerked as if he'd hit a concrete wall. He crumpled to the ground. A spiderweb of fiery cracks erupted from his wound. They spread across his entire body in a flash, turning him into glowing, human-shaped parchment. He arched his back and let out an unholy screech a second before he was consumed by a burst of bright flames and turned into a cloud of ash.

Artemus blinked and watched the creature's remains flutter gently to the floor. His gaze moved to the weapon in his hand.

He could have sworn he'd felt the inscriptions glow warmly against his skin when he'd pulled the trigger.

"Whoa," he said, his pulse thrumming. "I *like* this gun."

Elton and Shamus stopped beside him and stared at what was left of the demon.

"What just happened?" Shamus said.

"I have no idea," Elton muttered.

"Here they come," Callie warned.

Spectral shapes abandoned the battle taking place at the back of the warehouse and bounded across the floor toward them. Artemus looked past the amber-eyed creatures to where two men and a woman were engaged in a brutal fight with four demons.

His gaze met that of a figure holding a sword and a shield.

Artemus inhaled sharply when the strange resonance he'd experienced inside the ballroom reverberated through him once more.

It was the guy who'd stolen the cane from the auction house.

Smokey let out a low growl where he crouched next to Artemus. Shivers raced across his fur. He doubled then trebled in size as he bolted across the warehouse and flashed under the demons charging at them.

Artemus's fingers tightened around the knife in his left hand. He released the sword hidden within it, fired at the demon leaping toward Elton, and raised the blade.

It impaled the creature dropping down on top of him.

A foul-smelling black fluid oozed down the sword onto Artemus's hand before dripping onto his head.

Callie grimaced. "Yuck."

Her hair swelled around her face and her features shifted, giving her a leonine appearance, a second before a demon attacked her. She thrust her right hand out, grabbed the woman by the face, twisted on her heels, and hurled her as if she were throwing a javelin.

A faint shriek accompanied the female demon's hapless passage through the air. Isabelle jumped out of the way as the creature sailed past her before crashing into a BMW superbike.

She turned and scowled at Callie. "Hey, watch where you throw those things!"

Callie grimaced. "Sorry."

Mark walked up to the female demon and shot her point blank in the forehead.

By the time they'd dealt with the monsters who'd attacked them, Smokey had helped the two men and the woman at the back of the warehouse dispose of the remaining creatures.

Artemus came to a stop a few feet from the trio, heart pounding and chest heaving from the fight. He scanned the faces of the giant man and the woman, puzzled briefly by what he sensed from them, and focused on the dark eyes boring into him.

"Where's the cane?" he asked the man holding the sword and shield.

The thief glanced at his companions. "They took it."

The sword in the man's right hand shifted and transformed into a knife as plain looking as his own switchblade. Artemus blinked. The shield similarly morphed in the next instant, folding in on itself until it wrapped around the thief's left wrist and took on the appearance of a simple, leather watch.

Artemus's mouth went dry at the energy he could feel emanating from the two concealed weapons. They were similar to his knife in many ways, yet darker and more twisted at the same time.

He felt Elton's eyes on him.

"Is it magic?" Isabelle hissed to Shamus. "It's magic, right?"

The thief's dark eyes widened when Artemus's own sword resumed its original form.

"There are two of those things?" the woman next to the giant muttered.

Artemus frowned at the pair. "Are you with him?"

He tilted his head toward the thief.

The woman looked at Artemus as if he'd suggested she perform a sexual act in public. "What, this asshole?" She glanced at the thief. "Hell no!"

The thief sighed. "I really wish you would stop calling me names. 'Specially since I just saved your ass."

The woman scowled. "Oh yeah? Well, we didn't need your help. We could have finished them off on our own!"

"To be fair, he's right," the giant mumbled. "And the bunny helped too."

Callie took a step toward the large man. Her face and hair had returned to their normal appearance. "Where's the cane? He said you guys took it, but I can't feel it anymore."

Unease blossomed inside Artemus at Callie's strained voice.

"That's because it's not here," the woman replied. "Park took it and left while his people were attacking us. And what do you mean 'feel' it?"

Callie paled. "Park? Who is that?"

The woman shrugged. "The asshole who hired us to steal the cane." She glared at the dark-eyed thief. "Except *he* got to it first."

The man shrugged. "Hey, all's fair in robbery and misappropriation."

# CHAPTER SIXTEEN

"Who's your client?"

Drake studied the man who'd spoken.

Elton LeBlanc's eyes glittered coolly as he frowned at him from where he sat with his arms folded across his chest at the head of the kitchen table.

"I can't tell you that," Drake said lightly. "It would set a bad precedent. No one is gonna want to hire me if word spreads that I squeal like a little girl every time a job goes wrong."

"He's right," Nate muttered. He sat petting the rabbit on Drake's right. "Reputation is everything in this business."

Drake's gaze shifted briefly to the creature on the giant's lap. The bunny had resumed his benign disguise and seemed to be enjoying the attention, his limpid eyes half-closed and low purrs rumbling out of his chest.

Drake wasn't fooled for one second. The rabbit was a terrifying, powerful being. He'd seen what he could do up close when he'd come to his rescue back at the warehouse.

A faint frown marred Drake's brow. *Why did he do that?*

Serena drummed her fingers on the table where she sat next to Nate and let out an irritated sigh. "His client is Hugo Voggell."

"Voggell?" Elton jumped to his feet and leaned his hands on the table, a scowl darkening his face. "Why, that little weasel!"

Drake narrowed his eyes at Serena. "How the hell did you—?"

She smirked. "How do you think Park found out about the auction tonight?"

Elton started pacing the hardwood floor. "I thought Voggell was into Renaissance art these days. What the hell does he want with the cane?"

"Word on the street is some people want that piece real bad," Serena said. "That in itself was enough to generate considerable interest from the collectors who deal in the black market on all things rare and collectible." She hesitated. "I believe Erik Park was a representative of the main party interested in securing the cane."

Elton stopped and turned to her, his eyes filling with an intense light. "Do you know their name?"

Serena shook her head. "No."

A frustrated grimace twisted Elton's face. "Damn it." He sighed and ran a hand through his hair before assessing Serena with a brooding expression. "Did you know they were...demons?"

She raised an eyebrow. "Is that what you call them?"

"Yes."

Drake masked a frown. It was becoming clear to him that tonight's incidents at the auction house and the warehouse weren't the first encounters LeBlanc and his people had had with these creatures.

*What else do they know about them?*

"Interesting," Serena murmured. "No, we had no idea. We only met Park two days ago. And tonight's the first time we've ever seen those...things."

Elton narrowed his eyes. "Where did you meet Park?"

Serena exchanged a guarded glance with Nate.

The giant shrugged. "Our client broke our agreement when he tried to kill us. I think it's safe to divulge that information."

Serena pursed her lips and hesitated for a second before murmuring, "New York."

Elton had opened his mouth, likely to ask yet another question, when voices rose from the corridor outside the kitchen. Artemus Steele walked in, Callie Stone trailing behind him.

Drake tensed slightly. The connection he'd felt earlier that night with Steele back at the auction house, and more recently in the warehouse, still echoed within him. If anything, it was growing stronger the more time he spent in the man's company. He wasn't sure whether this was a good thing or a bad thing. There was only one thing he was certain of.

He'd never felt anything like it before.

"You sure you can't pick up on its energy signature?" Artemus said as he rubbed his hair briskly with a towel.

He'd showered and changed out of his bloodied clothes.

"No," Callie murmured, chewing her lower lip.

They stopped when they registered the people gathered in the room.

Artemus turned to Elton. "Why are we at my place again? You know I hate having people in my personal space." He glanced at Drake, Serena, and Nate. "Especially when they're not invited."

"Because the auction house will be buzzing with cops soon and this conversation needs to be private," Elton replied without a single trace of remorse. "Besides, may I remind you that this manor is as much mine as yours? It's only been in my family for ten generations."

Drake glanced at the dark wooden units, richly textured, aged wallpaper, and crown-molded ceiling of the kitchen around them.

Artemus Steele lived in a sprawling Gothic mansion sitting on a low hill inside walled grounds, some two miles west of Old Town and Lincoln Park. A private cemetery made up a third of the eight-acre estate. The rest was taken up by woodland that hid the property from curious onlookers.

The house itself was set over three floors and topped by steeply pitched gables with spires and decorative, wooden trimmings, brick chimneys, dormers, and even a tower with crenellated parapets. Tall, leaded-glass windows lined the irregular facade of the property and framed the south and east-facing porches with their slender posts and eldritch, cast-iron lanterns.

As if the location and exterior of the property weren't creepy enough, the inside would have made a perfect setting for some low-budget horror film. The place was a veritable maze of asymmetric rooms and passages covered in dark wood paneling and Victorian wallpaper. An eclectic collection of antiques and furnishings crowded the polished hardwood and checkerboard marble floors. Several of the tapestries and paintings looked like they belonged in a museum, while some of the larger pieces of furniture appeared reclaimed. They had been lovingly restored to their former glory with an attention to detail that spoke of hours of arduous labor.

"Why couldn't we have gone to your townhouse?" Artemus continued belligerently.

Elton sighed. "Because it's close to the auction house. And we would have had to drive past here to get there."

A bell rang somewhere inside the property. A thread of tension danced down Drake's spine at the sound. He sensed the same sudden edginess in Serena and Nate's bearings.

"Who the hell is visiting at this time?" Artemus headed over to an old-fashioned, black rotary-dial phone fixed to the wall next to the door, and lifted the handle. "Hello?"

Drake's pulse jumped when the blond man grew still and cursed.

"What the—? *Did someone order pizza?!*"

Artemus held the phone away from his ear and glowered at them.

"I did! I'll go get it!" Isabelle called out from another part of the house. "And really, Artemus? Briefs? I would have put you down as a boxer shorts kinda guy myself."

Serena arched her eyebrows. Drake swallowed an involuntary smile.

A vein throbbed in Artemus's temple. "Mark, kindly ask your woman to stop rifling through my underwear drawer!"

"You wish she was rifling through your underwear drawer," Mark scoffed in the distance. "Wait up, Belle. I'll go down to the gates with you."

Artemus looked at the ceiling. "God, give me strength. Callie, will you stop looking at my junk?"

Callie grinned and lifted her gaze from Artemus's groin.

# CHAPTER SEVENTEEN

"AGENTS OF THE VATICAN?" SERENA TOOK A SIP OF HER soda and arched an eyebrow. "So, you're saying you guys are priests?"

"No," Elton replied. "Most of us are regular citizens who've crossed paths with these demons at some time or another in our lives. We're part of the international task force scouring them out. Our organization discovered a while back that certain antiques and rare collectibles bear their—well, mark, you could say. The auction house is a perfect front allowing us to identify these items and find out more about these creatures."

It was four in the morning and the remains of their late-night meal lay scattered across the kitchen table.

Serena was surprised to find herself gradually relaxing in the company of the motley crew of individuals gathered in the room. Though she and Nate could have escaped from the warehouse after the battle with Park's people, they had elected to follow Elton LeBlanc's orders to accompany him and Artemus Steele to the mansion. So had Drake Hunter.

Serena didn't know what the thief's motive was in coming here but she suspected it mirrored her own. She was after information.

"And these creatures look like regular people?" she said. "Until they...don't?"

Elton nodded. "The first official sighting of a being that the Church would later go on to categorize as possessed by demonic forces took place in March 2018, outside the Cathedral of Saint John the Baptist, in Turin. It was a woman named Sofia Delcattori. She was a local primary school teacher and, according to the Vatican's investigation following her death, a deeply devout Catholic." Lines marred his brow. "She transformed in the middle of her niece's baptism. By the time a member of the public heard the screams coming from the church and raised the alarm, all thirty members of her family, their guests, and the priest and clergymen officiating the ceremony had been slaughtered."

"That's terrible," Callie murmured, her face pale.

"What happened to her?" Drake said.

"The police tracked Delcattori to a cemetery half a mile away," Elton replied. "It took an hour and twenty bullets to bring her down. The Vatican believes it was the armor-piercing rounds that finally killed her."

Artemus frowned. "Did her autopsy reveal anything?"

"No." Elton sighed. "They always go back to their human forms when they die. There's never anything in their bodies that hints at what they've become and, hence, no way to detect them." He looked pointedly at Artemus and Callie before glancing at the rabbit crunching on chicken bones in the corner of the kitchen. "Or there wasn't until tonight."

Surprise jolted through Serena. She stared at Artemus and Callie. "You guys can see what they are?"

Artemus hesitated before nodding.

"Yes," Callie murmured.

Artemus studied Drake steadily. "He can too."

Elton startled. "What?"

Everyone stared at Drake.

"You've seen his sword and shield," Artemus told Elton, his gaze still on the dark-haired thief. "They're similar weapons to my switchblade. He should be able to sense their auras."

Serena recalled Drake's expression when Park and his people had entered the warehouse. "Steele is right." Her gaze collided with Drake's cold stare. "This wasn't the first time you've encountered their kind. You looked pissed as hell when you saw Park and his entourage tonight."

Drake's mouth drew into a thin line. "So what if I can make out what they are? I want nothing to do with those people."

"I'm afraid it's too late for that," Artemus said. "Because all of us just landed dead center on their radar. What happened tonight was just the opening salvo. Trust me, this—whatever it is—it isn't over yet."

"Artemus is correct," Elton said. "This is the first time we have ever successfully engaged and defeated such a large group of these creatures. Their interest will no doubt be piqued."

"If the cane was what they were after and they now have it in their possession, why would they bother coming after us?" Nate said. "For revenge?"

Elton shared a guarded glance with Artemus before looking at the rest of them. "No. It's because they would have recognized we now have a way to find them and kill them."

Drake blinked. "I'm sorry, are you talking about me?"

Elton dipped his chin before staring pointedly at Serena and Nate. "And you too."

"Not interested," Serena said stonily. "We're only here because we want to know what we're dealing with."

"We've seen you fight," Artemus said. "You can take them on with your bare hands. We could use your skills."

Serena felt Drake's eyes on her.

"What's in it for us?" she said.

"I won't tell them what you are," came the quiet reply.

Serena stiffened. Nate tensed beside her.

She rose to her feet and glared at Artemus. "What do you mean by that?"

Artemus glanced at Elton. "I won't reveal your true nature to him or the organization he represents." He hesitated. "Not until you're ready to do so yourselves."

Elton frowned. "I don't understand—"

"What do you know?" Serena snapped.

For the first time in a long time, a sliver of dread stabbed through her. It had been a lifetime since she had last felt fear. And right now, her every instinct was telling her that this man could expose all her secrets in one fell swoop. That he could reveal to the world the abomination that she and Nate were.

Something that looked like sympathy flitted in Artemus's eyes. "You are not human. But neither are you demons." He looked around the room. "If it's any consolation, the only normal person in here right now is Elton." He grimaced. "Even then, there are days when I have my doubts about that."

Elton frowned.

Serena's heart thrummed against her ribs. *How? How does he know what we are?*

She clenched her jaw. "Speaking of that, we haven't addressed what you guys are either." She narrowed her eyes at Artemus and Drake. "How did you make your weapons change like that?" Her gaze shifted to Callie. "And what exactly *are* you?"

Artemus leaned against a kitchen worktop and crossed his arms. "I guess you could say that I'm a metalsmith. I can—" he waved a hand vaguely in the air, "—make things other blacksmiths can't make. And I can tell the age and origin of an object just by being in its presence." He paused. "I can also assess its true nature if it's an item of power."

"Its nature?" Nate repeated.

Artemus grimaced. "If it's good or evil."

Nate's expression mirrored the disbelief resonating through Serena.

*Still, we've seen what they can do with our own eyes. And our eyes do not lie.*

"And the sword?" she asked skeptically.

Artemus shrugged. "Something I came by when I was a child." He glanced at the rabbit. "I found it the night I met him."

Serena arched an eyebrow at Drake.

"Me? I'm just a regular thief," he said, deadpan.

"Regular thief, my ass," Artemus muttered. "I don't know whether he can forge things like I can, but I'm pretty certain he shares my other talents."

Drake eyed him stonily.

Serena turned to Callie. "And you?"

"I was normal until tonight." Lines furrowed Callie's

brow. "Well, I think I was anyway. All I know is that when those demons manifested themselves in that ballroom and went after the cane, something inside me...changed." She grimaced and rubbed a hand across the back of her neck. "And my marks started behaving strangely."

# CHAPTER EIGHTEEN

ELTON DREW A SHARP BREATH. ARTEMUS'S EYES widened.

"Marks?" Drake said in a stunned voice.

"Yeah, marks," Callie replied. "They're not...birth-marks. I woke up with them one day, when I was three."

She rose from her chair, turned, and swept her blonde hair to the side with one hand. She pulled the neckline of her blouse down.

Artemus's heart stuttered in his chest.

Imprinted in black pigment at the base of Callie's neck was the head of a lion. It had horns protruding through its mane at the front.

"And I have this one too."

She drew the rear waistband of her jeans down slightly and revealed a dark snake at the bottom of her spine.

Artemus's mouth went dry. "Shit."

He hesitated for a moment before slowly pulling his T-shirt over his head and showing them his back.

Only a handful of people had ever seen the marks that

appeared on his body the night he turned six. His parents, the doctor who'd examined him the next day, the detective in charge of investigating the allegations against his father, and Karl and Elton LeBlanc.

"Oh," Callie said, shocked.

The design was a simple and elegant pair of wings made of thick, black lines. They framed his shoulder blades and covered most of his back, the tips extending down to his loins.

A chair clattered to the floor.

Artemus turned.

Drake was on his feet, face ashen and hands fisted tightly at his sides. His dark eyes glittered with a flurry of emotions. Shock. Anger. Disbelief. And an agony so deep it seemed it would tear him apart.

Artemus's heart twisted with a sudden echo of pain. He took a step toward him, unbidden.

Drake moved back and stumbled against the fallen chair.

Artemus went still when he finally registered the astounding truth in the other man's tortured expression. "You have them too, don't you?"

BLOOD ROARED IN DRAKE'S EARS. FOR ONE WILD moment, he was back there again. At the orphanage. The night those loathsome blemishes had appeared on his back and he'd first heard the voice of the demon. The night he'd awoken a monster and burned the world he had known to ashes and bones.

*How? How is this possible? Why does he have—?*

Drake swallowed and dug his nails into his palms before glaring at Artemus. "So what? It doesn't mean a thing!"

His denial sounded fake even to his own ears.

"It means everything." Artemus's expression grew determined. "And I think it explains what I feel when I'm close to you."

Drake blinked. *The bond. He can sense it too?*

Callie's face fell. "Oh. You swing that way?"

Artemus blinked at her. Realization dawned in his eyes.

He scowled. "No, I do not *swing* that way!"

"You sure get a lot of attention from guys," Elton muttered. "And I've never seen you with a woman. You know I wouldn't think less of you if you were gay, right?"

Artemus swore. "Yes, I know that! I'm telling you I'm not." He pointed at Drake. "What I—*feel* for him is nothing like that!" He indicated the rabbit. "And I'm pretty sure *he* feels it too."

Drake's gaze shifted to Smokey. The rabbit had finished his meal and sat watching them with a focused gleam in his chocolate eyes.

*Is that why he helped me back at the warehouse?*

Serena grimaced. "By the way, what *is* he?"

Artemus rubbed the back of his head. "His and Callie's powers are similar. They're like us—" he glanced at Drake, "—yet different at the same time."

Callie dipped her chin in acknowledgement.

"Christ, Karl would have a field day if he were here right now," Elton muttered.

Drake frowned faintly. The name rang a faint bell.

"Who's Karl?" Serena asked.

A shadow crossed Artemus's face. "My mentor. And

benefactor." He looked around the kitchen. "This was his house."

Drake's shoulders slowly relaxed as he studied the man opposite him. He remembered now.

Karl LeBlanc was Elton LeBlanc's older brother. He'd owned a shop in Old Town and had been a notable blacksmith and antique dealer. His reputation as a recluse had nearly outmatched that of his metalwork.

*I wonder if that's where Steele gets his grouchy disposition from.*

Callie fidgeted in her chair. "This is all very interesting, but we really need to find that cane."

Elton gave Artemus and Callie a jaundiced look. "You guys never did explain why that thing is so special."

"It's powerful," Artemus said bluntly. "As powerful as my blade, I think."

Elton straightened in his chair. "Is it cursed?"

Artemus shook his head. "No. The opposite, in fact. It's—"

"—sacred," Callie interrupted. She frowned faintly. "That's the only way to explain it."

"It's touched by Heaven."

Drake blinked, surprised at the words that had just tumbled out of his mouth. He didn't know how he'd fathomed it. The truth had just come to him in that moment.

His heart sank as he finally acknowledged an unpleasant truth. Whatever had been set in motion tonight meant his fate was now linked to the people in this kitchen with him. He could hate it. He could deny it with all his might. But he knew in the very marrow of his bones that it was the cold, hard truth.

Callie stared at him. "I think you're right."

"What makes you say that?" Artemus asked.

Drake clenched and unclenched his fingers.

"Because I think the monster that lives inside me loathes that object with every fiber of his being," he said bitterly. "Because he—" he paused and swallowed convulsively, "—because *we* are touched by Hell."

# CHAPTER NINETEEN

ARTEMUS BLINKED AND OPENED HIS EYES. DUST MOTES danced in the rays of bright light filtering through a gap in the heavy drapes covering the tall, east-facing window of his bedroom.

He yawned, rolled onto his back, and looked at his watch. It was noon.

He tucked his hands behind his head and stared blindly at the richly colored hangings covering his four-poster bed.

It had gone six o'clock in the morning when Elton had finally left the mansion with Isabelle and Mark. Artemus had grudgingly given the rest of his guests a room for the night and had crashed out the moment his head hit his pillow. With the cold light of a new day washing over him, he wondered whether that had been such a great idea. Callie he didn't mind having under his roof. It was the other three that were still an unknown quantity.

The words Drake had spoken last night flashed through his mind. *Did he really mean that? About being touched by Hell?*

Drake had refused to elaborate on the matter after that. Artemus was still pondering his cryptic statement when he became aware of a warm weight on his feet. He lifted his head off the pillow.

Smokey was snoozing on top of the covers at the bottom of the bed.

Artemus glanced at the bedroom door. It was slightly ajar. He frowned.

He definitely recalled locking it last night.

Now that he knew what the rabbit was, he had to admit that the feelings he'd harbored toward the creature had changed. It wasn't the blind love his six-year-old self had felt for the pet he'd once had, but it wasn't hate either.

They were reluctant companions, of sorts. For what purpose, he still didn't know.

Smokey opened his eyes, yawned, and stretched. He blinked fuzzily at Artemus.

"You still haven't shown them your true form," Artemus said.

Smokey gave him a look equivalent to a shrug.

Artemus arched an eyebrow. "You should do it sooner rather than later. They'll freak out when they find out otherwise."

Smokey rubbed his muzzle and licked his paws. *What will be will be.* He paused. *Besides, there are worse things than me out there.*

Artemus grimaced as the rabbit's words rang inside his skull. "Great. Just the kind of pants-wetting news a guy wants to hear first thing in the morning."

He'd just pushed the covers off his legs and was climbing out of bed when someone knocked on the door.

"Wake up, Blue Eyes," Callie said briskly as she entered

the room. She stopped dead in her tracks and stared at his bare chest. Her gaze arrowed south. "Damn it." She stuck her head out of the door and yelled, "You were right, Serena! He's got pajama bottoms on!"

"Told you!" came Serena's faint yet smug reply.

"Get out!" Artemus growled at a smiling Callie.

The smell of freshly brewed coffee and a cooked breakfast wafted through the house when he made his way down to the kitchen minutes later. He walked into the room and stopped dead in his tracks.

Nate was wearing an apron and flipping perfectly shaped pancakes at the large, black cast-iron range to his right. Serena was munching on golden toast oozing butter and marmalade at the kitchen table dead ahead. Callie was feeding Smokey bits of bacon from her plate where she perched on a window seat to the left. Drake was leaning against the worktop next to Nate and sipping coffee.

It would have been a scene of domestic bliss were it not for the fact that Serena was also polishing a wicked-looking knife and Drake was cleaning his gun.

Artemus sighed, took a plate out of a cabinet, and helped himself to eggs and bacon from the serving dish on the table. "Where did that apron come from?"

The giant turned the stove off and brought a stack of steaming pancakes to the table. "I found it in the pantry."

A melancholic feeling rose inside Artemus. He remembered Karl had sometimes worn the thing when he cooked their Thanksgiving dinner.

Callie took a seat next to Artemus, poured maple syrup over her plate, and bit down on a mouthful of fluffy pancake.

Her eyes widened. "Oh my God, Nate. This is *so* good!"

Artemus finished his fried breakfast and tried the pancakes. Callie was right. They were the best pancakes he'd ever tasted.

"So, does cooking feature among the list of skills mercenaries must possess?" he asked a while later, patting his full belly.

Serena glanced at him distractedly. She'd finished cleaning her weapon and had taken out her laptop.

"Nate's always loved cooking. Father taught him how when—"

She stopped and bit her lip. A frown wrinkled her brow.

"It's okay to talk about it," Nate said quietly.

Serena looked at Nate, a muscle jumping in her jawline. "No. We made a promise when we left that place. We wouldn't speak about the past."

Artemus watched the exchange curiously. It was clear to him that the relationship between the two mercenaries was deeper than that of simple associates or friends. There was a bond that linked them. One as profound as his own connection with Drake.

He caught Drake watching the pair with an inquisitive gleam in his dark eyes.

Artemus turned to Callie. "I've been thinking about why you can't detect the cane anymore."

Callie frowned faintly. "So have I."

Artemus raised an eyebrow. "And?"

She hesitated. "I think it's no longer in the city. Whatever the—" she waved a hand vaguely, "—*thing* was that allowed me to figure out its approximate location mustn't work long distance."

Artemus nodded. "I agree. I also believe they must have a way of masking its energy signature." He shrugged in the face of Callie's stare. "It's the only thing that makes sense. Eric Park couldn't have been far from that warehouse when we got there last night. You should have been able to sense it."

Callie's expression grew wary. "If that's true, then we have a big problem."

"Okay," Serena said suddenly. She closed the laptop and rose to her feet. "I guess this is goodbye. Thanks for letting us stay the night. Let's go, Nate."

"What?" Callie said. "You're leaving?"

Serena eyed her coolly. "There's nothing keeping us here."

Nate climbed to his feet and opened his mouth to say something. He sighed when Serena flashed him a dark look.

Artemus frowned at the pair. "They'll come after you. You know that, right? We stand a better chance of defeating them if we stick together."

Drake stood up and tucked his gun into the back of his jeans. "I'm afraid it's adios from me too."

Something that felt like fear twisted through Artemus.

"You can't," he said in a hard voice.

He was surprised to find himself on his feet too.

Drake straightened to his full height and raised an eyebrow. "Who's going to stop me? You?"

The challenge echoed around the kitchen. The hairs rose on Artemus's arms as the air thickened with a faint thrum of power. That was when Smokey's voice rang inside his head.

*Let them go.*

Artemus and Callie stared at the rabbit.

"What?" Callie said, clearly stunned.

Serena frowned and looked from Artemus and Callie to Smokey. Drake's eyes grew hooded.

Artemus knew then that he too had heard the rabbit's voice.

*Our paths will cross again. This I am certain of.*

# CHAPTER TWENTY

Artemus looked around the grand hallway of the Victorian mansion.

Callie and Ronald Stone's elegant, limestone-facade townhouse was located in glitzy Rittenhouse Square, the most expensive neighborhood in Philadelphia. The nine-thousand-square-feet stately home was spread across four floors and boasted ten bedrooms, fourteen bathrooms, a state-of-the-art kitchen manned by a live-in chef, and a heated, indoor swimming pool.

"Your husband had good taste," Artemus murmured, eyeing the opulent furnishings and paintings he glimpsed in the rooms they passed as they made their way to Ronald Stone's study.

Callie grimaced. "I tried to convince him to buy an original Warhol once. He looked at me as if I'd committed a crime." She paused. "Yeah, kinda the way you're looking at me right now."

They'd left Smokey downstairs with Callie's butler and the housemaids. Judging from the way the rabbit had been purring in the hold of a heavy-bosomed girl, Artemus was starting to suspect he liked to put on a display of innocent cuteness in exchange for belly rubs and cuddles. His fangs also seemed to appear and disappear at will depending on his mood.

News of what had happened to Callie and her entourage in Chicago had evidently reached the ears of her house staff and they'd enquired after her health and that of her secretary and bodyguards at length when she and Artemus had arrived at the mansion. It was clear from the respect and affection they showed Callie that they truly cared for the young widow's welfare.

"By the way, won't you get in trouble with that detective?" Callie said as she headed for a bookcase masking a steel safe built into the wall of the study.

"Chase?" Artemus watched Callie input her biometric data and a twelve-digit code into the strongbox. "I think he and Detective Goodman will have bigger fish to fry than me when they take a look at the security videos from the auction house. Elton's team modified the recordings to mask what you, Smokey, and I did and make it look like a general robbery gone wrong. Considering most of those dead demons were regular citizens, Chicago PD is going to be a bit busy trying to figure out what the hell got into them." He paused. "Besides, we took your private jet to come here, so it's not exactly as if he'll be able to check flight manifests."

The safe opened with a soft hiss. Callie removed a stack of faded folders from inside and laid them on her dead husband's desk. "The paperwork for the cane should be in here."

She sat down and opened the first document holder.

Artemus took the seat opposite her, grabbed the second file, and started examining the aged records inside.

An hour later, they were still nowhere near finding any information pertaining to the cane.

"I don't get it." Callie frowned. "The documentation for the other antiques he told me to sell was in that safe."

"Is there anywhere else he used to keep important paperwork?" Artemus said.

Callie leaned back in the chair and pursed her lips. "He had a private safe at the bank where he stored his government bonds and stocks and shares certificates, but I looked at those two days ago."

Artemus raised an eyebrow. "How about your estate attorney? Any chance he or she is in possession of documents that haven't made their way to you yet?"

Callie shook her head. "No, I'm pretty sure Anthony gave me everything Ronald left for me when he read the will." She grew still and her eyes widened. "George."

"Who's George?" Artemus said blankly.

"George Canterbury, Ronald's former estate attorney and oldest friend," Callie said, her face brightening. "Ronald took Anthony on when George retired. He might know something about the cane."

Artemus glanced through the leaded glass of the oriel bay windows gracing the walls of the study. Dusk was falling outside.

"Where does he live?"

LIGHTS GLOWED WARMLY BEHIND THE WINDOWS OF THE red-brick house sitting on a five-acre plot at the end of a private road in Chestnut Hill. Callie stepped out of her Porsche and headed for the porch, Artemus and Smokey following in her steps.

The front door opened just as Callie reached it. A figure dressed in pajamas and a housecoat appeared on the threshold.

George Canterbury blinked myopically at her for a moment. Surprise widened his rheumy eyes. "Callie?"

"Hi, George." Callie leaned in and kissed his cheek. "Isn't it a bit early for bed?"

"Don't begrudge an old man his comforts," George said with a grunt. Sorrow clouded his face. "I must admit, I wasn't expecting us to see each other again so soon after the funeral."

A wave of sadness washed over Callie. "Neither was I." She hesitated and glanced at Artemus. "We have some questions we hope you can answer."

George studied Artemus briefly and considered Smokey with a puzzled expression before beckoning them inside the house.

"Would you like some tea?" the old man said, closing the front door.

"Tea would be nice," Callie murmured with a nod.

Her gaze swept over the photographs displayed on the sideboard and walls of the entrance hall. The pictures were all of George's family.

Callie had never met Amelia Canterbury, George's wife. She had died of bowel cancer a year before Callie married Ronald and was survived by her husband and their three children.

They made their way to the grand kitchen at the rear of the property and engaged in casual chitchat while the kettle boiled and the tea brewed. It wasn't until George had served the drinks in fine China cups alongside a plate of homemade cookies that the subject of their visit finally came up.

"You never did tell me the name of your friend," George said, eyeing them mildly.

Callie wasn't fooled by his benign expression. Despite his age, George Canterbury had maintained the sharp mind that had once made him one of the best estate attorneys in the country.

"My name is Artemus Steele," Artemus said.

George's gaze dropped to the rabbit sitting by Artemus's chair. "Does it have a name?"

"Its name—*his* name is Smokey," Artemus murmured.

George appeared temporarily satisfied with these answers. He looked at Callie. "So, what can I do for you?"

"The cane that Ronald kept as part of his antique collection in the basement. Do you know anything about it?"

George frowned faintly. "Why do you ask?"

Callie hesitated. "Because he told me to sell it, as well as everything else he kept in that vault, after his death."

George stared at her for a moment, wide-eyed and seemingly lost for words.

"I have to admit to being a bit flabbergasted," he finally murmured, fidgeting with his cup. "Of all of his antiques, that cane was the one Ronald treasured the most."

For the hundredth time in the last twenty-four hours, Callie wondered once more what it was that had driven her husband to request that she sell his most prized collection.

"He told me to take it to Elton LeBlanc's auction house in Chicago." She glanced at Artemus. "That's where I met Artemus. There was a robbery last night and the cane was stolen."

George drew a sharp breath. "What?"

"A lot of people died," Callie continued quietly. "We

know the cane's important enough to kill for. We just don't know why. I looked through all the paperwork Ronald kept about his antiques and couldn't find any purchase details for it."

She gazed at George steadily, hoping he wouldn't guess that she hadn't told him the whole truth about what had transpired at the auction house the day before.

"That's because there weren't any." A troubled expression clouded George's face. "I was there when Ronald bought it."

Artemus leaned forward. "Where? Whom did he buy it from?"

It was a moment before the older man spoke. "Well, it's not as if we committed a crime, but it sure felt like it at the time."

Callie exchanged a puzzled glance with Artemus. "What do you mean?"

George looked up and sighed. "It was twenty years ago. Ronald and I were on a business trip to the Middle East. He was investing in some new factories over there and wanted me to review the contracts. We visited Jerusalem on the way back." He faltered, his eyes growing unfocused. "We were in a market in the Old City when Ronald suddenly walked off without a word. I almost lost him he was moving so fast. He went down this deserted side street and inside a derelict shop. When I joined him, he was asking the owner if he had a cane. The guy went to the back of the shop and returned with one. It wasn't evident at first that it was made of ivory and plated with silver and gold; it was so dirty and covered in cobwebs. But Ronald evidently knew, somehow, that it was an object of value. He told me afterward that a voice had compelled him to go into that shop and purchase that item."

Surprise jolted through Callie. She remembered what Ronald had said to her in Baja four months ago. About how an angel had told him to sell his antiques and have the cane taken to Chicago.

She could see her amazement reflected on Artemus's face. She had told him about that incident when they were flying to Philadelphia.

"And that's it?" Artemus frowned. "That's all you know about the cane?"

"I'm afraid so," said George.

# CHAPTER TWENTY-ONE

DRAKE TYPED A CODE INTO THE DOOR'S DIGITAL LOCK, took a last look at the empty alley behind him, and carefully slipped inside the building.

Hugo Voggell's office was in a former slaughterhouse located half a mile from the South Brooklyn Marine Terminal. Although the antique dealer lived in a multi-million-dollar condo in Manhattan, he operated his business from the derelict depot overlooking the dark waters of Upper Bay. It allowed him to engage in some of his less than savory enterprises away from the eyes of the law, including the private auctions he routinely held for his black-market clientele.

Drake had discovered the code to the door some time back, when he'd first taken on a job for Voggell. He liked knowing where his clients lived and worked. Though he'd never officially been invited to Voggell's office before, the antique dealer preferring to hold their business meetings in hotels, Drake knew the approximate floorplan of the place from a trip to the NYC Department of Buildings two years ago. He hoped not much had changed since its original construction in the 1920s.

Beyond the door was a dimly lit corridor that stank of mildew and rat droppings. He ignored the digital cameras covering it and enabled the automode of the multispectral night vision function on his smart glasses. The retro-reflective hooded suit he wore and the low lighting would be enough to camouflage his presence on the video recordings.

He made his way down the passage to an intersection, took a left turn, then a right. A steel door bearing an industrial-grade electronic lock appeared at the end of the corridor. He slipped his knife out of the sheath at his hip, made sure his body screened the lock from the cameras at his back, and carefully removed the inner module. He connected a slim chip and transistor board to the exposed connectors and watched as the custom-made device cycled through hundreds of combinations. A soft electronic beep sounded a minute later.

Drake pulled the steel door oh-so-slowly open and slipped through a narrow gap into the room on the other side. He paused and looked around.

Locked away behind bulletproof and temperature-controlled glass and steel cages bolted into the walls and floor of the storage chamber was an extensive collection of antiques and rare objects. Drake's fingers grew itchy as he eyed the priceless items on display under a battery of small spotlights. He sighed.

*Now is really not the time to be thinking about stealing things.*

He passed two more similar storage spaces as he headed for where he thought Voggell's office would be. Pipes rattled overhead and around him when he entered the oldest part of the building, the central heating working overtime to fight the biting cold of a New York winter. He was navigating the shadowy fringes of the empty slaughter hall when the hairs rose on the back of his neck.

A low gasp left his lips and he ducked beneath the fist aimed at the side of his head. He spun on his heels and rose to face the attacker who had crept up behind him.

Serena Blake's cold expression appeared in washed out grays and whites on the night vision view of his smart glasses.

Drake cursed under his breath and danced out of the way of her lightning-fast blows. He blocked a knee strike to his groin, winced when her knuckles glanced off his jaw, and stopped her hand an inch from his left temple.

"It's me, goddammit!" he hissed, snatching the reflective hood off his head.

Serena froze, pupils dilating. She recovered, scowled, and brought her face up close to his.

"What the hell are you doing here?!"

"Same thing you're probably doing," Drake muttered. "Looking for information on Park." He let go of her hand, straightened, and looked around. "Where's Nate?"

"I'm here," the giant murmured behind him.

Drake twisted around. He hadn't heard the man move in behind him.

He grimaced. "What are you, a cat?"

Nate shrugged. "I'm light-footed for a big man."

Drake frowned. He was pretty sure there was more to it than that. And he was certain it had everything to do with what he had witnessed these two do in the warehouse in Chicago the night before.

"You found anything yet?" he said, checking the

gloomy space around them to see if their scuffle had attracted any attention.

Serena shook her head. "We just got here."

"Voggell's office is that way," Nate said.

He indicated a corridor that led toward the far side of the building.

"How do you know that?" Drake asked suspiciously. "You guys been here before?"

"No," Nate said. "There's a light on at the back. And his car is here."

Drake stilled.

"What?" Serena said.

"That light wasn't on before, and his car wasn't on the premises."

Serena frowned before reaching for her gun. "You sure?"

"I've been watching the place for the last two hours," Drake said quietly.

He slipped his own weapon out of the holster on his thigh.

Unease coiled through him as they made their way toward the back of the slaughterhouse. He had yet to see any sign of the three guards he'd observed come on the night shift an hour ago. Although the men could very well be sipping cocoa and watching a rerun of *It's a Wonderful Life* in a security room somewhere, the eerie silence inside the building told him otherwise. The gloom dissipated as they approached an opening into what looked to be Voggell's auction hall. They hugged the walls of the concrete passage and inched slowly forward. A low murmur of conversation reached Drake's ears as they approached the corner. His skin prickled.

One of the voices rose in volume, its tone growing more agitated. A scream rendered the air in the next instant. Serena stiffened beside Drake.

They dropped on their haunches and peered around the edge of the wall.

# CHAPTER TWENTY-TWO

A WHITE, MODULAR OFFICE STOOD ON A ONE-STORY concrete and steel mezzanine at the far left corner of the auditorium. The light from the open doorway of the cabin washed across the group of people gathered around the bottom of the metal staircase beneath it.

Drake clenched his jaw.

The three security guards he'd seen enter the warehouse earlier lay dead on the floor, their mangled bodies lying at unnatural angles that spoke of broken necks and limbs. Sprawled on the concrete next to them was one of Voggell's bodyguards. Fresh blood pooled out from beneath the man's chest where he lay face down, his body twitching in his final death throes. His figure grew still and a deadly rattle sounded as he took his last breath.

A second bodyguard gurgled and choked where he struggled in the grip of a large man, hands clawing futilely at his attacker's wrist and legs kicking out helplessly where he dangled two feet above the ground.

A cry left him as he was flung violently to the right. The sound stopped when he struck a metal pillar twenty feet away. He crumpled to the floor, his broken skull leaving gory streaks on the surface of the column.

A low whimper escaped Hugo Voggell where he stood frozen next to the staircase. His gaze moved from his dead bodyguards to the six figures facing him.

"What do you want?" he mumbled, his face ashen. He started backing away. "Is it money? I can give you money!"

The large man and his companions followed Voggell as the latter stumbled into the shadows of the auction hall. Their figures faded in the gloom. Drake frowned.

Serena touched his shoulder and pointed to their right. He saw the metal gangways crisscrossing the roof space of the auditorium and dipped his chin.

They moved into the auction hall, located the closest staircase, and headed up onto a walkway overlooking the center of the hall. Voggell and his attackers came into view some twenty-five feet below them.

"What do you know about the cane?" the large man was saying in a dispassionate voice.

He and his companions had surrounded the antique dealer.

Confusion clouded Voggell's face for a moment. "Cane? What—?" He stopped abruptly, his expression clearing. "Wait! Is this about Chicago?"

"Indeed it is," the large man replied. "Mr. Park would very much like to have any data you may hold about the antique that went up for auction last night on Mr. LeBlanc's premises."

Drake glanced at Serena and Nate and saw his own puzzlement reflected on their faces.

*Why the hell does Park need information on the cane when it's in his possession?*

"Look, I don't know anything about that thing apart

from the fact that it's valuable and one of a kind!" Voggell said, his tone desperate. "And I don't have it, so I can't help you!"

The large man cocked his head to the side and studied Voggell for a silent moment. "Do you speak the truth?"

Voggell swallowed convulsively, his chin jerking up and down as he nodded. "I swear on my mother's life!"

"What of the man you sent to steal it?" the large man said coldly. "What do you know about him?"

Drake drew a sharp breath.

The large man and his five companions turned and looked straight up at the gangway where he, Serena, and Nate crouched.

Voggell followed their gazes. His jaw dropped open when he saw Drake.

The eyes of Voggell's attackers flashed amber.

"Get them," the large man said.

~

*SHIT!*

Serena's fingers tightened around her gun as she watched the large man's five companions leap onto the closest pillars and scale them at inhuman speed before launching themselves into the air. The gangway shook and rattled when they landed upon it a couple of seconds later, their wicked talons curving around the railings where they crouched atop the metal bars. They dropped down languidly onto the walkway.

Her shots struck the first two point blank in the chest. The creatures stopped in their tracks for a fleeting moment before moving toward them, faces distorted into garish masks.

"When are you going to learn that normal bullets don't work against these things?" Drake said.

He'd holstered his gun and taken out his dagger. The blade glinted and transformed into a sword at the same time his watch flashed and morphed into a shield.

"Next time, some warning would be good!" Serena snapped.

She put her gun away and snatched a pair of knives from her weapons belt.

"I'm sorry, I was trying not to make a sound so as not to attract the attention of the demons," Drake retorted.

Serena scowled. *One of these days, I'm going to shut him up!*

"There's more of them," Nate said quietly behind her.

Serena looked over her shoulder and saw five more creatures spring up the staircase.

*Where the hell did they come from?*

Then, the monsters were upon them.

THE BEAMS FROM THE PORSCHE'S HEADLIGHTS CUT through the foggy darkness as Callie pulled into the empty parking lot. She rolled to a stop and killed the engine. Silence fell inside the car.

She eyed the dark building before them skeptically. "You sure this is the place?"

Artemus studied the SUV parked in a reserved spot five feet from the rear access door. "That's Voggell's car."

It was Elton who'd provided them with the address of Hugo Voggell's office earlier that evening, after they'd left George Canterbury's house.

"What do you want to go there for?" Elton has asked when Artemus had spoken to him.

"Philadelphia was a dead end. We need to know where that cane came from and why Park was after it. Voggell may have some answers."

"Well, don't stay away too long. Detective Chase called. He wants to interview us again on Monday."

Artemus had frowned at the news. "Why?"

"I think he suspects something. He's struggling to understand how we escaped the attack at the auction house relatively unscathed."

"I should be back in Chicago by Monday."

The rank smell of human waste washed over them from the nearby waters of Upper Bay and the Hudson River. They were halfway to the rear entrance when Smokey suddenly stiffened between them.

Callie frowned. "What is it?"

Artemus's skin tingled. His pulse started to race as he finally detected the energies Smokey had sensed coming from the warehouse.

The rabbit moved swiftly toward the building. *We need to hurry*.

# CHAPTER TWENTY-THREE

D RAKE GRUNTED WHEN A DEMON'S FIST CONNECTED
with his shoulder. Heat flared across his skin as claws
carved vicious tracks into his suit and flesh. He gritted his
teeth, blocked the creature's next strike with his shield,
and slashed him across the thigh with his sword. The man
shrieked and sagged. Drake stabbed him in the chest and
pushed him over the railing before turning to face the rest
of the demons crowding the gangway, his pulse hammering
away in his veins. Four feet behind him, Serena and Nate
were holding off a second group of demons.

Movement below caught Drake's attention. More creatures swarmed the auction hall from the shadows.

*What the—?*

"Damn it!" Serena deflected a couple of lightning-fast
blows to her head and glared at the horde of demonic
figures heading for the gangway. "There are too many of
them!"

Drake clenched his jaw. He could feel the energy inside
him straining to break loose in the presence of the

demons, his power resonating once more with their corrupt aura. Though it sickened him, he realized he had no option but to access it if he wanted to get out of there alive with Serena and Nate. There would be no Artemus, Smokey, and Callie to save them this time around.

*Shit. That blond bastard was right. We should have stuck together.*

Drake took a shallow breath before concentrating on the walls restraining the darkness suffusing his soul. They appeared in his mind's eye, tall, indomitable barriers that contained the evil within him. He allowed them to flex slightly.

A gasp left him as the ungodly force spilled over and swept through his body.

The marks on his back trembled. A coppery taste filled his mouth. Coldness swamped his consciousness. In his hand, the sword thickened and lengthened, the metal growing a shade darker.

The demons blinked, their amber eyes widening.

Drake moved.

SERENA CAST A QUICK GLANCE OVER HER SHOULDER AT Drake. She could sense something different about the dark-haired thief. Something ominous.

She crossed her knives and slashed the neck of the demon before her. Wetness sprayed the back of her hands and arms as black blood gushed out of the creature's wounds. She kicked her attacker into the man behind him, sidestepped to avoid the clawed fist heading for the back of her head, and drove her right elbow into the gut of the demon behind her. A guttural noise left the creature. It turned into a shocked sound when Nate lifted him and threw him over the railing.

The demon smashed into the ground twenty-five feet below the gangway with a sickening thud. He lay still for a moment before slowly sitting up and shaking his head.

Serena's knuckles whitened on the blades in her hands.

*These assholes just won't stay down!*

Her chest heaved as she turned to confront the demons facing them. She glanced at Nate and was alarmed to see him also panting.

In all their years as soldiers of fortune, they had never come across an adversary they couldn't defeat in hand-to-hand combat. That they had nearly been overcome twice in the space of twenty-four hours was an unpleasant surprise. She narrowed her eyes.

*This fight is far from over.*

She stretched out the kinks in her neck, twisted her heels into the ground, and focused. The air thickened next to her as Nate similarly tapped into the core of what made them inhuman.

DRAKE'S BODY TINGLED AND HUMMED WITH POWER AS he slashed, stabbed, and cut through the crowd of demons surrounding him. Though the sword in his hand dripped with blood, he could feel the monster inside him hungering for more. More chaos. More destruction. More death. He shivered at the potently addictive feeling.

A strange undercurrent pierced the red bloodlust clouding his vision. He became conscious of the vibrations shaking the walkway and looked over his shoulder.

Ten feet away, Serena and Nate fought a group of demons with a tactical precision and speed that more than matched their adversaries, their strikes so powerful they left imprints in the bodies of the creatures attacking them.

Three shadowy figures lunged up from beneath the railing to Serena's left and launched themselves at the mercenary. A grunt escaped her as they lifted her off her feet and carried her over the opposite railing.

Drake's stomach twisted. The darkness inside him abated. He moved instinctively toward her, arm outstretched, knowing he would be too late to stop her fall. His eyes widened.

Serena spun and twisted elegantly through twenty-five feet of empty air before landing nimbly in a low crouch on the floor of the auction hall. A grim smile curved her lips when she looked up at the demons slowly rising to face her. She straightened and bolted toward her attackers. Her fists and feet blurred as she danced between them, her blows and kicks catching them unawares.

Admiration flickered through Drake. *Jesus, that woman is—*

"Behind you," Nate said.

Drake turned and saw a giant hand heading for his face.

Artemus, Callie, and Smokey rushed into a shadowy hall at the far end of Voggell's building. Twenty feet ahead of them, Serena was fighting a group of demons with brutal speed and strength, her face a mask of pure focus while her bloodied knuckles delivered powerful blows. High up on a gangway to the right, Nate was similarly engaged in a fierce battle with another horde of demonic creatures.

Artemus's stomach clenched with fear.

A few feet behind Nate, Drake was clawing at the arm of the large demon choking him, his sword lying uselessly on the walkway by his feet.

Artemus raised his gun and fired.

His shot struck the creature in the thigh. The demon staggered back a step, grip loosening slightly around Drake's throat. He looked down at the shallow depression in his flesh and the faint orange cracks spreading from it before locking eyes with Artemus. The demon frowned.

Artemus's heart sank.

*Shit. Why isn't he turning into ash?*

Callie transformed next to him and opened her mouth on an unholy roar. The sound immobilized the four demons charging toward them from the left of the hall. More appeared from the right.

Artemus unleashed his sword and started firing at them. His bullets tore holes in their chests and limbs. Their uncanny screams echoed to the rafters as they were consumed by flames. Ash thickened the air along with the smell of death and blood.

More demons appeared from the gloom.

Up on the walkway, a group of creatures swarmed Nate and lifted him over the railing. He gasped and reached out as he started to fall. His right hand closed on the edge of the platform while the demons plummeted to the floor of the hall around him. He grabbed the railing with his other hand and started hauling himself up.

Artemus caught movement on the columns supporting the grid of gangways. He slashed the creature before him in the neck and turned to shoot at the two figures launching themselves through the air toward the mercenary.

His bullets missed them by a hair's breadth.

# CHAPTER TWENTY-FOUR

THE DEMONS LANDED ON TOP OF NATE, THE DARKNESS wreathed around them wrapping around the large man in suffocating clouds. All three swung precariously for a moment as the mercenary tried to hold onto the walkway. His fingers slowly slipped.

They crashed down fifteen feet to Serena's left.

"Nate!"

She started toward him, only to stagger to a stop when a group of demons blocked her path.

*Shit.* Artemus clenched his teeth as he took down the creatures swarming out of the shadows around him. *Where the hell are these bastards coming from?*

A low growl sounded to his left. He blasted two demons in the head and slashed one across the gut before glancing at Callie. Surprise flashed through him.

She'd killed the creatures who'd attacked her and stood breathing heavily, her eyes a vivid green and a scowl marring her brow. Something was poking through the mane covering her forehead. Something else was peeking out the back of her jeans. She moved just as the demons around Nate rose and surrounded the large man climbing to his feet, a broken arm dangling by his side.

Motion high up drew Artemus's gaze a second before Callie stormed the crowd of snarling creatures.

Smokey had climbed the stairs to the gangway and was darting between the legs of the demons in his path. He lunged just as he reached Drake and the giant demon, his body swelling in size a second before he made contact. His jaws locked viciously around the creature's arm, breaking the latter's hold on Drake's throat.

Drake sagged and coughed violently as the demon finally let him go. He swooped to grab his sword from the walkway and turned to face the monsters at his back.

The giant demon clutched at Smokey with his wicked claws and tried to wrench the rabbit from his body. Smokey held fast. The demon frowned, glanced at the drop next to him, and leapt from the walkway, the rabbit still in his grip. Their shapes blurred and twisted as they fell.

They struck the floor hard and rolled toward the mezzanine.

Concrete exploded as they smashed into two of the columns supporting the structure. The modular office trembled and groaned before collapsing down on top of them in a cloud of debris and plaster dust.

A shiver raced down Artemus's spine. The air in the hall grew heavy.

"*Smokey!*" Callie cried.

She started for the wreckage, her face pale. Behind her, the demons who'd attacked Nate lay dead.

"Wait!" Artemus said.

She stopped and glanced at him. Her eyes widened

when she finally sensed the change in the energy inside the hall. Her gaze shifted to the rubble just as it moved.

The demon rose first, bloodied figure swaying slightly as he shook his head, his expression stunned.

The wings on Artemus's back trembled violently as a pile of concrete and steel stirred a few feet from the creature.

Smokey slowly emerged from the remains of the mezzanine, a low growl rumbling from his throat.

His body had grown. His fur had shrunk. His color had darkened.

For the second time in his life, Artemus gazed upon the true form of the creature he had met all those years ago, on the night his destiny had changed forever.

Up on the gangway, Drake froze, his eyes locked on the beast rising to face the giant demon atop the mound of debris. The fine tremors racking the thief's frame told Artemus he was experiencing the same violent surge of power thrumming through his own body. A power that was originating from Smokey.

Callie blinked. "Oh."

The hellhound stood four feet tall and was black as night. An unholy red glow filled his pupils and his lips peeled back to expose two rows of wicked fangs almost as long as Artemus's switchblade. He stepped toward the demon, four hundred pounds of coiled, compact muscle and sinew moving with lissome, deadly grace under his shiny coat. Drool fell from his jaws in thick globs that sizzled when they hit the chunks of concrete beneath his paws. Holes appeared in the blocks, the spit burning through the cement like acid.

Smokey's true name echoed inside Artemus's skull like a long lost song. *Cerberus*.

Surprise flashed in the demon's amber eyes. The hell-hound lunged.

The pair collided violently before smashing into the debris. The demon grunted as they plowed down the uneven mound. He sank his claws into Smokey's flank, scoring red lines into the hound's flesh.

Smokey snarled and snapped his jaws at the demon's head. A choked noise escaped the creature when the hell-hound's fangs found his throat. The sound of the demon's neck snapping echoed across the hall like a gunshot. He went limp in the hellhound's grip, his body resuming his human form once more.

Smokey growled and shook the corpse like a rag-doll before flinging him violently aside. The mangled remains of the dead demon sailed through the air and landed with a splat a few feet from Serena.

The mercenary slowly stared from the corpse to Smokey.

Callie smiled at the hellhound, her expression relieved. "It's nice to finally meet you."

Smokey padded over to her and bumped his burly head gently against her shoulder.

Artemus sighed and put away his blade and gun.

Drake pointed an accusing finger at the hellhound. "What the hell is that?"

"Your knight in shining armor," Artemus said with a frown. "What happened here?"

He indicated the auction hall and the scores of dead demons.

"We came to find some answers," Drake said, glancing at Serena and Nate. He narrowed his eyes at Artemus. "What are *you* doing here?"

"Saving your ass, by the looks of it," Artemus said. "Again."

Drake scowled.

"Is he a demon?" Serena said, her gaze still on Smokey's new form. "He looks like a demon."

"No." Callie stroked the hellhound's head and scratched him behind the ears. "His name is Cerberus."

Smokey's eyes rolled back slightly in his head and he huffed with pleasure.

"As in, the mythical hound that guards the gates of the Underworld?" Serena said with a look of disbelief.

Callie nodded. "Uh-huh."

"That's one badass dog," Nate mumbled.

Smokey trotted over to the dead demon, cocked his hind leg, and released a steaming flow of acid urine all over his adversary.

Drake wrinkled his nose. "Sweet Jesus, what *is* that smell?!"

"Callie, what's that poking out of your back?" Serena stared. "And your head?"

Callie touched her forehead. Her eyes widened. She cast a wild look over her shoulder.

The color drained from her face. "*Noooo!*"

# CHAPTER TWENTY-FIVE

ERIK PARK STARED AT THE WOUNDED DEMON ON THE other side of the desk.

"They're dead?" he said incredulously. "All of them? Even Ramos?"

The man nodded, his face pale. He'd assumed his human appearance and was clutching at the bloodied laceration in his abdomen.

Park swiveled his chair around and frowned at the dazzling lights of the city spread out beyond the glass facade of his office. That one of his strongest generals had been defeated during what should have been a straightforward recon mission was not news he welcomed.

Taking care of Hugo Voggell and his entourage should have been a walk in the park for someone of Ramos's caliber. When Park had felt the dark call for reinforcements a while back, he'd been startled but had sent more demons to Brooklyn nonetheless, the creatures' bodies melting into the night to emerge out of the shadows in the slaughterhouse in a matter of seconds. He hadn't expected the fight that had taken place there to wipe out Ramos's entire squad.

He turned and narrowed his eyes at the only survivor to return to their headquarters. "Tell me exactly what happened."

Surprise filled him as the demon started to talk. When the man described the three intruders Ramos and his team had uncovered in the slaughterhouse and the three more who had come to their assistance shortly after, a thread of trepidation wormed its way into his bones. But when the demon related what he had witnessed at the end of the battle, before his timely escape, Park's misgivings turned into a mixture of alarm and excitement.

"Are you certain?" he said stiffly. "You saw them transform?"

The demon nodded. "Yes."

Park gazed at him blindly for a moment. "Thank you." He waved a hand at the demon. "Why don't you go take care of those wounds?"

The man turned and left the office, his expression relieved.

Park signaled to the two bodyguards standing by the door. "I need a moment."

They exited the room.

He rose to his feet and brought up a number on the smartband on his wrist. The call connected a moment later.

"Sir? It's Park." He turned and stared out over the city. "I think I've found the Guardian."

❧

"SERIOUSLY, IT'S NOT AS BAD AS IT LOOKS."

Callie glared at Artemus and hiccupped between sobs. "Oh yeah?! Well, I'd like to see how you'd react if you suddenly grew horns and a tail!"

She looked over her shoulder.

"*And it isn't even a normal tail!*" she finished in a high-pitched howl.

Artemus stared from the stubby, white horns protruding through the front of Callie's hair to the baby snake peeking out the back of her jeans. The creature had coiled in on itself and gone to sleep, evidently bored by the incessant wailing of its mistress.

Smokey sniffed at the reptile a couple of times where he perched on the leather couch next to Callie and gave it a tentative lick. The hellhound had assumed his disguise once more, all signs of the deadly monster from the slaughterhouse masked behind the limpid, chocolate gaze and fluffy fur of the Rex rabbit.

The infant snake opened one lazy eye and flicked its tongue at the bunny with a friendly hiss.

Drake walked into the lounge and came to an abrupt halt.

"I cannot tell you how disturbing that is," he said dully as he stared at the two creatures nuzzling each other. "I've seen some weird shit in my life, but this takes the cake."

Callie's eyes rounded, her face crumpling and a fresh wave of tears flooding her eyes.

"See?" she bawled. "Even *he* thinks it's weird! I'm a freak! An ugly, horned, tailed freak!"

Artemus grimaced as her sobs rose in volume once more. He narrowed his eyes at Drake. "Way to go, asshole. I'd just managed to calm her down."

"Really?" Drake said sarcastically. "'Cause that's not what it sounded like from the bedroom, Goldilocks."

Artemus decided to ignore the 'Goldilocks' comment. "Has he talked yet?"

"No." Drake grimaced. "And if she keeps working him over the way she is, he won't be in a fit state to say anything either."

Artemus sighed. "Stay here."

He headed for the corridor Drake had appeared from.

"And do what exactly?" Drake said sullenly.

Artemus shrugged and indicated Callie. "I don't know, use your charms to cheer her up."

He navigated the dingy passage toward the bedroom of Hugo Voggell's safehouse.

It was Drake who'd told them about the antique dealer's hideout in Harlem a couple of hours back. When they'd failed to find any traces of the man or his car after the demons' attack in Brooklyn, they'd gone searching for him at his condo in Manhattan.

"Give me a second," Drake had said as they stood in Voggell's extravagantly furnished and very empty apartment. He'd slipped his smartglasses on, touched the controls on the right rim, and grinned at whatever came up on his viewscreen. "I know exactly where he is."

"How long ago did you bug his place?" Artemus had asked when they'd parked in the alley backing the dark building where the antique dealer had taken refuge.

They'd left Callie's Porsche and Drake's bike at Voggell's condo and taken Serena and Nate's SUV for the ride to Harlem.

"Long enough," Drake had replied.

Artemus had eyed him suspiciously as they stepped out into the wintry night. "You bug my place too?"

Drake had smiled wordlessly in response.

Artemus recalled the thief's annoying smirk with a

frown as he walked into the bedroom. He stopped and stared from Voggell's bloodied face to the woman towering over the man strapped to a chair.

"Whoa," Artemus muttered. "Easy there. We want the guy to be able to speak."

Serena cast a cold look his way.

Nate was perched on the edge of the bed next to her, busy checking their weapons.

Artemus was unsurprised to see that the man's broken arm had already healed.

Voggell hawked out a glob of blood-streaked spit and looked wildly at Artemus. "Will you tell this crazy bitch to get off my case? I don't know anything about Park and his organization! I'm telling you the truth!"

"Really?" Artemus arched an eyebrow. "'Cause they sure seem to know a lot about you. That's how they found out about the auction in Chicago."

Surprise flashed on Voggell's weasel-like face. Anger darkened it in the next instant. "You know what? Fuck you!" He scowled up at Serena. "*Fuck all of you!*"

The mercenary backhanded him across his cheek so hard the chair nearly toppled over. Artemus winced.

Voggell choked on his breath as he slowly brought his head back around. He spat out a broken tooth. It joined the other three on the floor.

Artemus crossed the bedroom and dropped down on his haunches in front of the bound man. "The sooner you talk, the sooner this will be over. Pretty soon, she's gonna break something that can't be fixed." He glanced at Serena. "Like your skull."

Voggell's chest heaved as he glared at them, fear a dark light coiling in the depths of his eyes. "You've seen what those people can do! They're—*they're monsters!* They'll kill me if I talk!"

"They'll kill you anyway," Nate said flatly from the bed. "In our experience, they don't like leaving witnesses."

The color drained from Voggell's face. He gnawed the inside of his cheek for a silent moment.

"Look, if I—" he gulped and swallowed convulsively, his eyes shifting from Serena to Artemus, "if I tell you what I know, can you guarantee my safety?"

Artemus shook his head. "We can't."

Voggell's face fell.

"But I know people who could," Artemus added.

Voggell sagged in the chair, relief flooding his eyes.

Drake walked into the bedroom. He was grimacing and wriggling his jaw from side to side with one hand.

Artemus rose to his feet and eyed the red marks on the thief's left cheek. "What happened?"

"Let me guess." Serena narrowed her eyes. "She slapped you."

"All I did was tell her that the snake looked cute all coiled up on itself," Drake muttered. "Like a little pig's tail."

# CHAPTER TWENTY-SIX

DRAKE STUDIED THE TWO BURLY BOUNCERS GUARDING the entrance of the low-key building some hundred feet from the narrow alley where they'd parked the SUV. A woman in a thigh-length, red sequin dress stood between the men. She was checking guests off on the paper-thin tablet in her hand as they turned up on the doorstep of the property.

"I still think this place is too modest looking for what it's supposed to be," Serena said in a dubious tone from her position in the driver's seat.

"I don't think Voggell would lie to us," Drake murmured from the backseat. "And I couldn't find much in the NYC Department of Buildings' archives about this joint. Besides, one of my contacts just confirmed he's heard about the place in the last couple of minutes. He said rumors are rife that some pretty extreme stuff goes on in there. And he confirmed admission is by invitation only."

"Well, it's a good thing I got us access then," Serena muttered.

It had taken the mercenary most of the afternoon to trace and hack the database of the private BDSM dungeon Voggell had told them about the night before at his apartment in Harlem. Artemus had contacted Elton LeBlanc that morning to ask if the Vatican organization he belonged to had agents in New York who could protect the antique dealer. A team of dark-suited men had landed on a shell-shocked Voggell's doorstep an hour later and whisked him away to a safehouse.

Drake, Artemus, and Callie had caught a few hours of shuteye while Serena and Nate checked out the club where Voggell had told them he knew members of Erik Park's entourage hung out. The two mercenaries seemed to be able to survive on little sleep, something Drake suspected had everything to do with what they were.

The club was in a building that looked as empty and derelict as half the apartment blocks on the rundown Chinatown backstreet it was located on. Which made the limos and luxury sedans pulling up to the curb and the glamorous patrons piling out of them appear all the more out of place.

The few locals they'd seen in the area since they'd gotten there had walked past swiftly with their eyes cast down, giving the place a wide berth. Some even went so far as crossing the road to do so.

Drake didn't blame them. From where he sat in the rear of the SUV with Callie, Smokey, and Artemus, he could sense a faint thrum of dark energy coming from the building.

Artemus grabbed the door handle and stepped out of the vehicle. "Okay, time to get this show on the road."

Drake joined Artemus, Serena, and Smokey in the alley.

Artemus passed the brand new, black leather leash attached to Smokey's collar to Serena. "Here, it'll look better if you hold him."

The leash matched the spandex, lace-up catsuit and open-toed platform ankle-boots the mercenary had donned for their visit to the sex dungeon.

"Can you even breathe in that outfit?" Drake had asked when she'd stepped out of Voggell's bathroom an hour ago.

The catsuit hugged her lithe curves like a second skin and left little to the imagination. Add to it her kohl-rimmed eyes and crimson nails and lips, and she looked every inch the dominatrix she was pretending to be.

"Yeah," she'd replied coolly before raising an eyebrow at him and Artemus. "And what the hell is with the preppy look? We're going to a sex club, not Sunday mass."

Drake had glanced down at the expensive boots, ripped jeans, black shirt, and short, brown leather jacket he wore. Artemus was dressed in a similar outfit, except his shirt was white and his boots and jacket wine red.

"What's preppy about it?" Drake had asked irritably. "It's all the rave right now."

"Serena's right, you know." Callie had pursed her lips and examined them critically. She'd calmed down some-what since she'd woken up and seemed resigned to her newly acquired body parts. "You should have gone with the leather chaps."

"What, and expose our butts to the icy weather?" Artemus had snapped. "No, thank you." He'd glanced at Serena's catsuit. "Besides, we need *somewhere* to hide our weapons."

The mercenary had smiled thinly at that. "Oh, believe me, choirboy. I have weapons under this suit."

"Where?" Artemus had asked dully. "Wait. On second thought, don't answer that."

Callie wound the rear window of the SUV down a fraction as they started up the alley. She was staying back in the vehicle with Nate as their backup.

"Be careful," she called out, a trace of anxiety underscoring her voice.

"We will," Artemus said.

Smokey let out a reassuring huff before eyeing the leather leash attached to his collar. He gave it a tentative nibble.

"Don't even think about it," Artemus warned. "That thing was like a hundred dollars!"

Smokey pasted a moue across his face.

The queue outside the club had died down by the time they cut across the street. The woman in the red dress eyed them curiously when they strolled to a stop in front of her.

Drake clenched his fingers slightly and saw a muscle jump in Artemus's cheek out of the corner of his eye. Both of them could see the black tendrils of corrupt energy crowning the heads of the woman and the two bouncers.

"Hello, Miss—" the hostess glanced at the screen of her device, "Van Dyke." She flashed them a dazzling smile. "I see this is the first time you're visiting us."

"It is," Serena said. The seductive smile that curved the mercenary's lips nearly had Drake's jaw dropping open in shock. She cast a slow glance his way, as if she'd read his thoughts, and he saw the warning light in her pale blue eyes. She looked back at the hostess. "I've heard a lot of good things about your club. I hope it won't disappoint me and my...companions."

The hostess studied Drake and Artemus appreciatively

before looking down. Her eyes widened. "Oh my gosh, I see you brought a third pet! He's *so* cute!"

She dropped down on her haunches and stroked Smokey's head and ears. A hint of redness flashed in the rabbit's pupils for a second before he wrinkled his nose sweetly at the woman.

Serena arched an eyebrow at the woman when she straightened. "He's the *only* pet I've brought." She took hold of Artemus and Drake's jacket collars and jerked the two men close. "These two are my slaves."

Drake swallowed a curse as Serena ran her tongue lazily up his right cheek.

The hostess's face glazed over with a look of pure lust. "Let me check you in so you guys can go have some, er, fun."

Serena looked into the retinal scanner on the woman's tablet and typed in a code. She'd installed fake biometric data and a cypher on the club's servers a few hours ago and was wearing nano contact lenses that matched the ID she'd just inputted.

A green light flashed on the tablet screen.

The hostess smiled. "You're all checked in. Have fun."

The bouncers stepped aside and pushed the doors open, their faces impassive. A dingy corridor appeared beyond the threshold.

Serena stepped inside the building first and headed down the passage to an old-fashioned, industrial-sized cage elevator at the end. The accordion door rattled loudly when she pulled it open. Drake glanced at the discreet motion sensors and cameras covering the ornate metal enclosure as they followed her inside the cabin. Artemus closed the elevator behind them and pressed the only button on the chrome plate to the right. The mechanism controlling the cage kicked in with a faint whine. Gray brick walls rose around them as they started their descent.

It was almost a minute before the elevator clattered to a stop at the bottom of the shaft.

"How far down are we?" Artemus said quietly.

"About two hundred feet," Serena murmured.

Drake frowned. "That's deep."

They stepped out in a brightly-lit, white-tiled, circular foyer. Black and crimson leather couches dotted the gleaming floor of the lobby in an artful arrangement that framed a path leading to a red metal door at the opposite end of the pristine space.

Serena started toward it, Smokey at her side.

A dull, rhythmic vibration worked its way through the soles of Drake's boots as he and Artemus headed after her. Goosebumps broke out across his skin.

He slowed and clenched his teeth. "You feel that?"

Serena stopped and frowned at him. "What, the music?"

Drake fisted his hands, his nails biting into his palms. "No. I mean the energy."

"I do," Artemus said, his eyes cool.

Serena stared at them. "There are demons behind that door?"

"Yeah," Drake said. He flexed his right hand slightly and sensed the reassuring weight of his knife where he'd tucked it inside the sleeve of his jacket. "Lots of them."

# CHAPTER TWENTY-SEVEN

THE MUSIC STRUCK ARTEMUS FIRST. IT CRASHED OVER him in solid waves, a steady, pulsing vibration that made his eardrums throb and his teeth tremble in his jaws. Next came a sultry, suffocating heat that wrapped around his body and brought with it the heady scent of expensive perfume, cigars, and sex. He blinked as his eyes adapted to the low lightning.

They were standing on a narrow mezzanine over-looking a cavernous space. The metal platform extended on either side of them and wrapped halfway around towering cherry wood and purple velvet-paneled walls before ending in stairs that spiraled down into the smoke-wreathed, split-level club below.

Artemus stared.

Men and women in leather outfits that left little to the imagination danced and writhed under colored spotlights inside metal cages on podiums and sunken decks scattered across a backlit, black and white, checkered floor. Some of the enclosures were large and featured live sex and BDSM shows, the multiple male and female partners engaged in the carnal acts seemingly oblivious to the captive audience watching them from islands of shadowy tables and booths framed by the circular bars dotting the space.

It took seeing an elegantly dressed couple rise and strip before climbing inside a cage to join two men for Artemus to realize that the participants were all guests of the club.

"How many?" Serena said.

Artemus glanced at her distractedly. "How many what?"

"Demons," the mercenary replied.

Artemus observed the ominous shroud of darkness twisting and snaking above the club. He didn't even have to focus his mind to see it, so thick was the evil clouding the place.

"About a hundred, give or take," he said quietly.

Serena narrowed her eyes. "We took down about forty of them in Brooklyn. And that was with Nate and Callie too."

Artemus looked past her to Drake.

Sweat beaded the thief's forehead and a muscle jumped in his cheek. An echo of something that felt like pain danced through Artemus's consciousness from the dark-haired man.

Smokey was also staring at Drake.

"You gonna be okay?" Artemus said with a faint frown.

Drake met his gaze, surprise flashing briefly on his face. "I—" he paused and clenched his jaw, "I think so. Let's just get this over and done with."

They headed down into the pit.

Dozens of pairs of eyes focused on Serena as she descended the spiral stairs ahead of them, her leisurely pace and cool expression drawing as many curious and admiring gazes as her seductive outfit. Artemus had to hand it to the mercenary. The woman knew how to make an entrance.

Smokey got "oohs" and "aahs" when they stepped onto the crowded floor. Pets were obviously not a normal sight in the BDSM dungeon, something Artemus was grateful for; he didn't think he could have tolerated it if the sex shows included any form of bestiality. Although the rabbit put on the ultimate show of cuteness with his limpid brown eyes and adorable twitchy nose, the thrum of energy pulsing through him told Artemus he wasn't exactly happy to be in the presence of so many demons.

Covetous glances followed Artemus and Drake's own passage through the club as they headed to a bar, the patrons appraising them just as closely as they had Serena and evidently liking what they saw. Artemus masked a shudder at the hunger in their eyes and fought the urge to find the closest shower.

Serena ordered drinks and looked pointedly at Drake. He sighed, slipped his cell out of his back pocket, and tapped it against the bartender's smart band.

"Would you like to open a tab?" the man asked with a friendly smile.

He was one of the few humans in the club.

"Sure," Serena said before Drake could utter a reply.

The thief frowned.

Someone touched Artemus's shoulder in a languid caress. He turned and looked into the face of a beautiful brunette and her movie-star-handsome male companion.

"Hey there," the woman said with an alluring smile. "You're new. Wanna play?"

She indicated a cage that had been vacated by two men and a woman who had just finished a loud and unbridled session of intercourse.

Artemus ignored the vile aura surrounding the woman's partner and pasted a demure smile on his face. "I'm afraid that's up to my mistress."

The brunette looked past him to Serena.

"You have an obedient pet," she murmured, envy underscoring her mild tone.

Serena arched an eyebrow, her expression benevolent. "I trained him well."

Artemus almost rolled his eyes.

The brunette pursed her lips and stared at Drake. "Is this one off limits too?"

Serena shrugged. "It depends what you want to do with him."

Drake stiffened slightly.

The brunette walked slowly around the thief, her gaze roaming the hard planes and angles of his body like a starving man eyeing up a feast. "Is he a good sub?"

Serena's gaze grew hooded for an instant. "He has his moments."

"Oh," the brunette's companion murmured. "He likes to put up a fight?"

Artemus saw the dark coils crowning the man's head thicken, his interest in Drake piqued. Drake took a slow sip of his drink and met the demon's stare unflinchingly.

"He does." Serena glanced at Drake. A lazy smile curved her lips. It never reached her eyes. "In fact, he loves nothing more than being tied down."

A choked sound escaped Drake. He coughed and wiped his mouth, a warning light dancing briefly in the depths of his dark gaze as he glanced at Serena.

Lust darkened the male demon's face. He moved until he practically stood toe-to-toe with Drake and studied the thief with a heated expression. "I'd very much like to see that."

Smokey's fur quivered where he crouched by Serena's feet, the small burst of savage energy flashing from him resonating inside Artemus.

Serena shared a guarded glance with Artemus where he'd positioned himself just behind the woman and her companion. This was their chance to isolate one of the demons and question them about Erik Park.

"Sure," the mercenary murmured with a shrug. "But we like to play privately." She stepped up to Drake and placed a proprietary hand on his chest. "That's when he's at his...loudest."

Drake stared at her, a muscle jumping in his cheek.

The woman smiled. "We have a private room out back."

They followed the couple through the club and into one of three corridors that branched off the main floor. The music dwindled as they negotiated a series of twisting, dimly-lit passages. Peep rooms appeared, the clusters of guests gathered in front of the glass walls avidly watching the sex shows beyond while they sipped champagne and nibbled on canapés. They passed velvet-padded doors beyond which moans and cries of pleasure echoed.

The couple's suite was a sumptuous chamber decked out with all the playthings the BDSM dungeon had to offer, including a red, leather-padded restraining cross and a spanking bench.

The sounds of the club faded when the demon closed the door behind them and twisted the lock.

# CHAPTER TWENTY-EIGHT

ERIK PARK BLEW OUT A CLOUD OF EXPENSIVE CIGAR smoke and eyed the Triad gang member sitting opposite him with a neutral expression.

The man was leaning back lazily against the leather couch, one foot crossed atop the opposite knee while he drank a hundred-year-old single malt Scotch whiskey and studied the crowded BDSM dungeon through the glass wall to his right. His three associates braced the floor behind him, faces somber and cool stares locked on Park's own bodyguards where the two men stood framing the door of the VIP room.

The suite was one of several located above the main floor of the club. It was where high-powered, elite members in need of privacy could enjoy the live sex and BDSM shows on offer from behind the one-way-glass wall and indulge in their own sick fantasies in the fully equipped playroom that came with it.

It was also where Park sometimes held business meetings.

He stifled an amused smile. Judging from the erection

the Triad gang member was subtly trying to hide, the pretty redhead in the black leather catsuit whipping a naked man chained to the wall of a cage on a podium directly below them was doing a fine job of distracting him. The guy was also high on something; from his dilated pupils and the fine beads of sweat on his forehead, Park was willing to bet he'd taken a hit of a potent drug to hide his nervousness before attending their face-to-face.

The man's trepidation didn't surprise him. The reputation of Park's organization had grown to legendary status since they started making their mark in the city's seedy criminal underworld a decade ago. It was the Triad gang's leader who'd contacted Park's secretary a week back to discuss the terms of a potential alliance between their groups. With Park's organization now controlling the majority of the drug and human trafficking routes on the east coast, most of the other big players in the area had conceded large sections of their turf to Park and signed up to work under him. Once they saw what Park and his people were capable of, many were more than eager to join the fold.

The few who weren't never lived to see another day.

Park took another puff on his cigar, draped an arm across the back of the couch he sat on, and looked steadily at the Triad gang member. "Let's talk business, shall we, Mr. Chan?"

The man startled slightly at the sound of his name. He dragged his gaze reluctantly from the redhead in the cage and met Park's stare with a slight flinch.

"I believe my secretary forwarded you the relevant documents a few days ago," Park said.

He signaled to one of his bodyguards. The man opened the door.

Park's secretary entered the suite, a folder in hand. Chan's eyes widened.

"All that remains is for you to sign on the dotted line," Park continued in the same light tone.

The Triad man carried on staring at Park's secretary. The woman was wearing black stilettos and a purple leather outfit that matched that of the redhead in the cage beyond the glass wall. Her luxuriant blonde hair was piled in a bun held by sticks at the back of her head and bore violet highlights that matched her lipstick and the eye-shadow framing her gray eyes.

She took a seat next to Chan, opened the folder on the coffee table, and uncapped a beautiful fountain pen.

The man finally seemed to register what Park had just said. He blinked and looked distractedly from the blonde to the contract in front of him. Lines furrowed his brow. He raised his chin defiantly at Park.

"I'm sorry, but I think you misunderstood my leader's intentions," he said in a clipped tone full of false bravado. "I came here to negotiate the terms of an alliance, not sign your contract blindly."

Park raised an eyebrow. "What is there to discuss? The conditions of the offer are identical to those your competitors accepted when they agreed to work for us."

Chan's frown deepened. "Here's the thing. We don't *work* for anybody. We are looking to become your partner, not your underling."

Park rolled his cigar carefully between his fingers and studied the glowing embers at the tip. "Mr. Chan, let's cut to the chase. What is it that your leader wants, exactly?"

"A fifty per cent cut of the revenue of our shared business enterprises," Chan replied.

The faint throb of the club's music filled the room in the silence that followed.

Park sighed. "I don't think your leader quite understands how this is supposed to work, Mr. Chan." He crushed the cigar in the ashtray on the side table next to him, propped his elbows on his knees, and steepled his hands beneath his chin. "You see, we can wipe out your group like that."

He snapped his fingers loudly.

Chan jumped at the sound.

"Instead, we are choosing to give you the chance to show us what you can do for us before we decide whether to kill you or not." Park paused and smiled faintly as Chan turned pale. "I'm sure you've heard on the grapevine by now the...*things* we can do. Would a demonstration help convey the seriousness of our intent to your leader?"

Chan swallowed and started shaking his head. "No, that won't be—"

Park looked at his secretary. "Jade?"

The blonde moved so fast her body blurred. She jumped over the back of the couch, stabbed the first of Chan's associates through the throat with her right stiletto, and gored the second man in the eyes with the fountain pen.

Blood bubbled and gushed out of the Triad members' wounds as they fell to their knees with choked screams. The third man staggered back a couple of steps and whipped a gun out of his coat, panic flaring across his face.

Park smiled as his secretary transformed, her exquisite features distorting into the demonic shape that lived beneath her skin. A guttural cry escaped her. She leapt on the man just as he fired.

The bullet struck Chan in the left temple where he sat

frozen on the couch. A comical expression distorted his features for a moment, as if he couldn't quite believe what had just happened. The light faded from his eyes. He fell face down on the coffee table.

Park ignored the sounds of his secretary feasting hungrily on the flesh of the dying bodyguards and stared at Chan. "Well, that's unfortunate," he muttered.

He sighed, rose, and walked over to the dead Triad man. He grabbed a handful of his hair and lifted his head off the table before crouching down and looking into the dead man's open eyes.

"I know Mr. Chan is wearing video contact lenses so you've seen what just happened to your men," Park said quietly. "This was your one and only chance to ally yourself with our organization." He smiled thinly. "We do not offer second chances."

Chan's smartband started chiming as Park let go of him and straightened to his full height. He wiped his hands on a napkin and looked over at his secretary where she now stood staring at him, a hungry expression on her once more human face.

"How many times have I told you to wipe your mouth after you finish eating?" Park said with another sigh.

He cast the napkin at her and watched with a benevolent half-smile as she dabbed primly at the crimson stains on her lips and chin.

There was a reason he liked keeping Jade Q close to him. Not only was she an excellent secretary, she was also one of his strongest generals, stronger even than Ramos. She was also the only woman who had ever been able to keep up with his sexual appetite. Being possessed by a demon meant she didn't break like human females did under the strain he put their bodies through in the bedroom.

"Would you like us to take care of the Triad group tonight, sir?" Jade asked demurely after she finished cleaning herself.

She stepped over the remains of Chan's men and put away the unsigned contract.

Park nodded. "Please do. And make the message...loud. A couple of our recent associates are nervous about their new working relationship with the organization. Show them what will happen to them if they renounce their agreements."

Jade flashed him a wicked smile.

A shiver of sexual excitement danced through Park. "And come see me after."

Jade's pupils flared amber for a moment before she bit her lower lip with her pristine white teeth. Park knew she would satisfy him in the dark and twisted ways only she could.

A frantic knocking came at the door of the suite. Park frowned.

Jade tapped her smartband and studied the feed from the camera outside the door. "It's Ramos's man." She looked up at Park. "The one who came back alive from the South Brooklyn slaughterhouse."

Park's frown deepened. *I wonder what he wants.*

He hesitated before dipping his chin at his bodyguards. They opened the door of the suite.

Ramos's man rushed in, face flushed and expression agitated. "Sir, they're here! I just saw them!"

Park shared a puzzled glance with his secretary.

"Who's here?" he asked with a trace of irritation.

"The people from the slaughterhouse! The ones who killed Ramos and our men!"

Park stiffened. "Where?"

Ramos's man swallowed and lowered his gaze in the face of Park's intent stare. "They went out back, sir. To one of the private rooms."

# CHAPTER TWENTY-NINE

DRAKE BIT THE INSIDE OF HIS CHEEK AND CURLED HIS fingers into fists.

Artemus met his gaze from the other side of the room. The blond was leaning against the wall next to the door with his arms folded across his chest. He narrowed his eyes fractionally, his expression clearly telling Drake to relax.

Drake swallowed a curse and glared at him for a second. *I'd like to see you relax if you were standing here strapped to a fucking cross about to be tortured by a demon in some kind of sick sex play!*

Artemus's lips twitched in a mildly amused smile for an instant, as if he'd read his mind. Serena studied Drake with a carefully detached expression where she sat in the chair next to Artemus.

A sound distracted Drake. He looked over to the right and saw the demon remove several items from the hooks lining the interior walls and doors of a wardrobe.

The man's companion straightened where she sat on the edge of the bed, Smokey in her lap. "Oh." She bit her lip at the demon's choice of playthings, arousal bringing a flush of color to her cheeks. "I *like* those."

Drake stared at the contraptions the demon placed on a side table next to the cross. There were two floggers, a wicked looking whip, a liquid wax kit, nipple clamps, and what looked like some kind of electrostimulation device. His gaze focused on the leather item in the demon's right hand. It was a red ball gag.

A shudder raced through Drake when the man stepped up to him. He fought down the foul energy boiling inside him as the demon's aura resonated with the darkness within his soul.

"Open up," the man commanded in a hard voice.

He took Drake's chin in a brutal grip and forced his lower jaw down.

"Easy," Serena said coldly. "Don't mark him."

Drake stiffened when the man placed the ball gag inside his mouth before fastening the leather ends tightly at the back of his head. The man's breath washed across Drake's face as he leaned back slightly and stared into Drake's eyes, the light inside his dark gaze bright with depraved sexual excitement. Drake didn't have to look down to know how turned on the guy was.

*I think I'm going to be sick.*

The man slipped a knife out of his dress pants.

Artemus straightened slightly. Serena narrowed her eyes.

The demon looked over at them and smiled faintly at their expressions. "Relax. This is just for his clothes."

Cool air washed across Drake's chest and midriff as the man cut the buttons off his shirt one by one, the fasteners pinging softly when they landed on the wooden floor. The demon parted the ends of the shirt to expose Drake's torso and stepped back to admire his handy work.

"Pity," he murmured. "Whip marks would suit your skin."

Drake bit down on the ball gag. *And my sword would suit your heart, asshole.* He stiffened when the man turned and attached the wires on the electrical device to the nipple clamps. *Oh shit.*

"Allow me," Serena said coldly from the other side of the room.

She rose, crossed the floor, and took the items off the demon. Drake glared at her when she stopped before him.

"You need to loosen up a bit," she murmured in a low voice only he could hear. "You're not exactly conforming to the image of a submissive pet."

He glowered at her. His pulse skittered a second later when she ran her left hand all the way down his chest to the buckle of his belt. She leaned into him and brought her lips to his right ear, her fingers clenching slightly on the toned muscles of his abdomen.

"You can play pretend, can't you?" she whispered.

Drake blinked. Her breath on his skin and her touch were evoking a wholly different feeling to that of the demon who'd just manhandled him. He gasped around the ball gag in the next instant when he felt the cool bite of the nipple clamps on his flesh. Something flashed in Serena's eyes before she handed the electrostimulation box to the demon and headed back to her chair.

The demon reached for the controls, a hungry smile on his lips.

Drake hissed when the first electric current stabbed through him. The woman on the bed let out a low moan and squirmed, her eyes feverish with lust, her gaze locked on him and her companion.

Drake panted through his nose while the demon adjusted the controls on the device, sending stronger and stronger pulses coursing through him. His knife trembled against his forearm where it lay hidden under the sleeve of his shirt. He gritted his teeth and felt sweat bead his forehead as he resisted the urge to unleash the wicked force threatening to rip itself loose from inside his body.

"I don't think he's enjoying that," Serena said in a warning tone.

The demon ignored her and ramped up the current.

Drake let out a grunt. Smokey stirred and hopped off the lap of the woman on the bed. Artemus stepped away from the wall, his expression darkening.

It was Serena who reached the demon first. She clamped her fingers on his wrist and stayed his hand as he went to increase the intensity of the electric current once more.

"I said, I don't think he's enjoying that!" she snapped.

The man glowered at her, his features shifting and his eyes flaring with an amber light, the vile creature within him emerging for a fleeting moment.

"Babe?" The woman had risen from the bed and stood watching her companion and Serena hesitantly, her teeth worrying her lower lip. "Is everything okay?"

The man took a shuddering breath. He clenched his jaw and smiled at the woman. "Everything is fine, sweetheart. Why don't you sit down and enjoy the—"

Drake's eyes widened. Artemus drew a sharp breath from the other side of the room. Smokey's fur shivered and trembled at the same time a low growl escaped his throat.

Serena turned and met Drake's stricken stare. "What is it?"

Drake's stomach twisted as the air inside the room thickened with a suffocating aura of pure evil. *They know. They know we're here!*

The man tilted his head toward the door, as if listening to something. He scowled, transformed into his full demonic form, and stabbed Serena in the chest with his knife.

# CHAPTER THIRTY

SERENA GASPED AS THE BLADE SLIPPED BETWEEN HER RIBS and pierced her lung. She dug her fingers into the demon's wrist, twisted it violently until he let go of the weapon, and front kicked him in the gut. He flew across the room with a grunt and crashed into the wardrobe.

The demon's companion screamed. She dashed toward the door, only to freeze when the tip of Artemus's sword met the hollow at the base of her throat.

"Lady, trust me when I say you're not gonna want to go out there right now," Artemus said coldly, fingers clenched tightly around the gun that had appeared in his left hand.

Serena yanked out the dagger embedded in her flesh just as the leather straps binding Drake to the cross tore open with an explosive force. He ripped the ball gag out of his mouth, his pupils flashing red for a moment. She drew a sharp breath when he brought his fist toward her head as if to strike her.

The watch on his wrist extended into a full shield in the blink of an eye and blocked the vicious talons heading for her throat.

The demon snarled and scraped his claws against the metal where he stood to her left, his eyes glowing embers. His companion blubbered and stumbled to the farthest corner of the room, her face white with terror as she stared at the creature who was once a man.

Drake engaged the demon while Serena stemmed the flow of blood from her wound. The cut was deep and, judging from the brightness of the crimson fluid staining her hand, had lacerated an artery. She heard a whistle of air escape her punctured lung.

*Shit.*

Drake leaned out of the way of the demon's swinging arm and thrust his sword up beneath the creature's rib cage and into his heart. The demon gasped and stiffened. The knife clattered out of his hand. He clutched at the sword in his chest with bloodied fingers before thudding slowly down onto his knees and toppling over onto his side. His breathing turned shallow and irregular before stopping entirely, his features assuming their human appearance in death.

Artemus and Smokey turned to face the door. A shiver shook the rabbit seconds before his shape swelled and he shifted into his hellhound form.

The dead demon's companion started screaming again where she cowered next to the bed. She scrambled onto her hands and knees and crawled beneath the metal frame, her shrieks growing muffled.

"They're coming," Artemus warned.

"Who's coming?" Serena said.

She picked up the electrostimulation device Drake had cast to the floor, yanked the top of her catsuit open, and clamped the electrodes on the laceration above her right breast. She twisted the controls and bit her lip as electricity surged through her body.

Drake grabbed her left wrist. "What the hell are you doing?!"

"This will accelerate my healing," Serena said between gritted teeth.

Drake scowled. "How?"

The chandelier on the ceiling shivered as a powerful force shook the room. The hairs rose on the back of Serena's nape. She could feel it now. The energy that Drake, Artemus, and Smokey had evidently sensed moments before. It was more powerful than the force she and Nate had experienced back at the slaughterhouse in Brooklyn and the warehouse in Chicago. A lot more.

"It will stimulate them," Serena bit out as she sent another powerful pulse into her flesh.

"Stimulate what?" Drake asked.

Serena looked from the doorway into his dark, penetrating gaze. She hesitated for a second. *There's no point avoiding the truth anymore. They're bound to find out what Nate and I are sooner or later. Hell, I think Artemus already knows.*

"The nanorobots in my body," she admitted in a low voice.

Drake let go of her hand as if he'd been burned.

Something twisted inside Serena at the look on his face. Something that felt very much like pain. She squashed the distracting feeling, dropped the electrical device onto the floor, and removed the daggers taped to the hollows between her shoulder blades and spine.

She could feel the nanorobots working deep inside her body, cauterizing bleeding vessels and knitting together torn tissues.

*Faster! Hurry!*

The vibrations shaking the room intensified. A low rumble echoed above the tinkling of the crystal chandelier hanging from the ceiling.

The door exploded in a thick cloud of darkness.

~

CALLIE SCRATCHED HER FOREHEAD. HER FINGERS bumped against her horns. She pursed her lips and sighed.

Nate glanced at her in the rearview mirror. "You okay?"

Callie grimaced. "Yeah. I still can't get used to my new —body parts."

The infant snake stirred at the base of her spine. She scratched the itchy spot just above it and felt it flick its tongue at her fingers in a friendly gesture.

"I've lived with these marks for most of my life and never minded them before," she murmured. "Now, I'm not so sure."

Nate was silent for a moment.

"They are part of who you are now," he said quietly, his eyes meeting hers fleetingly in the mirror. "Like the marks on Artemus and Drake, and the rabbit's hellhound form." He paused. "The four of you are pretty unique."

"The four of us are monsters," Callie said bluntly.

A stillness came over Nate then. "No, you are not."

Callie narrowed her eyes slightly. She couldn't help but notice the large man's slight emphasis on the 'you.'

"You know we're going to have to talk about it at some point or another, don't you?"

Nate's expression turned inscrutable.

"It's time you told us exactly what you and Serena are," Callie continued.

"It's up to Serena to decide that matter," Nate said stiffly.

Callie stared at the back of Nate's head. She shifted forward and propped her folded arms atop the headrest of the front passenger seat.

"See, I'm puzzled by that. Technically speaking, you're stronger than her. So, why aren't you the leader of your team?"

"Because we made a pact, a long time ago. Serena, me, and…Ben. We decided she would be the one to guide us. She may not be as physically strong as me but she's the better fighter and the smarter one."

"Who's Ben?" Callie said, puzzled.

Something shifted in Nate's eyes for a moment. An echo of an age-old pain. "He was our brother. We lost him a few years ago, in an accident." He hesitated. "Serena still blames Drake for his death."

Callie's eyes widened. She was about to ask him to tell her more when something outside the SUV drew her gaze. She looked past Nate to the building where the BDSM dungeon was located.

The air around it was shivering, the night thickening to the darkest black, as if all light was being sucked out of the immediate vicinity.

A suffocating pressure filled Callie's mind. Instinct made her look over her shoulder, toward the rear of the alley. Her eyes widened at what she saw.

"Nate, start the car!"

A low growl erupted from her throat and underscored her words. She could feel her hair thickening around her face and her horns and snake tail growing.

Her marks knew what was coming.

"What's wrong?" Nate asked.

"*Just start the car!*" Callie snarled, gnashing her teeth at the oppressive evil bearing down on them.

Smokey's faint cry resonated inside her mind. Fear filled Callie. Her gaze locked on the building now enveloped in a thick billow of swirling, foul clouds.

Nate fired the ignition and gunned the engine. The vehicle started to shake as he pulled away. Callie fisted her hands.

*Too late!*

The demons swarmed the SUV in a heavy mantle of darkness.

# CHAPTER THIRTY-ONE

ARTEMUS GRUNTED AS A FIST CONNECTED WITH HIS LEFT loin. He deflected the wicked claws heading for his eyes, fired at the creature behind him, and cut the throat of the monster trying to gouge his chest. Ash fluttered around him when the demon he'd shot self-combusted in a burst of flames and a dying scream. He raised the gun at the creatures trying to bring Smokey to the ground eight feet to his right.

The weapon clicked on an empty magazine.

"*Shit!* I'm out of ammo!"

He jammed the gun into the rear waistband of his jeans and grasped his sword in a two-handed grip, body humming with tension.

"Great!" Drake blocked a blow to his thigh where he stood on a bar some ten feet to the left. He repelled the demon trying to emasculate him, kicked him in the head, sliced another across the face with his blade, and scowled at Artemus. "Why didn't you bring more?"

Artemus brought his sword around in an arc as he headed toward the hellhound where he fought the creatures atop him. The blade carved through the neck of the demon running toward him, cutting short its deep-throated ululations and lobbing its head off cleanly.

"Well, excuse *me* for not predicting the shitstorm we would end up in tonight!" He kneed a demon in the groin and punched a second in the face before glaring at Drake. "And where was I supposed to hide them? Up my—"

"Will you two clowns shut the hell up and concentrate on finding a way out of this place?!" Serena shouted as she stabbed a demon in the eye and sucker-punched another one in the stomach.

She was standing with her back against a cage up ahead and showed no signs that the wound she had suffered a short while back had slowed her down in the slightest. If anything, the surges of electricity she'd delivered to her body seemed to have spurred her to a whole other level of physical violence.

The humans who'd been in the club had long since fled the premises. When the fight had first broken out and spilled over into the main club, many had assumed it was a show put on for their entertainment. It wasn't until Drake decapitated a female demon that the reality of what was unfolding inside the BDSM dungeon became brutally clear. The gory head went spinning through the air in a spray of arterial blood before landing in the lap of a laughing blonde in a white dress. Screams of terror and a desperate rush for the exits ensued.

The blade in Artemus's hand trembled when he finally reached Smokey. He slashed and stabbed at the creatures swarming the hellhound, the metal shivering and sparking with flashes of golden light as power pulsed from his core into the weapon.

Smokey shook himself free of the last two demons

with a snarl. His thick jaws snapped on bones and crushed flesh as he fell upon the creatures. He shook them violently from side to side and batted at them with his deadly claws until they went limp in his hold. Blood dripped from the wounds on his flanks. He straightened in the middle of the corpses, a low, continuous growl rumbling from his throat and his eyes aglow with an unholy light.

Artemus stood by the hellhound's side and studied the crowd of demons blocking their path to the stairs and the fire exits. *Fifty down. Fifty to go.*

Something gnawed at his mind as they engaged the remaining creatures with blades, fists, claws, and fangs. Something that had been troubling him ever since they got out of the private room at the back and reached the floor of the main club.

The demons weren't attacking them *en masse*, as they did at Voggell's place. Instead, they were coming at them in small groups, like they were tag teaming each other. It was almost as if—

*They are testing us.*

Artemus swooped beneath a wicked talon, elbowed his attacker in the face, and glanced at Smokey.

Drake stabbed a demon in the gut before looking over at the hellhound. He met Artemus's uneasy gaze.

"I think he's right," he said grimly.

Serena wiped a sliver of blood from her mouth before casting a frown their way, her chest heaving. "Who's right? And about what?"

"Smokey thinks these guys are playing with us," Artemus said in a low voice. "I have to agree. They could have overwhelmed us by now. And they haven't."

Serena stared at the dead bodies around them. "*This* is playing?"

Artemus's skin prickled a second before the coils of darkness swirling through the air thickened. The demons around them stopped in their tracks, amber eyes focused unblinkingly on them. A deathly hush fell over the club.

A shudder coursed through Drake where he stood to Artemus's left. He fisted his hands and looked up. Artemus followed his gaze.

An elegantly dressed Asian man was watching them from the mezzanine. He was flanked by two bodyguards and rolling a cigar between his fingers, his pose as relaxed as that of the blonde in the skin-tight, purple leather outfit next to him.

"That's Erik Park," Serena said in a hard voice.

"Who's the chick?" Artemus muttered.

Serena narrowed her eyes at the blonde. "I don't know."

Artemus appraised their enemy with a steady stare.

There was something different about Erik Park. Something that set him apart from the other demons in the club. It took Artemus a few seconds to figure out what it was.

Unlike the creatures they'd fought in Chicago and Brooklyn, Park's aura was a thick, obsidian black, as if it had never been touched by the light of day. The blonde's was almost as nasty.

A faint smile curved Park's lips when he met Artemus's eyes.

"You have my heartfelt gratitude, Mr. Steele," he drawled. "Thanks to you and your friends, we appear to have found the Guardian."

Artemus frowned.

Smokey stiffened and took a step forward. His growls deepened and flecks of acid drool dripped from his jaws as he glared at the demon on the mezzanine.

*Callie.*

Surprise jolted through Artemus. Before he could ask the hellhound what he meant, Park spoke once more.

"You know what to do," he told the blonde next to him.

# CHAPTER THIRTY-TWO

Park's words were like a match to a fuse. A veil of darkness smothered the lights, bringing a pall of gloom to the entire club. Amber flashed all around them.

The demons finally attacked.

"Shit!" Drake said between clenched teeth.

Artemus grunted as a flurry of fists and talons rained down on him. He blocked the vicious onslaught with his sword, the blade juddering in his grip while claws slashed and sliced through the leather covering his arms.

"We have to make it to those stairs!" Serena shouted.

Blood oozed out of the cuts on her face and body as she fended off the strikes of the demons swarming her, her wounds healing almost as quickly as they appeared.

"Easier said than done!" Drake snarled, deflecting a storm of wicked blows with his shield before counterattacking with his blade.

Artemus's heart thudded against his ribs. He eyed the twenty feet separating them from the metal steps spiraling up toward the mezzanine and the primary exit.

*Serena's right. Our only chance is to get to that door!*

There was only one thing left to do.

Artemus repelled another wave of attack and concentrated. Heat flared inside his chest with his next breath. Power surged through him and danced down his sword. The blade broadened and lengthened in his grip, the metal vibrating until it shimmered with a faint, white haze.

An echo of the savage energy running through his veins resonated inside his consciousness a heartbeat later, startling him. He looked over at Smokey and Drake, sensing the same strange bond. The bond he had felt the day he first met the two of them.

The hellhound's eyes flared and brightened to molten gold. His hide trembled and shivered as his body swelled, adding another foot to his height and girth.

Drake's sword darkened and thickened, the edges of the blade twisting into wicked, jagged teeth. The shield covering his left arm grew dull, the metal losing its luster as if all light had been sucked out of it. His eyes, when they met Artemus's, were blood red and filled with a feral light.

Artemus's pulse stuttered. *Is this Drake's true form?*

There was no more time to think.

SERENA FELT THE CHANGE IN THE AIR AND SAW THE demons falter for a split second. She followed their surprised gazes. Her eyes widened.

They moved as one, every step, every gesture, every strike synchronized, as if they were parts of a single, well-oiled machine. When Drake ducked, Artemus attacked. When Artemus stepped back, Smokey pounced. Blades, claws, and fangs flashed as they advanced through the crowd of demons, the sheer brute force of their assault felling the creatures where they stood, their passage often too fast to be gleaned.

Something glittered out of the corner of Serena's eye. She leaned sharply to the side. A faint draft sent the hair fluttering at her right temple. A single lock slowly spiraled to the floor.

She turned and studied the blonde who'd just sliced the dark strands with her blade.

The woman in the purple leather outfit smiled, her teeth sharp fangs that matched the dagger in her hand, her pretty face distorted by the evil that lurked beneath her skin.

Serena inhaled sharply as the woman's blade danced toward her once more, the motion so quick she would have missed it had she been an ordinary human. She blocked the attack a hair's breadth from her stomach and gritted her teeth as her own knives were knocked violently out of her grasp. She swooped, spun on one heel, and aimed a reverse roundhouse kick at her attacker's head as she rose.

The demon blocked it with one hand.

Numbness bloomed up Serena's leg as the woman curled her fingers into her limb with a sadistic grin, crushing flesh and grinding bone. Serena scowled, lifted herself off the ground with her right leg, and hooked her foot around the demon's neck. She braced her hands upside down on the ground, twisted, and flipped her over.

The demon pivoted in the air in a gravity-defying turn. She landed firmly on her feet, grabbed a stunned Serena by the throat, and hurled her bodily across the club.

Air whooshed out of Serena's lungs as she smashed through two chairs and a table before crashing into one of the bars. Bottles exploded around her, drenching her in expensive liquor, the shards slicing her exposed skin. Pain shot through her spine and sent tingles sparking down her legs. Her knees sagged.

The neural implant in her brain and the nanorobots that lived inside her took over, dulling the feeling to a barely noticeable ache. She braced a hand against the counter and straightened.

A fist slammed into her solar plexus.

Serena bent over with a grunt, alarmed at how rapidly the blonde had closed the distance between them. She deflected the next blow with her left forearm. Heat erupted along her skin as the woman sliced a line from her elbow to her wrist.

Serena snatched a piece of broken glass from the countertop and stabbed the blonde in the chest and gut with lightning fast strikes.

The woman stepped back, her amber eyes narrowing as she looked down and slowly fingered her wounds. Her features shifted, the ugly mask sharpening and becoming more grotesque, as if the demon inside her was threatening to break loose.

The hairs rose on Serena's arms. Her ears popped as the pressure dropped around her.

A deep growl erupted from the blonde's throat. A shudder shook her from head to toe. She grew in size in the blink of an eye, gaining two feet in height and some hundred and fifty pounds in weight.

Serena stared at the monster now towering over her.

*Oh crap.*

The next thing she knew, they were in the air. The demon touched down on the mezzanine, lifted Serena above her head, and hurled her over the railing at a metal cage below. The world spun around Serena in a dizzying kaleidoscope as she fell toward the evil black spike atop the enclosure. She gritted her teeth.

*This is gonna hurt like a bitch!*

Something flashed below. A dark shape leapt toward her.

There was a sound like thunder.

Black wings filled Serena's vision and carried her into darkness.

# CHAPTER THIRTY-THREE

CALLIE OPENED HER EYES. BLACK AND WHITE SPOTS swam fuzzily before her. She blinked. The spots blurred before coalescing into a dull, gray surface some five feet above her. She stared at it groggily for a moment. Memory returned in a burst of violent sounds and images. She tensed and bolted upright.

*Nate!*

She regretted the movement instantly. Fire pulsed through every inch of her body and her head throbbed with the most vicious pounding. She bit her lip and fought down a wave of nausea, her fingers curling on the edge of the stone bench she was lying on.

The last thing she remembered was the demons swarming the SUV. Although she and Nate had put up a fight, they'd had little chance of winning in the face of such overwhelming numbers.

She noted the bruises and cuts on her forearms absent-mindedly while she focused on her surroundings.

She appeared to be in some kind of cell. Bare stone made up the ceiling, floor, and three walls of her prison.

Metal bars lined the fourth wall, with a door in the middle. Flames flickered in a sconce in the corridor outside, the yellow light casting dancing shadows across the ground.

Callie rose from the bench and took a step toward the cell door. Metal clinked. A heavy weight gripped her right leg. She looked down.

There was a shackle and chain around her ankle. She frowned.

A noise distracted her. Footsteps sounded in the passage. Callie stiffened as they drew close. She could tell from the way her skin was prickling that someone powerful was approaching. Shadowy figures appeared beyond the cell bars a moment later.

"I see you're up."

Callie studied the man who'd just spoken. From Serena's description, she was pretty certain she was in the presence of Erik Park.

She narrowed her eyes at him. "Where's Nate? And what did you do with my husband's cane?"

An amused smile danced across Park's thin lips. "Walk with me."

Callie stood motionless while one of Park's bodyguards opened the cell and unlocked the fetter around her leg. She stepped out of her prison and reluctantly followed Park as he led the way up the corridor. They passed a row of empty cells and negotiated a couple of turns. An opening appeared up ahead. They emerged into a shadowy space.

Callie slowed to a stop, her eyes widening as she took in her new surrounds.

The cave rose some eight stories tall and was nearly half as wide, the ceiling lost in gloom. The walls were bare rock and dotted with flaming torches that cast a hazy, yellow light over the lower levels of the chamber. Rows of seats carved out of black stone rose in tiers in a semicircular gallery to her right, much like an ancient Roman amphitheater.

Callie's stomach lurched when she looked to the left.

A stone arch some twenty feet tall and fifteen feet wide rose from the middle of a low stage that appeared to be the focus of the auditorium.

Nate stood bound to a metal cross some five feet in front of it.

His face was badly swollen and bruised, and cuts covered his bare arms and chest. He lifted his chin and squinted at her.

"Callie?" he whispered hoarsely.

Callie darted up a flight of stone steps and rushed over to him, heedless of Park and his bodyguards. She stopped in front of him and raised trembling hands to his face.

"Are you okay?"

Nate licked his cracked lips. "Nothing time won't heal. You? They hurt you?"

"No." She shook her head and smiled tremulously. "I'm fine."

"Your marks," Nate mumbled, staring. "They're back to normal." His eyes grew hard as he studied the wounds on her arms. "And you don't look fine to me."

Surprise bolted through Callie. She touched her forehead and the base of her spine. Nate was right. Her tail and horns were gone.

"Those are from when they attacked us in the alley." She fingered a fresh cut on his left cheek. "This looks new."

Nate glanced past her. "They don't play nice."

A fresh wave of anger surged through Callie. She

twisted on her heels and glared at Park where he stood watching them. "What did you do to him?"

Park shrugged and tucked his hands into the pockets of his expensive suit trousers. "We just asked your friend some questions, that's all."

Callie straightened, her fingers curling into fists at her sides. "What do you want? And where's my husband's cane?"

Park smiled again. "Funny you should mention that."

The hairs rose on Callie's arms. Her pulse started a rapid thrumming in her veins. She looked around, an ominous foreboding swamping her.

Flames started flickering wildly around the cave, as if in the midst of a storm. Shadows oozed out of the rock walls and ground until they filled the chamber, wreathing coils of darkness that doused the light to a paltry glow.

Callie gasped and heard Nate draw a labored breath. The very air around them grew heavy, making it hard to breathe. Her gaze found Park once more.

She froze, every muscle in her body turning to stone.

Something was happening next to the Asian man. Something that defied the laws of physics and nature. Something impossible.

The shadows next to Park were merging. The blobs of darkness collided and pooled until they formed a solid, rippling line several feet above the ground. A loud ripping noise echoed through the cave, as if the very air were being torn asunder.

The black line split in the center. Blood-red light spilled out of the thin, jagged opening that appeared.

Bile rose in Callie's throat at the foul energy that flooded the chamber. She knew without a doubt that it was coming from the crimson glow. Her marks trembled. Her hair thickened. Her nails lengthened.

Park reached inside the light. His hand vanished all the way to his wrist, his limb swallowed by whatever lay on the other side of the rift in space. Lines appeared on his exposed forearm. They snaked up his skin lightning fast and spread across his neck and face, a spiderweb of darkness that throbbed as if it were a living thing. His features shivered for a moment.

Callie caught a glimpse of the demon that lived within him and shuddered.

A grimace distorted Park's lips as he slowly pulled something out of the pulsing, red fissure. The opening closed seconds later.

Callie's eyes widened.

Park was holding the ivory cane in his hand.

Except it no longer resembled the cane that had gone up for auction in Elton LeBlanc's place in Chicago a few days ago. Veins of gold and silver now suffused the shaft in a complex, spiraling pattern of symbols that shone faintly, as if they were lit from within.

*Thump.*

Callie blinked.

*Thump-thump.*

It came again. A jarring thud deep inside her, so loud she wondered if the others in the chamber had heard it.

*Thump-thump. Thump-thump.*

Callie raised a trembling hand to her chest. It was as if a second heart had started to beat inside her, alongside her human one.

*Thump-thump. Thump-thump. Thump-thump.*

Something stirred deep inside the bowels of Callie's consciousness as the strange pulsation continued, the rhythm rising in speed and ferocity until she could no longer distinguish it from her own heartbeat. Something ancient. Something sacred.

In that moment, Callie finally glimpsed the true nature of the creature who lived within her and the purpose of the cane. Ice filled her veins. Her gaze moved from Park's triumphant expression to the stone archway on the stage behind her.

# CHAPTER THIRTY-FOUR

*SHE WAS DREAMING. AND IN THE DREAM, SHE WAS THERE again. In that place of eternal cold and darkness. A place of pain and terror. The fortress where she and Nate had lived the first six years of their lives. Although 'live' was far too generous a word for what they had endured in that time.*

*There had been a third. Their brother in arms. The one their father, the man who had helped rescue them the day their prison fell, named Benedict. The baby who would grow up to be Ben. Her Ben. The first man she had ever come to care for. To love, even, although love was an emotion her kind had not been engineered to feel. The one who would eventually be taken from her by a monster called Drake Hunter.*

Serena's eyes snapped open. She grabbed the hand of the woman about to press a dressing against her left flank.

Isabelle stilled and stared at her. Her eyes grew hooded. "You're awake."

Serena slowly uncurled her fingers from around the woman's wrist. Blood filled the pale marks she had left on her skin. Isabelle finished fixing the dressing to her wound, pulled her T-shirt down over the waistband of her combat trousers, and rose wordlessly from the bed.

Serena pushed herself up onto her elbows and looked around the unfamiliar room. "Where are we?"

"A safehouse," Isabelle replied stiffly.

She turned and headed for the door.

Serena studied her as she swung her legs over the edge of the mattress, muted echoes of pain shooting through her from her recent injuries. "You don't like me, do you?"

Isabelle stopped, her hand on the doorknob. She hesitated before sighing and twisting on her heels. She took a couple of steps toward the bed, folded her arms across her chest, and lifted her chin belligerently.

"No, I don't," she said bluntly, her gaze cool. "I know what you are."

Serena rose to her feet. Someone had stripped her out of the catsuit and dressed her in a fresh change of clothes —her own. She pulled her T-shirt up to examine the latest wound on her body.

Something had stabbed clean through her flank from front to back. She couldn't recall how exactly she had gotten the injury. The last thing she remembered was falling toward the club floor and the wicked spike on the roof of a cage growing closer.

Serena blinked. Something flashed before her mind's eye. A fleeting memory. Of black wings and arms wrapping her in a warm, protective cocoon.

"And what am I?" she murmured distractedly as she pondered what exactly she had seen in that ephemeral moment.

"A super soldier."

Coldness squeezed Serena's heart at Isabelle's icy words. The same coldness that had been with her since she, Nate, and Ben had left the only home they had ever known and ventured out on their own, determined to carve their own lives and fates. That they had cast aside a man who had loved them unconditionally was something that still filled Serena with pain and guilt, and she had asked herself the same questions a thousand times over since Ben's death.

Would he still be alive today if they had never left the estate that cold winter's morning? Would they still be living under the same roof as the man who had raised them and who had been determined to erase the grim future meant for them from birth and forge them a new destiny?

Time and time again, Serena revisited the fateful decision she had made. It had come the day she overheard an altercation between the man they had called father and one of his subordinates. An altercation that had revealed what the others their father presided over as leader truly thought of them. Others who had gazed upon her, Nate, and Ben with the same chilling expression Isabelle was offering her right now.

Serena met the other woman's stare unflinchingly. "Do they know?"

"You mean Artemus and Drake?" Isabelle shrugged. "Yeah, they do. So do Elton and the Vatican. Your—*kind* aren't exactly easy to find these days."

Serena clenched her teeth. It had been inevitable that the truth of what she and Nate were would be uncovered, especially after what had happened at the club. Isabelle's next words made her stomach twist with an uncommon jolt of fear that rooted her feet to the ground.

"I lost friends in Greenland," the blonde said quietly. "Friends who had been with me for a long, long time."

Serena's eyes widened. She unfroze in the next instant and took a step toward the other woman. "You are one of them!"

Isabelle frowned. "I think that's my line."

Serena marched up to her and grabbed the front of her shirt.

"I was six years old at the time!" she hissed in Isabelle's face. "I was a *child!* All of us who were rescued that day were children! It wasn't our fault we were—" she faltered and swallowed, "we were born! We never *asked* to be made this way!"

Isabelle watched her from fathomless eyes.

"That may be true," she said after a short silence. "But I still don't trust you."

The door opened behind her. Artemus walked in and stopped at the sight of them.

He narrowed his eyes. "What's going on?"

"Nothing," Isabelle said in a mild tone while Serena slowly released her shirt. "Just getting to know one another, woman to woman."

"Really?" Artemus said. "'Cause it looked like she was thinking of punching your lights out."

He glanced at Serena, his eyes unreadable.

Isabelle's expression grew affronted. "No one punches my lights out!"

"Demons do," Artemus countered.

Isabelle scowled. "No non-supernatural entity punches my lights out."

Mark appeared behind Artemus. "What's taking so long? You were just changing her—oh." He paused and studied Serena with a carefully neutral expression. "You're up." He hesitated. "How're you feeling?"

"I'm okay," Serena replied, appraising Elton LeBlanc's guard with fresh eyes.

*I wonder how many of them are like Isabelle. Is Elton one of them too?*

"No, Elton isn't," Isabelle muttered.

Serena blinked at her, surprised she had read her mind.

Isabelle grimaced. "It was only logical you would think it. And neither is Shamus."

Serena indicated Mark with a tilt of her head. "But he is?"

Isabelle's silence answered her question.

"What are you talking about?" Artemus said with a puzzled frown.

"Nothing you need to concern yourself with, Goldilocks," Isabelle said.

She headed out of the room, Mark following in her footsteps.

Artemus scowled and stormed out into the corridor. "Don't call me that!"

Serena stared at the empty doorway.

Artemus reappeared. "Well, are you coming?"

Surprise flashed through Serena. She could sense no animosity in his gaze or his voice. It was as if he simply didn't care about the fact that she was a monster.

"Yeah," she murmured.

She followed him out of the bedroom and down the passage to a large, open-plan, living-dining room over-looking Central Park. Sunlight streamed through the large, east-facing bay windows up ahead.

Elton LeBlanc turned from where he stood gazing out over the city.

Drake sat on a couch to the left. She could see the outline of a dressing under his shirt, over his right flank.

He met her stare steadily, his eyes as inscrutable as Artemus's, yet devoid of any hostility. If anything, he looked curious.

"It's time we talked," Elton said coolly.

A door opened and shut in the distance.

Shamus appeared through a doorway to the right. "I got us bagels, doughnuts, and coffee." His expression brightened when he saw Serena. "Oh. You're up." He stopped and placed the box he was holding on the dining table. "Want a bagel?"

# CHAPTER THIRTY-FIVE

Park took a bite of his steak and lifted a crystal glass to his lips. He swallowed a sip of rich, red wine and flashed a benevolent smile at the woman opposite him.

He indicated the untouched plate before her. "Come, eat."

Callie Stone stared at him coldly, her arms folded across her chest. Her gaze occasionally flickered to the ivory cane leaning against Park's chair.

They were in his suite, on the tenth floor of the organization's headquarters in Lower Manhattan. The cave where the secretive and more often than not grisly activities of the group took place was over two hundred feet below them, deep beneath the silt and sediment and inside the very marrow of the bedrock that made up the city.

Even now, sitting in the comfort of his private dining room, Park could feel faint waves of sordid energy pulsing from the giant stone arch that had been one of the organization's most prized possessions for the last two decades.

He'd been twenty-two when the artifact had been dug out of a valley outside the city of Jerusalem. A member of the group for a mere four years, he'd answered the dark call at the age of eighteen, after the demon inside him awoke one night and killed his entire extended family in a frenzied rage in their tiny home in a village in Gyeongbuk Province, in South Korea.

It was the organization that had found him hours later, wandering aimlessly through the rice fields fifteen miles from what had once been his home, his clothes, hands, and face drenched in blood and his mind a vacant space filled with the voice of the demon.

It was later that Park learned that the moment a demon awoke inside a human, it triggered some kind of signal inside the closest organization members. They were almost always the first to reach the new fledglings and guide them into the fold of the group.

Moments after the men who'd helped excavate the site outside Jerusalem had carried the heavy relic onto a truck bound for the port, they had been slaughtered, their bodies torn asunder, and their flesh feasted upon by the group members who'd been in attendance at the long-awaited unveiling.

More than the triumphant accomplishment of having finally located one of the artifacts they had been scouring the Earth for, Park's lasting memory of that night remained the compelling sight of his master. Naked, bathed in blood and gore, his demonic shape completely exposed and his eyes glowing with the light of Hell itself, the leader of their group had towered over them in all his unholy glory, his presence so overpowering the lesser demons among them had fallen to their knees and been unable to meet his gaze.

Park had not known then what it must have cost his master to commune so fully with the other side that night.

The first time he was taught how to open a rift between this world and the place where demons dwelled, the pain had rendered him unconscious. Even now, after a decade of practice, he still bit his tongue to stop himself from screaming in agony when he delved into the eternal crimson light of the demons' plane of existence.

*And now, we finally have the key.* Park glanced from Callie to the cane. *Or should I say keys.*

Callie watched him in silence while he finished his meal.

He swallowed the last of his wine, dabbed his mouth primly with a linen napkin, and sighed. "You really are stubborn, Guardian."

Callie stiffened in her seat. Her green eyes narrowed. "What did you call me?"

Park smiled and rose to his feet. Callie watched him warily as he walked around the table. He stopped behind her and placed his hands on her shoulders. A shudder ran through her. Park's smile widened.

"You, my dear, are the Guardian of the Gate. And that —" Park leaned down until his lips were level with Callie's left ear, "is your key."

He indicated the cane with a tilt of his chin.

Callie twisted her head until she was looking straight into his eyes. "What are you talking about?"

Park knew that she was lying. He could smell it on her skin. He curled his fingers into her shoulders until she whimpered in pain.

"Unlock the key, Guardian," he hissed.

"I don't know—I don't know what you mean!" Callie said, her knuckles white where she gripped the armrests of the chair.

Park stilled, surprise shooting through him. He sensed

an element of truth in her words. He let go of her and headed back around the table. Heat flared from the cane and threatened to singe his skin when he took hold of it. He masked a grimace and carried the artifact over to Callie.

"Only you can decipher the sigils that have appeared on the key," Park explained. He laid the cane on the table before her. "Once you utter the words, its true form will be revealed and the Gate will open."

Callie turned to stone. She stared unblinkingly at the cane, her hands frozen on the armrests, as if she were afraid to touch it.

"What is behind the Gate?" she finally said in a tremulous voice.

Park smiled, his body trembling as the demon inside him threatened to break free. He grabbed Callie's hair, ignored her shocked cry, and tugged her head back viciously until she was looking up at him.

"*You know what's behind the Gate, Guardian!*" he spat, his face an inch from hers. Her pupils widened until he could see his demonic reflection deep in their dark depths. "*So spare me your lies and unlock the key!*"

For a split second, something stared back at Park from behind Callie Stone's eyes. A sliver of unease darted through him. He let go of her abruptly, grabbed the cane, and marched out of the suite, certain he'd imagined the slithering shapes he'd just seen.

Jade was waiting for him outside.

"Take her back to the cave," Park ordered with a scowl. "I think she's going to need a certain kind of inspiration to give us what we want."

Jade smiled.

# CHAPTER THIRTY-SIX

Serena took a shallow breath. "In the 1950s, following the discovery of DNA and the birth of genetic engineering science, a...man by the name of Jonah Krondike aligned himself with a rogue faction of the U.S. Army and started what was effectively the first human enhancement experiment."

Drake watched Serena closely where she sat looking absentmindedly at her half-empty coffee cup on the couch opposite him.

It had been half a day since the extraordinary events at the private BDSM dungeon in Chinatown had unfolded, and Callie and Nate had gone missing. After the battle had ended, Artemus, Smokey, and Drake had fled the premises with an injured Serena, moments before the first patrol cars screeched to a stop outside the building. A manhunt was now on to identify and track down the perpetrators behind what the NYPD and the FBI were describing as the worst nightclub massacre of the century.

Drake had masked a grimace when he'd seen the police news conference that morning on TV.

*They're gonna have to work extra hard to find us, seeing as all the security camera recordings in the club and the surrounding neighborhood were mysteriously destroyed by a power surge. It's a pity they didn't get to witness the true forms of all those dead demons.*

"A man?" Elton narrowed his eyes at Serena. He was sitting to Drake's left. "You hesitated for a moment there."

Serena met his gaze steadily. "Let's just call him a man for the time being."

Elton's frown deepened.

"By human enhancement, do you mean—?" Shamus started.

"Super soldiers," Isabelle interrupted in a taciturn tone. "She means super soldiers."

Elton arched an eyebrow. "I thought that dubious honor belonged to Hitler and his Aryan race aspirations of the Second World War."

"You would be wrong," Serena murmured.

Drake exchanged a glance with Artemus where he sat on the couch next to him. Smokey polished off the remains of a doughnut at their feet before leveling limpid brown eyes at Serena. Unlike Elton and Isabelle, who were watching the mercenary with a distrustful expression, the hellhound seemed more intrigued than suspicious about her, a sentiment Drake and Artemus shared equally.

They now understood what it was they had sensed in Serena and Nate's presence—the nanorobots that lived within their bioengineered bodies.

When the blonde demon had thrown Serena from the club's mezzanine, Drake had acted instinctively. What it was he had done exactly in those precious few seconds though, he wasn't sure.

When Artemus had described what he and Smokey had seen, Drake had told him to pull the other one.

"If that really happened, then why the hell did I get skewered by that spike?" he'd said mutinously as he dressed his wound.

The metal stake on top of the club floor cage had sliced clean through his flesh and Serena's left flank when they'd landed atop it, missing their spines by scant inches.

Artemus had studied him for a thoughtful moment. "Because I don't think you were in full control of your powers."

Drake had frozen and stared at him, surprised at the other man's undertone. "Wait. Are you saying that—" he'd clenched his jaw, "that something like that has happened to you too?"

Artemus had hesitated. "Yes." He'd shrugged. "So I've been told, anyway."

Drake had frowned. "You don't remember?"

"No," Artemus had replied in a troubled voice.

Drake shook his head and focused on the present.

Serena met his gaze briefly.

"Over the decades that followed, Krondike recruited more scientists specializing in the fields of eugenics and biotechnology into the program," she continued. "One of those enlisted was a brilliant and disgruntled American scientist by the name of Professor Ian Serle. Krondike and Serle built a company called AuGenD, with the primary intent of working on genomic engineering technologies to advance their goals of producing the first batch of genetically enhanced super soldiers at a secret facility in Yuma. That facility was destroyed in 2013. Jonah Krondike died during the battle that took place there. The super soldiers who made it out alive were apprehended and placed in a rehabilitation program. Some managed to reintegrate back into human society and went on to live fairly normal lives. Those who didn't were kept in a facility where they could not harm themselves or others." She paused, a cynical smile twisting her lips for a moment. "Chemical lobotomization, they called it. They said it was for their own good. That they wouldn't suffer anymore."

"Who are *they*?" Elton said.

Serena leaned back against the couch and crossed her left leg atop her right knee, her expression unreadable. "I'm afraid I cannot reveal that information."

Elton scowled. "Cannot? Or *will* not?"

Drake glanced at Isabelle. A muscle jumped in the blonde's jawline as she glared at Serena.

*She knows something.*

"I made a promise," Serena said quietly. "We all did. So the answer to both your questions is yes. I cannot and will not tell you more. Now, do you want the rest of this story or are you going to keep bitching about every single little detail?"

A muffled snicker escaped Artemus. Drake bit his lip.

He had to hand it to the chick. She had balls of steel.

Elton looked like he was about to say something. He hesitated and swallowed his words with a glare. "Please, continue."

"Thank you," Serena said drily. "Unbeknown to Serle, Yuma turned out to be only a secondary program. Krondike and his son Vlado Krall had a primary facility elsewhere, where their scientists had been working on even more advanced human enhancement technologies. That facility was in—Greenland."

Elton straightened in his seat. "Wait a minute. Greenland?" His eyes widened. "Are you talking about the place where that nuclear explosion happened in 2017?"

Drake stiffened.

Artemus went still next to him. "What nuclear explosion?"

Drake's heart started drumming rapidly in his chest.

"Not many people know of it," Elton explained reluctantly. "The government of Denmark, in conjunction with the U.S. and the United Nations, decided to keep the details of what happened that day under wraps. It's only because the Vatican has access to that information that I came to find out about it."

Serena glanced at Isabelle.

"About what?" Artemus said with a scowl.

"In the early morning hours of August 14$^{th}$ 2017, a task force consisting of troops from several NATO allied countries infiltrated the primary research facility in Greenland," Serena said in a cold, detached voice. "They successfully overpowered Vlado Krall's army but were unaware of the four nuclear devices he had activated before his death. Three of those devices detonated deep enough underground not to cause any major damage on the surface. Shortly after dawn, the fourth device went off. That one was on the surface." Serena's fingers clenched around the cup in her hands. "The resulting nuclear explosion was carefully curtailed by some of the people who came to that facility that night. No signs of radioactive debris or radiation were ever found at the site. All that was left was—"

"A one-mile-wide dome of ice and rock that still stands to this day," Elton finished in a voice full of wonder. A frown marred his brow. "And what do you mean, *curtailed?* Who the hell can stop a nuclear explosion?!"

# CHAPTER THIRTY-SEVEN

A RINGING STARTED IN DRAKE'S EARS. HE COULD FEEL the room closing in around him, the air becoming too thick to breathe. Darkness started to encroach on his vision. Artemus's voice reached him from a distance.

"August 14th?" the man at Drake's side said in a lifeless voice.

Elton blinked. "Oh. That's right. Your birthday is August 13th."

Drake's mouth went dry. He turned to stare at Artemus, his head moving almost mechanically atop his body.

"In the early hours of August 14th 2017, on the night of my sixth birthday, I woke up in the field behind my house to strange lights in the sky. It was the first and only time I ever sleepwalked." A muscle jumped in Artemus's cheek. "That was the night I met Smokey and found my switchblade." He lifted his knife from inside his right boot and studied it with a frown before tucking it back in its place. "It was also the night the marks appeared on my back."

The ringing grew until it filled Drake's entire world.

*The demon was back. It roared inside him. Whispered*

*unspeakable things. Raged in a wicked voice full of wrath and despair. It had been with him so long Drake could barely recall a time when he had been free of it. And yet, as he listened to Artemus's words, Drake relived every single second of the night he first met the creature. The night that had haunted him all of his life. The night he awoke a monster and burned the only world he had ever known to ashes and bones.*

"—ke! *Drake!* Hey, snap out of it!"

Drake startled at the sound of Artemus's voice.

Artemus's hands were on his shoulders. He was shaking him, his face full of concern.

Drake heard the harsh breaths wheezing in and out of his throat and realized he was hyperventilating. A warm weight landed on his lap, distracting him from his first panic attack in almost two decades.

Smokey raised his forepaws and pressed them gently against Drake's chest, his chocolate eyes bright with a comforting light.

Drake uncurled his fists, wrapped his hands shakily around the rabbit's soft body, and buried his face in his neck. The creature's strong pulse drummed against his cheek and his steady heartbeat echoed between his finger-tips. Drake squeezed his eyes shut and concentrated on the sensations until his ragged breathing slowed.

It was a while before he felt able to let go of the hell-hound. He took a deep breath, opened his eyes, and raised his head to face a battery of stares.

"What the heck was that?" Isabelle said.

Serena and Elton were frowning at him. He thought he read a trace of unease on the mercenary's face. Drake swallowed hard. He hesitated before turning to look at Artemus.

The other man was watching him warily. Yet, in the

depths of the blue eyes opposite his, Drake saw something that gave him the final bout of courage he needed to admit something he had never told another living soul in all his life.

"In the early hours of August 14th 2017, outside a little-known town in Texas, a boy woke up to find the orphanage he had grown up in on fire around him. Scattered on the three levels of the institution, still in their beds, were the burnt and twisted remains of the nuns and the children he had known all of his life. They had perished where they lay, the moment of their death so sudden they never even knew it had come upon them."

Drake's voice dropped to a whisper. He stared blindly at his hands where they lay limply on his lap. "That night, as he walked through the fire unscathed and watched flames dance on his fingertips, as he picked up the watch and the blade that he found in his path, the boy realized he was the one who had caused the devastation around him. Because he heard a devil talk to him. A devil that has lived inside him since. A demon gifted to him by Hell." He raised his head and met Artemus's shocked stare. "That boy was me. That night was the night I turned six. And that demon?" He pressed a hand to his chest and felt the old, familiar guilt twist so tightly around his heart he feared it would rip it apart. "He's still here."

Something beeped in the stunned silence that followed.

All eyes turned to Serena as she stared at the flashing smartband on her left wrist. She froze a heartbeat later, her entire body going rigid, the color draining from her face. She jumped to her feet and ran out of the room.

Smokey trembled on Drake's lap. The rabbit leapt onto

the floor and morphed into his hellhound form as he dashed over to the bay windows.

Elton let out a grunt of surprise and stumbled out of his chair. "What the—?"

Isabelle, Mark, and Shamus yanked their weapons from their holsters and aimed them at the hellhound.

Artemus bolted from the couch and placed himself squarely between the beast and his friends. "Whoa!"

Drake found himself on his feet and at his side.

"Put the guns down," Artemus ordered in a calm voice. He motioned gently with his right hand and glanced from Elton to the hellhound. "He won't hurt you."

Smokey whined and started pacing the floor, his giant claws clicking against the tiles and his breath misting the windows as he stared out over the park.

"What the hell is that?" Elton asked shakily.

"That's his true form," Artemus replied. "His real name is Cerberus. He's a hellhound."

Isabelle's jaw dropped open. "Huh?"

The hand holding the gun fell limply at her side.

Mark and Shamus hesitated, their eyes shifting briefly to Elton. The latter nodded reluctantly. They lowered their weapons.

*I can hear her!*

Drake turned and looked at Smokey just as Serena strode back into the room.

Artemus frowned at the hellhound. "Hear who?"

Smokey shook his head and pawed the floor, leaving gouges in the marble. Serena opened her laptop on the dining table and started frantically working the keyboard.

"Who are you talking to?" Elton asked, puzzled.

The older man still looked wary as he gazed between the hellhound and Artemus.

Serena looked wildly from the computer to Smokey. "What did he say?"

Coldness filled Drake at the dread reflected in her pale eyes. He had never seen her look so afraid before.

Artemus exchanged a glance with Drake. "He said something about hearing her."

"He means Callie," Drake murmured.

"Wait," Isabelle said. She holstered her weapon. "You mean the dog's talking to you?"

Smokey threw his head back and let out an unholy howl. The room shook. Glass trembled and shuddered. A porcelain vase shattered on a sideboard.

*"I think you pissed him off!"* Mark shouted, his hands over his ears.

Artemus cursed as he closed the distance to Smokey. He took hold of the trembling beast's head, hushing noises tumbling out of his lips. Drake found himself following the other man once more, at a loss as to why he felt the same undeniable urge to comfort the hellhound. He laid his fingers on the creature's right flank and shivered at the energy rumbling beneath his hide.

A deep shudder shook Smokey from his head all the way to his tail. He stopped howling and lowered his head to stare into Artemus and Drake's eyes.

Drake's stomach twisted at the agony he read in the hellhound's red gaze.

"Found him!" Serena barked.

She turned the laptop around.

A satellite map of New York was displayed on the screen. More precisely, a red dot was flashing at what looked to be an address in Lower Manhattan, the light blinking on and off in tandem with the beeping from her smartband.

Drake frowned. "What is that?"

"That's Nate's GPS chip," Serena said grimly.

Artemus's eyes widened. "You mean you know where they are?"

He let go of Smokey and strode over to the dining table.

"Yes." Serena turned to Elton, her hands fisted at her sides. "How many agents does this organization of yours have in New York?"

Elton frowned. "Right now? About a hundred, give or take."

"Shit!" Serena tapped her smartband and scrolled rapidly through the display. "How many more can you get here within the next hour?"

"Another eighty to a hundred, maybe," Elton replied. "Why?" He glanced at Artemus and Drake. "What's going on?"

"That place?" Serena indicated the flashing dot on her laptop before typing out a message on her smartband. "It's crawling with demons. We're gonna need all the help we can get if we want to go in there and rescue them!"

Smokey huffed and whined.

Elton stared at the satellite map. "You mean *that's* their headquarters?"

"I don't know," Serena said. "But whatever it is, Callie and Nate are there."

"We need floorplans for that building," Drake said grimly.

"Somehow, I don't think we're gonna find any real information about what's in there," Artemus said. "But we do need a game plan before we walk in blind."

"We haven't got time for a game plan!" Serena snapped.

An alert came through on her smartband. Relief flashed in her eyes. "Reinforcements will be here soon."

Artemus stilled. "What's the rush?"

Drake frowned. "What reinforcements?"

A muscle jumped in Serena's cheek. "That chip? It only activates when Nate's—" she paused and closed her eyes briefly, "—when Nate's biosystem is shutting down."

Ice prickled Drake's skin.

"He's dying?" Artemus said in a dangerously calm voice.

Serena nodded stiffly, her eyes filled with an equal measure of rage and distress. "I have a very clear signal on his trace. Which means that chip is currently exposed to air."

"What does that mean?" Isabelle asked.

Serena glanced at the blonde. "The only way to get such an unobstructed trace is if they carved that thing out of his brain."

"What reinforcements?" Elton repeated in a bewildered tone.

Smokey started pacing the floor once more. *They are hurting her.*

The hellhound's tortured words echoed inside Drake's skull.

*They are hurting my sister!*

# CHAPTER THIRTY-EIGHT

A SCREAM RENDERED THE AIR AND ECHOED AGAINST THE rock walls. It took a moment for Callie to realize it had come from her own throat.

She bit her lip and panted as Park's secretary finished carving another cut across her abdomen. Agonizing pain gave way to fiery throbbing. Crimson wetness ran down her legs in rivulets before dripping into the expanding dark pool at her feet.

She was chained to a metal cross in the cave beneath the high-rise, the manacles binding her wrists and ankles slick with blood where they had torn her skin while she struggled against her torturers.

Lying on a pedestal ten feet before her was the cane. Beyond it, Nate hung limply on a cross, his eyes closed and his head drooping forward. Blood was congealing in a thick, sticky mess on the left side of his head, where they had drilled into his skull.

Park turned away from the stone arch looming above them on Callie's left. "Say the words, Guardian."

He headed toward her at a leisurely pace.

Callie blinked sweat and blood from her eyes before glaring at him. "Even if I knew them, I would never tell you in a million years!"

Park smiled thinly. "Oh, you *will*. On this, you have my word."

"Oh yeah?" Callie mumbled. "Well, you can take your word and shove it where—"

Her eyes widened a second before a guttural scream tore out of her. She whimpered and looked down at the wicked dagger Park's secretary had just wedged beneath her right ribcage.

Callie choked on her next breath, blood bubbling and frothing past her lips.

The blonde smiled at her, her features trembling violently as the demon inside her phased in and out of view.

"I believe Jade just punctured your right lung," Park said in a conversational tone. "I hear that can hurt like a bitch." He crossed the stage and stopped next to Nate. "But I think this—" he lifted his right hand and formed a clawed fist, his fingers and nails extending into wicked talons, "will probably hurt more."

He turned, met Callie's eyes, and punched through the left side of Nate's chest, his hand disappearing inside the large man's body through a miasmic dark cloud.

Nate woke up with a shocked shout. Rage burned through Callie when his tortured gaze collided with hers.

Park twisted his wrist slightly.

Nate's eyes rolled back in his head, his face and throat growing flushed, the tendons and veins in his neck straining to bursting point. Pink-stained froth burst out of his mouth and dribbled down his chin.

"Right now, I'm holding your friend's heart in my hand," Park said.

He moved his wrist again.

"*Stop it!*" Callie screamed as all color drained from Nate's face.

Her breath locked in her throat. She froze before looking down to where Park's secretary's own clawed hand was now wedged inside her abdomen.

It felt like someone was ripping her apart from the inside out.

Callie threw her head back and screamed.

Heat exploded inside her chest.

A raspy voice reached Callie dimly through the buzzing in her ears. It said strange words, the likes of which she had never heard before. Words that rang with power. It took a moment for her to realize the voice was coming from her own mouth. And that the words were a holy incantation.

An incandescent light flashed on the pedestal. The first sigil on the cane glowed gold. It turned crimson a second later.

A faint rumbling rose inside the cave. The cross trembled and shook behind Callie. She blinked, her tortured breaths echoing inside her skull.

Everything was shaking around her. Her gaze found the stone arch dazedly.

Darkness was pooling around it.

~

PARK STIFFENED.

*It's happening!*

Elation flooded him as a foul energy suffused the air,

the evil force thrumming out of the Gate resonating with that of the demons within this plane of existence. His lips peeled back in a snarl, the creature inside him shivering with anticipation while his brethren answered the dark call and started to gather around him.

He could feel his master coming.

# CHAPTER THIRTY-NINE

THEY CAME IN BANDS OF THREE AND FOUR, THEIR VANS
and SUVs pulling smoothly into the car park behind
the building where Elton and the Vatican organization
had set up a temporary command and control center,
some two hundred feet around the corner from their
target.

A hulking, bearded man with red hair walked over to
Serena and engulfed her in a giant bear hug. "Hey, girl. It's
good to see you. How have you been?"

"Hi, Lou," Serena mumbled against his chest. She was
conscious of Drake's gaze on her as she stepped out of the
other man's hold. "I'm okay, thanks."

Lou frowned slightly, his pale eyes appraising her.
"Here, I brought you something."

He took a dark combat uniform out of a duffel bag and
handed it to her. It glistened slightly in the light.

"Thanks," Serena said, avoiding his stare.

The mercenary knew her too well to buy the barefaced
lie she'd just told him.

Her pulse jumped when he removed a flat, round metal

disc the size of a tennis ball and what looked like a pen from the bag. "Compliments of the doc."

He dropped them into her hands.

Serena stared at the gadgets in her palm. "Are these—?"

She looked up at him, hope flaring inside her.

Lou smiled faintly. "Yeah. The prototypes he's been working on." He grimaced. "He said, and I quote, 'Tell her if she destroys them, I will skin her alive and feast on her remains.'"

Serena sighed at the threat.

Lou turned to face the silent group watching their exchange. "Hi, I'm Lou."

He held out a hand to Elton.

Elton hesitated before shaking hands with the mercenary. He looked past him to the men and women busy removing crates of weapons from their vehicles and suiting up for combat. "You all super soldiers?"

Lou smiled, clearly unoffended by Elton's suspicious tone. "Yup. And you guys are—" he glanced from the hordes of armed men and women behind Elton to Serena, "what was it again?"

"Agents of the Vatican," Serena muttered.

"Oh." A super soldier with dark hair and brown eyes finished loading his twin Berettas and headed over toward them, a friendly grin on his face. "So, you guys are, like, priests?"

"No," Elton replied coolly. He turned to Lou and indicated the troops of super soldiers. "You're the one in charge of them?"

"Well, technically, she is." Lou cocked a thumb at Serena. "I'm second in command and this little guy right here, God save our souls," he rolled his eyes and patted the shoulder of the shorter, dark-haired mercenary next to him with a heavy hand, "is our next XO. His name is Tom. Say hi, Tom."

"Ha-ha, asshole," Tom muttered with a grimace. Chuckles erupted from the other super soldiers. "Hey, I'm Tom."

He shook a wary Elton's hand.

"You're their boss?" Drake asked Serena gruffly.

He glanced at Lou and Tom before staring at her.

She narrowed her eyes. "I'm not the boss of anyone."

"She may not look it, but this little lady here is likely the best fighter of all of us," Lou said, flashing a good-natured smile her way and blatantly ignoring her warning glare.

"And she pretty much always takes charge whenever we get together for our larger operations," a female super soldier said. "She can't help it. It's like a disease."

"Yup, our very own Miss High and Mighty," someone else said teasingly.

"I am not high and mighty!" Serena snapped.

"Oh yeah?" another super soldier called out. "What about Guatemala? And El Salvador."

"El Salvador was fun." The first super soldier scratched her nose with an amused expression. "Hey, wasn't that the time she whooped Tom's ass so hard he peed blood for, like, a day?"

Tom pulled a face.

Lou grinned. "That's what you get for trying to feel her up."

"For the last time, I was not feeling her up," Tom grumbled. "There was a blood-sucking leech on her butt. I was being a *friend* and getting rid of it for her."

"Yeah, keep telling yourself that," someone scoffed.

Serena sighed again as the super soldiers continued

exchanging teasing banter. It was something they always did before a mission. To remind themselves that they were more than just monsters.

"I thought your kind weren't meant to have a sense of humor," Isabelle muttered, eyeing Tom and the laughing super soldiers curiously.

Serena glanced at her before checking her Glocks. "Someone's hand evidently slipped in the lab when they made us. Besides, we were freed before our brains could be conditioned for mindless obedience, unlike the previous generations of super soldiers."

Isabelle's eyes grew thoughtful. "You're all children rescued from Greenland?"

Serena hesitated before dipping her chin.

Isabelle raised an eyebrow. "And you all became mercs?"

Serena hesitated. "Not all of us. One is the world's current leading neurosurgeon. Another is an ace at stocks and shares. A third is a tech billionaire. And one is—" she grimaced, "a top pastry chef in France."

"What are we dealing with exactly?" Lou asked briskly, slinging a pair of assault rifles across his chest. "All you said was Nate and your friends are in trouble."

"Big guy's in trouble?" Tom narrowed his eyes. "We can't have that."

"Yeah," another super soldier muttered. "He makes the best pancakes in the world."

"Exactly," Tom said, nodding vigorously.

"That's all you think about, isn't it?" Lou muttered. "Your stomach." He turned to Serena. "Who's the enemy?"

"Demons," Artemus said behind them.

He jumped out of the back of the van where he'd been gearing up and eyed the super soldiers curiously.

Drake stared at the bandoliers and ammunition belts wrapped around the blond man's chest and thighs. "You got enough ammo there?"

Tom raised a hand, a sickly expression dawning on his face. "Hmm."

Artemus grimaced and looked down. "What? You guys think it's too much?"

"Not if you want to walk like the Hunch Crotch of Notre Dame, it isn't," Serena muttered.

"Did you say demons?" Lou said dully.

Smokey leapt out of the van behind Artemus.

"Oh!" Tom blinked. He took a step forward, his lips curving into a smile. "What a cute—"

A shiver raced along the rabbit's body. His fur trembled, as if a storm were raging inside him. He transformed.

Tom froze. The rest of the super soldiers stiffened behind him, their expressions growing hard as they stared at the powerfully-built, midnight-black creature facing them.

"Whoa," Lou mumbled, his eyes locked on the hellhound.

"It's okay," Artemus said. "He's with us."

"What *is* he?" Tom said, fascination slowly replacing the dread on his face.

"His name is Smokey, AKA Cerberus." Artemus hesitated. "He's a hellhound. Well, *the* Hellhound."

"That's so cool," Tom said in a voice filled with awe. He cast an eager look at Artemus. "Can I pet him?"

Smokey's eyes flashed red.

"It's gonna be like El Salvador all over again," one of the super soldiers muttered behind Tom.

"Yup," another super soldier mumbled. "He's gonna get

another ass whooping." The woman studied the hellhound. "Or, in this case, torn from limb to limb."

Shamus appeared with a group of Vatican agents and dumped four metal crates on the ground. He dropped down on his haunches and flipped the lids open. "We have some spare ammo for you. Standard bullets don't work against these things."

Lou crouched down and examined an assault rifle magazine.

"What are these little beauties?" he muttered, fingering a casing.

"Silver-leaded slugs impregnated with Holy Water from Rome," Shamus replied.

Lou stared at him. His startled gaze shifted to Serena. "He's kidding?"

"I wish he were," she murmured.

Tom was studying Shamus with a puzzled frown.

"Hey," he said, his expression clearing, "you're Shamus Carmichael. The three-time world-heavy-weight boxing champion!"

Shamus blinked. "Yeah, I am."

The black man rose to his feet, ears reddening as he found himself suddenly surrounded by a horde of enthusiastic super soldiers all jostling to shake his hand.

"So, hmm, could I get an autograph?" a man half a foot taller than Shamus mumbled with a shy smile.

The hairs rose on Serena's arms. She looked up just as twilight fell across the car park.

Storm clouds were gathering in the darkening sky above them. They roiled and whirled in strange, twisting shapes, their centers pulsing with flashes of gold and red light. Static filled the air with crackles and pops.

Lou followed her gaze. "So, demons, huh?"

"That does *not* look natural," Isabelle muttered.

A low growl drew their eyes to Smokey. Flecks of drool dripped from the hellhound's jaws. He pawed at the ground and looked from Artemus to Drake, a silent message passing between them.

A muscle jumped in Artemus's cheek as he listened to words only he and Drake could hear. "We have to go. Now!"

He pulled his switchblade out of his boot.

Lou's eyes widened when the knife transformed into a sword. His gaze moved to the shield now covering Drake's left arm and the sword in the thief's right hand.

"Okay," he muttered in a resigned voice. "So, you guys got any tips on fighting these things?"

"Aim for the head," Serena said as she headed rapidly for the back of the van to change into the combat suit.

Drake made a slicing motion across his throat with his left thumb. "Just take the whole thing off."

"Alrighty then, decapitation it is," Tom said brightly.

# CHAPTER FORTY

NATE WAS DYING. HE KNEW THIS AS CLEARLY AS HE knew that he was a monster and that he loved Serena more than just as a sister.

His head pounded viciously, the nanorobots inside him too busy repairing the extensive damage the demons had inflicted on his brain and body to curb the pain from where his tormentors had bored into his skull. A raspy gasp left his throat when Park withdrew his talons from inside his chest. The fire that had gripped his heart dulled to hot prickles.

Park stared unblinkingly at Callie, a triumphant light blazing in his dark eyes.

The widow looked frail and helpless where she hung on the cross opposite Nate, her clothes ripped to shreds and her slender body covered in cuts and bruises. Unfamiliar words tumbled from her lips and her face glistened with a sheen of sweat. Nate could tell from her glazed expression that her mind was elsewhere.

The cane vibrated and hummed on the pedestal between them, the symbols on the shaft slowly flashing from gold to crimson, one by one. The tremors shaking the cave intensified.

Nate stared at the giant stone arch to his right.

The structure was throbbing as if it were alive, the shadows around it pulsing with threads of macabre red. Darkness started to merge in the center, black tendrils arching across the empty space between the vertical columns to fuse into a thickening spiderweb.

The hairs rose at the back of Nate's neck. He looked around.

The entire cave was filling with demons, their bodies emerging out of thin air, their hungry eyes fixed on the stone arch on the stage.

Nate's gaze found Callie once more. His eyes widened.

Something was happening to her. Her hair was lengthening and thickening around her face, the blonde strands turning the color of spun gold. Ivory stubs appeared on her forehead and grew into long, curved horns that protruded through her spreading mane.

The snake appeared from behind her back. It was fully grown, its golden body as tall as Nate and as thick as his forearm, its slit-like eyes shining with a ferocious light.

A faint glow appeared in the middle of Callie's abdomen. It expanded and brightened, working its way under her skin toward her throat in a kaleidoscope of dancing lights edged with orange and red.

CALLIE SHIVERED AS HER SKIN PRICKLED AND HER BODY twitched, an unholy energy surging through her with every beat of her heart.

*No. Not just mine. It's the heart of the one who lives inside me too!*

She gasped when an incandescent heat bloomed inside her belly. Her frantic gaze found the cane while words she did not want to speak continued falling from her lips.

*Get ready. It is almost time.*

Callie stiffened.

It was the first time she was hearing the voice of the beast that resided within her.

"Why are you translating the sigils?" she whispered hoarsely, the quakes reverberating across the cave masking her voice from the demons crowding the stage around her. "You're giving them what they want! You're unlocking the key!"

*Because the cane is not just a key. It is also a weapon.* Our *weapon.*

Callie stared at the artifact where it thrummed and rattled on the pedestal. "What kind of weapon?"

*You will soon see. Whatever happens, we must not allow the Gate to open.*

Callie gazed dazedly at the vile creatures materializing out of the ether around the cave. "There are hundreds of them! We won't be able to defeat them all! Not just the two of us!"

*They are almost here.*

Callie swallowed, confusion dancing through her. "Who are almost here?"

*Your kin.*

The last incantation left her mouth. The final symbol flashed gold before turning crimson.

Callie blinked.

The cane levitated off the pedestal. It thickened and lengthened into a golden scepter before twisting and arrowing through the air toward her, so fast it pierced the heads of five demons before they knew what had struck them.

Callie found her right hand opening automatically. The scepter spun upright and slapped into her palm with a sound like thunder, as if it had always belonged there. She closed her fingers around it.

Power filled her, so bright, so sudden, so gloriously intense, all her senses were blinded for an instant. The manacles holding her prisoner tore open before clattering to the ground, the metal sheared by the muscles she had suddenly acquired. She dropped down onto the stage, her claws clinking against the stone, and slowly opened her eyes.

Her hair moved and hissed around her head, her lustrous locks replaced by hundreds of tiny, golden snakes, their movements controlled by the serpent growing from her tailbone. A primitive growl rumbled up her throat. Smoke curled out of her nostrils and mouth. The tips of her horns glowed with an orange light.

Callie smiled savagely.

She knew what the heat was for now.

# CHAPTER FORTY-ONE

"Where the hell are they?" Serena murmured.

The same question resonated through Artemus as he trained his gun around the empty lobby, his pulse thumping rapidly in his veins.

They'd been inside the high-rise for ten minutes and had yet to see a single demon.

Elevator doors opened on their left. A team of super soldiers and Vatican agents walked out of the cabins. More came through the doors leading to the stairs.

"Upper levels are clear," Lou said briskly.

"So are the lower levels, including the boiler room and the underground garage," Isabelle said.

Elton frowned at Serena. "Are you sure this is the right location?"

Serena glanced at the silent, flashing dot on her smartband.

"Positive," she said in a steely voice.

Artemus slowly lowered his gun.

The building belonged to a firm of lawyers, one of the largest and richest in the country. From the limited infor-

mation they had managed to glean about them thus far,
the company was notorious for representing some of the
more unsavory members of the criminal underworld on
the east coast.

"Hey!" Tom exclaimed. "What the—?"

Artemus turned and looked where the super soldier
was staring. A rat had just scampered across the man's
boots and was heading rapidly for the revolving door that
opened onto the street outside. More followed, their dark
bodies streaming across the white tiles in a growing tide
from the stairs, the creatures scrambling over one another
in their haste to escape. They piled against the glass door
with high-pitched squeaks until their combined weight
slowly pushed it open.

"Now I've seen everything," Lou said leadenly.

*They are below us.*

Artemus looked at Smokey, tension humming through
every fiber of his being once more. The hellhound was
staring at the floor.

"What's our ground-penetrating radar saying?" Serena
asked with a frown as she gazed at Smokey.

Lou touched the side of his smart glasses and viewed
the data streaming from the satellite above New York.

"I got nothing," he said with a shake of his head as he
studied the display. "Just a whole lot of rocks from the
garage down."

"Let's check it out," Drake said stiffly, his fingers
clenching and unclenching around his sword.

Artemus frowned. The metal of Drake's blade had
darkened again, like it had done back at the club.

He met the man's grim gaze. "That demon talking to
you again?"

"Bastard's practically singing in my ears," Drake

muttered, a muscle jumping in his jawline. "They're here, alright."

They headed for the underground garage.

"Now what?" Elton said as they spread out around the gloomy, echoing space.

"There," Drake said after a moment.

He pointed at a dark area of the carport.

Lou shone a light onto it. Rats were pouring out of a tiny hole at the base of the wall.

"Hey, guys," Tom murmured. The super soldier was staring at something on his smart glasses. "Infrared is picking up a structure behind that wall."

"What kind of structure?" Serena said.

"An elevator shaft."

"Great." Isabelle stared at the solid concrete. "Anyone pack a jackhammer?"

"We won't need a jackhammer." Serena snatched three tiny black balls from a pouch on her thigh and threw them at the wall. The devices attached themselves to the surface with a faint whine before flashing red. "Get down!"

The floor and walls trembled around them when the bombs exploded seconds later.

Artemus coughed and waved at the billows of particulate matter clouding the air in front of him as he slowly straightened to his feet. The dust cleared. He stared.

The detonation had blown a four-foot hole in the concrete wall. Cables glistened in the space beyond the dark opening.

"Let's go!" Serena barked.

She climbed through the gap, pulled a zip line from her combat suit, hooked it onto one of the cables, and dropped out of sight. Lou, Tom, and the other super soldiers followed suit, the Vatican agents lining up behind them.

Smokey snarled.

*This will take too long. We are running out of time!*

The hellhound's eyes flashed from red to gold. His body expanded, taking on the monstrous shape he had assumed at the club. He raised his forelegs and smashed his giant paws violently down upon the ground.

The resulting boom resonated across the garage. A crack appeared in the concrete floor.

"Hmm," Artemus said, a sick premonition dawning inside him.

The hellhound struck the ground again. The fracture expanded and spread, a jagged spiderweb of cracks radiating from the point of impact until it formed a perimeter around Drake, Smokey, and himself.

"The heck is he doing?" Elton said with a scowl from where he stood outside the circle.

"Creating a shortcut," Drake replied.

His sword had transmuted once more, the blade's edges gaining serrated teeth. A shiver danced down Artemus's spine when he gazed into the thief's glowing red eyes.

"Get ready," Drake growled.

Artemus blinked at the raspy echo that accompanied the other man's warning. The hellhound smashed into the floor a third time. The ground shuddered.

Artemus's fingers clenched on his gun and sword a second before the floor gave way beneath them.

*Oh crap!*

THE HOLE LED TO THE ROOF OF A YAWNING SPACE. Drake's stomach lurched as he, Artemus, and Smokey smashed through the last layer of rock and started falling through what looked to be some hundred feet of empty air.

He caught a glimpse of a mass of red-tinged darkness beneath him, fired off the hook line attached to his left wrist, and grunted as the metal claws smashed into the remains of the ceiling above him, slowing his descent. He swore when Artemus collided violently with him a second later. Their cables intertwined as they plunged toward the sea of demons.

The lines suddenly sagged. They stared at one another.

"Shit," Artemus said dully.

The hooks holding them secure broke loose from the rock with a judder. Drake's gut twisted as they plummeted toward the roiling shadows below.

Smokey broke their fall, his giant body shoving some dozen demons out of his way as he skidded to a stop below them. The hellhound braced himself and grunted when they landed heavily on his back.

"Ow," Artemus muttered.

He lay under Drake and had taken the brunt of the impact. Drake rolled off him and slid down Smokey's back. Artemus joined him on the ground a second later.

They stiffened when they finally registered their surroundings.

They were standing in the middle of an enormous, semicircular gallery, at the rear of a cave. Filling the rows all around them were hundreds of demons. The creatures were pushing and surging toward the center of the auditorium, their zealous, red eyes focused unblinkingly on the opposite side of the cavern. They seemed oblivious to the

newcomers in their midst, the air above them fairly thrumming with a heavy, choking miasma of pure evil.

Drake's pulse spiked when he followed their gazes.
"What the—?"

A giant stone arch wreathed in pure darkness domi-
nated the low stage that formed the focal point of the
cave.

Nate was lying on the ground a few feet to the right
of it.

Standing protectively in front of him and the arch,
wielding a golden scepter with an effortless grace and skill
that belied the strength and violence behind her every
move, was something that bore a dim resemblance to
Callie Stone.

The creature's head was a mane of vicious, glittering
snakes that bit and tore into the demons before her. At her
back, a large golden snake dipped and bobbed its head, its
powerful body swatting away any attempt to slip around
behind its mistress. The horns on her forehead dripped
with blood and were tipped with flames above her leonine
features.

A wave of demons surged toward her. The creature
opened her mouth and roared, her eyes a dazzling, jade
green. A sonic vortex wrapped around a dozen demons and
immobilized them.

A river of fire flowed out of Callie's jaws next. The
demons caught in the path of the blaze shrieked, the
flames engulfing them in orange fireballs that consumed
their flesh in seconds, much like the rounds from Artemus's gun.

"Chimera," Artemus whispered in a voice full of admiration, his eyes locked on the monster defending the arch.

*Not defending.*

Drake looked at Smokey. The hellhound glanced between him and Artemus.

*She is the Guardian of that Gate. And she must not allow it to be opened. We must help her.*

"A Gate to what?" Artemus said, bewildered.

Smokey growled. *A Gate to—*

"—Hell," Drake finished in a voice filled with dread.

He finally knew what Park and his organization were attempting to do.

The demons around them paused. Hundreds of heads pivoted toward them. They became the focus of a sea of glowing red eyes.

Movement to the far right caught Drake's gaze at the same time as guttural shouts tore through the air. He caught a glimpse of the super soldiers and the Vatican agents emerging through the mouth of a corridor before focusing on the two large demonic shapes bellowing out a warning on the other side of the cave.

Park and the blonde from the club stood on the stage some twenty feet from Callie. They towered above the other demons, their eyes radiating rage and indignation as they registered the enemy among them.

Drake gritted his teeth when the corrupt energy filling the cave thickened, making his very bones tremble. "Here they come!"

# CHAPTER FORTY-TWO

SERENA DROPPED TO HER KNEES, SLID BENEATH TWO clawed fists, put a round of bullets through the heads of the demons above her, and jumped to her feet. She swooped, roundhouse-kicked another demon in the gut, and stabbed him in the eye.

Ten feet to her left, Tom punched a demon in the jaw and shot him in the head before flashing a grimace her way. "You forgot to mention how fugly these things are!"

"He's right!" Lou shouted from somewhere behind them.

"Ewww! Gross!" another super soldier said, shaking foul demon blood off her dagger with a disgusted expression.

Serena leaned out of the way of a set of deadly talons, heel-kicked the demon at her rear in the groin, and fired at the one trying to disembowel her. The creature fell. She caught a glimpse of Nate some twenty feet away, amidst the crowd of hellish shapes swarming the cave.

A large shadow drifted over her. Smokey landed at her side

with a violent thud that shook the stage, his paws crushing the skulls of two demons. The hellhound glanced from her to Nate. Serena nodded grimly when she grasped his intent.

He took the lead as they cleared a path to the fallen super soldier, the demons around them falling beneath claw, fang, bullet, and blade. Serena dropped down by Nate's side while Smokey carried on toward the arch and the creature that looked like Callie. The giant super soldier blinked his eyes open when he felt her presence.

"Serena?" he said between cracked, bloodied lips.

Serena's heart twisted as she beheld his broken body. She removed the devices Lou had given her from a pouch on her thigh, slammed the disc onto the center of Nate's chest, and gently turned his head to the side.

"Sorry," she mumbled, her eyes meeting his startled gaze, "this is gonna hurt."

A choked scream left Nate when she stabbed the pen into the base of his neck. She depressed the button atop it and pushed the one in the middle of the disc.

Nate gasped, his back arching off the ground as two thousand volts of electricity and a surge of new nanorobots entered his body from both devices. His eyes glowed silver for an instant, the miniature machines in his retina supercharging with power. The disc on his chest trembled before rapidly expanding and covering his frame with the same dark combat suit she wore.

Nate sat up and stared at his gloved hands.

"How you feeling?" Serena said above the sound of the battle raging behind her.

Nate looked at her and blinked. "Good." Determination filled his face as his cuts and bruises started healing at an accelerated speed. "Better."

His eyes widened a moment before something struck Serena in the back. She looked over her shoulder.

The giant blonde demon from the club was standing over her, her fiendish features locked in a triumphant expression. The creature's gaze dropped to where her clawed fist had smashed into Serena's combat suit. The material rippled and shifted around her talons, blocking and diffusing the energy of the impact. The demon stepped back, surprise flashing in her red eyes.

Serena smiled grimly. She straightened to her full height and turned to face the monster towering over her, her left hand finding the second blade in the sheath on her thigh. "This is a nanorobot, liquid-armor suit, bitch."

The blonde scowled and charged.

THE CHIMERA GLANCED AT SMOKEY WHEN HE STOPPED at her side.

"Hello, brother," she growled.

The hellhound snatched a demon from the air with his strong jaws, crushed the creature's neck, and tossed him to the side.

*Sister.*

"Come now," she admonished, smoke coiling out of her mouth while she staked two demons through the head with the scepter and flung them at the churning crowd. "Here I am, exposed in all my glory, and you have yet to take your final form."

Smokey's lips peeled back in a wicked grin. The snake at the base of the Chimera's spine butted heads with him gently.

*I cannot let you take all the credit now, can I?*

With that, the hellhound shook himself with a grunt, grew another two feet, and assumed his ultimate manifestation.

The Chimera smiled.

"That is more like it," she murmured as she beheld the monstrous, golden-eyed, three-headed creature standing next to her.

～

"HOLY SHITBALLS," ARTEMUS SAID DULLY.

Drake panted as he slashed the throat of a demon and blocked a strike to his head with his shield where he and Artemus stood at the bottom of the auditorium. His eyes widened when he followed the blond man's gaze to the stage.

The beast that fought beside the Chimera was the mythical animal from the legends of old. Black as night, fierce gazes radiating a holy light, his three heads and powerful body gleaming with powerful muscles, Smokey was one breathtakingly fearsome killing machine.

"I can't believe I put a leash on him," Artemus muttered, elbowing a demon in the face and shooting another in the chest.

"Not that I mind hearing about your heartwarming memories of the rabbit, but do you mind concentrating on the fight?" Drake snarled, narrowly evading a set of wicked talons headed for his eyes.

Demons swarmed the cave around them, the shadows wreathing their bodies so thick he was struggling to see the super soldiers and Vatican agents engaged in the battle around them. He gritted his teeth, his hands shaking and his heart pounding violently as he struggled to contain the darkness threatening to rip his very soul apart.

The devil in him was getting stronger.

Before he could even begin to contend with the forces swirling inside his body, an enormous shape collided into him, lifted him off his feet, and carried him toward the back of the cave.

# CHAPTER FORTY-THREE

PARK GROWLED WITH RAGE AND TIGHTENED HIS TALONS around the throat of the dark-haired man with the glowing red eyes. The cave wall loomed ahead of them.

He swung his arm back and smashed the thief violently into the rock.

The man grunted, blood staining his lips. His sword fell from his grasp and clattered to the ground some ten feet below where they hovered in the air.

Park fisted his right hand and aimed it at the man's heart. The thief raised his shield and blocked the strike a second before it reached his chest.

Fury burned through Park.

*How dare they?! How dare they try to keep us from opening the Gate?!*

He could feel his master's approach slowing in the transdimensional space where the demons moved, the leader of their organization evidently detecting that all was not right at his final destination.

*They're ruining it! They're ruining it all!*

"Die!" Park roared.

He reached clawed talons under the shield and pierced the man's gut all the way through to his back.

SMOKEY STIFFENED. HE TURNED HIS HEADS, HIS GOLDEN eyes finding the two shapes at the rear of the cave. He snarled, thick flecks of acid drool dripping from his jowls and burning the bodies of the dead demons he stood upon.

ARTEMUS FELT THE JOLT AS IF THE DEMON'S FIST HAD punched through his own body. He gasped, heat flaring through his abdomen, his shocked gaze focusing on the fiendish form of Park and the limp frame of Drake, heedless of the demons attacking him.

His skin prickled as the pressure inside the cave dropped.

Something was coming. Something evil.

SERENA'S EARS POPPED. SHE CAST ASIDE THE decapitated skull of the blonde demon, leapt down from the headless torso a second before it thudded to the ground, and turned. Her eyes widened. Something that felt very much like fear grabbed hold of her heart.

Park had Drake in his grip where they hovered above the uppermost tiers of the gallery at the back of the cave. The demon's hand was embedded deep inside the unconscious thief's body.

Night fell around Serena. Vertical, crimson lines

flashed into existence in the shadows boiling above the battlefield. Her stomach plummeted when she saw the creatures that emerged from them.

Tom swore where he stood fifteen feet to her left.

"Hey, you never said they had wings!" he yelled a second before one of the new arrivals snatched him up in wicked talons and lifted him into the air.

FIRE CONSUMED HIM. IT ROARED INSIDE HIS VERY BEING, a torrent of red flames that burned him to the core. Yet, despite the blazing inferno engulfing his body and the agonizing pain searing his every sense, Drake could only perceive darkness around him. A darkness so profound it was as if he had gone blind.

He was dimly aware that Park had impaled him with his clawed fist. And at the back of his mind, so distant he could barely make it out, he could feel Smokey and Artemus's anger. Drake blinked blood out of his eyes.

*I'm dying.* A shocking sense of relief flashed through him at the thought. *Finally. I will have my peace.*

Something moved in the shadows in front of him. A shape appeared out of the gloom. Drake stared, his heartbeat a thunderous drumming that drowned out all sound.

The demon stopped a few feet away and watched him with a cold expression. *You are weak. Let me lend you my strength.*

Drake shuddered, bile rising in his throat as he fought the corrupt energy pushing against the barriers of his mind. "Never!"

The demon smiled at his vehement reply, his red eyes

glowing wickedly. *Your defenses will fall. You* will *accept me. And you will become what you were* meant *to be.*

Surprise jolted through Drake at the demon's words. "What do you mean—?"

He stopped and blinked when he saw movement behind the creature.

A low growl escaped the demon. He turned to watch the ethereal shape emerging out of the darkness, his fiendish features radiating hate.

The woman was tall and willowy, her slender form hidden by a gauzy white dress, the long hair wrapping around her body so pale it glowed and cast a faint, golden halo around her.

Her eyes were the light of the stars themselves.

She came silently toward them, her movements graceful, her expression peaceful.

The demon took a step back, his disgust plain to see. The woman walked past him with nary a glance and stopped in front of Drake.

Drake took a shaky breath as the fires burning inside him started to abate.

*It is not yet time for you to die, child.*

He startled at the sweet, melodious voice ringing in his ears. The woman placed her hand over his heart. A feeling very much like love washed over him in a strong, warm wave.

She leaned in until her lips were close to his right ear. *You will have to embrace his strength.*

Drake stiffened, knowing she meant the demon.

*But do not fear. For I am with you too.*

Light bloomed around the woman's hand. She pushed her fingers straight through his rib cage until she had a hold of his heart.

Drake's eyes flared. He tipped his head back and screamed at the unholy power erupting inside him. The marks on his back quivered, as if caught in a storm.

They unfurled with a clap of thunder.

~

SOMETHING BOOMED AND FLASHED IN THE DARKNESS. A point of light somewhere at the back of the cave. Artemus clenched his teeth where he crouched under the dozens of demons pummeling him with their fists. He fired into the milling crowd, his skin and hair coated with the ashes of the creatures he had killed.

*Too many! There are too many of them!*

~

PARK BLINKED WHEN SOMETHING PIERCED HIS BACK AND sheared open the front of his chest. One moment he was holding the dark-haired thief in his hand, the next the man had disappeared from his grip.

*What—?*

Black blood bubbled out of his mouth as the weapon that had impaled him was wrenched from his flesh. He clasped the gaping wound in his rib cage and twisted in the air, shocked that there was something in this world that had managed to hurt him. He froze at the sight that met his eyes.

Black wings rose from the back of the thief's body. He was poised motionless in the air a few feet away, the color of his new appendages matching the armor that covered his frame like a second skin. He raised his chin and met Park's shocked gaze.

Park's stomach lurched.

The man's face had hardened into a fearsome mask and his eyes shone with a fiery light that was both crimson and gold. Tiny flames danced on the tips of his fingers.

Park drew a sharp breath when he saw the sword in the man's right hand. It was the one he had dropped earlier, when Park had attacked him. Except it looked different. His heart thumped painfully in his chest.

Though he had only ever seen it in the treasured, archaic scripts owned by the organization, he recognized the blade instantly.

The broadsword was nearly as tall as the thief himself and made of a black metal that did not belong in this world, its edges wicked serrations that flickered with the orange glow of a smoldering fire.

Park's gaze gravitated to the large, dark shield engraved with glimmering cryptic runes now covering the man's left arm.

*It's him!*

He gazed wildly at the being he had been erroneously trying to kill, conscious of the grave mistake he had been about to commit. "You are Samy—"

The dark angel stabbed him through the heart.

Park gasped as the blade ripped his flesh asunder. A tortured grunt left his throat, his demonic form shuddering violently before shrinking to his human frame once more.

He gazed imploringly at the being who had delivered the fatal blow.

"But why?" he mumbled, choking on blood.

The angel's expressionless face blurred as blackness started encroaching on Park's vision.

His last breath left him in a near silent wheeze.

# CHAPTER FORTY-FOUR

TALONS TORE INTO ARTEMUS FROM ALL SIDES, BRINGING wave after hot wave of pain that shredded his nerves until his body was a river of fire. Blood dripped into his eyes and mouth. He knelt with his arms over his head on the cave floor, his blade and gun lying uselessly several feet to his right where they had been wrenched from his grasp.

They were losing the battle. He knew this as well as he knew that he was reaching the limits of his endurance.

Despite the brutal strength and efficiency of the super soldiers and the deadly firepower of the Vatican agents, demons kept emerging from the shadows in their dozens to replace their fallen brethren, their winged brothers similarly materializing out of the rifts that had appeared throughout the cave. Even Callie and Smokey were struggling on the stage, their bodies virtually hidden by the creatures swarming them.

Darkness had completely filled the stone arch behind them.

Artemus's stomach twisted when he glimpsed the faint,

thin, crimson line that had appeared in the center of the solid blackness. Tremors started shaking the cave.

*Shit!*

He gritted his teeth and curled his hands into fists as he desperately called upon the lifeforce that dwelled inside him, his heart thumping violently against his ribs.

*More! Dammit, I need more power!*

A memory suddenly danced through his mind. Of a dark alley and a rainy night. Of a boy who had heard the voice of the girl he loved seconds before something extraordinary happened. Of the word that had been spoken.

Artemus blinked.

Someone was standing in front of him. For a moment, he thought it was the girl from his dreams. His eyes widened.

The woman was tall and beautiful, her sylphlike figure covered in a delicate, pale dress. Her long hair was the color of light and her pupils fathomless depths where stars swam.

Artemus swallowed hard. He could see her through the crowd of demons as clear as day, as if their shapes had suddenly become insubstantial.

The apparition smiled at him gently, her face radiating love. Her lips moved, framing the same word the girl had spoken to him in his vision that night in the alley, all those years ago.

The word that fell from Artemus's lips in a near silent whisper as he reached inside himself one more time to the core of what he was.

"*Rise.*"

Power exploded within him. He choked on his breath as it flooded every fiber of his being with a single beat of his shuddering heart. His marks quivered and grew.

SERENA GRUNTED AND DEFLECTED ANOTHER ATTACK with her forearms. Nate blocked the clawed foot heading for her head, snatched the winged demon from the air, and slammed the creature into the ground.

"There are too many of them!" Serena shouted as he crushed the shrieking demon's head under his boot.

She looked over her shoulder. Alarm filled her.

She could barely see Callie and Smokey where they stood surrounded by demons in front of the arch. Her eyes widened when she registered the thin red line splitting the solid darkness between the stone columns.

"That does not look good!" Lou shouted.

Light exploded in the center of the cave, so bright she had to shield her eyes. Serena's pulse hammered in her veins as she slowly lowered her fingers from her face.

"Is that—?" Nate said beside her, his voice full of rising wonder.

The being that floated effortlessly in the air some fifteen feet above the floor of the cave bore only a passing resemblance to Artemus Steele. His hair was the color of the sun. His skin glittered like silver where it was exposed beneath his golden armor. His eyes, when he slowly opened them, were the clearest, most breathtaking blue Serena had ever seen in her life.

In his right hand was a broadsword almost as tall as him, the pale flaming metal matching the color of the elegant wings framing his body.

Serena's heart leapt into her throat when she saw the

black-winged figure who appeared next to Artemus from the back of the cave.

"Whoa." Artemus stared at Drake's wings. "Those are bigger than the ones you had at the club." His gaze dropped to the broadsword in Drake's right hand. "Hey, how come yours has teeth and mine still doesn't?"

Drake narrowed glowing eyes at him. "For a guy with white wings and golden armor, you sure ask stupid questions."

"Huh?" Artemus looked over his right shoulder. His shocked gaze dropped from his wide, snowy wings to the metal suit covering his body from the neck down. It lowered farther to the empty space beneath them. "Shit! We're floating!"

His wings beat in panic, feathers thumping the air like wood striking a skin drum. He shot up so fast his stomach dropped.

Drake's hand closed around his left ankle seconds before his head came close to striking the ceiling of the cave. "For Christ's sake, will you stop acting like the world's biggest asshole and focus?"

"Sorry," Artemus mumbled.

He blew out a shaky breath and levitated gently back down to Drake's side high above the cavern floor.

It was exactly as Karl had described happening in the alley back when he'd found him all those years ago. Except Karl hadn't mentioned that he'd flown. He shivered at the feverish energy buzzing under his skin.

This was a whole other level of power.

Artemus's racing pulse slowed as he came to terms

with what had just happened. The bond he could feel linking him to Drake and Smokey had never felt as strong as it did in that moment; this, whatever they were right now, was what they were truly meant to be.

He wondered who the woman was that he had seen before his transformation.

*I can't think about that right now.*

Artemus studied the sea of demons watching them from the bottom of the cave.

"So, I guess this makes us, what—" he grimaced, "angels?"

"If that's the word you want to use, then, yeah," Drake muttered.

Artemus hesitated. "Should angels be swearing? You just called me the world's biggest asshole. And you took Christ's name in vain. I'm pretty sure that's blasphemy in, you know—" he raised his eyes heavenward, "*that* place."

Drake scowled. "One of these days, I'm going to stab you."

His sword roared with flames. He moved, his body dropping toward the cave floor so fast Artemus would have missed him had he been watching with human eyes.

"Hey, wait up!"

# CHAPTER FORTY-FIVE

SERENA KNEW SHE WOULD NEVER FORGET HER FIRST sight of the two warrior angels engaged in battle for as long as she lived.

They swooped through the cave like wrath itself, their attacks so blindingly swift the faint echoes of supersonic booms accompanied their movements. Their holy blades carved effortlessly through the swarms of demons, the creatures' bodies bursting into fireballs and clouds of ash in their path, their shrieks fading into nothingness.

They were Yin and Yang. Darkness and Light. Power and Glory.

And on the stage, their life forces reinvigorated by the incredible beings that now shared the same air as them, the two beasts roared and renewed their defense of the arch.

THE END CAME WITHIN MINUTES.

Drake watched as Artemus landed on the stage and

took care of the last wave of demons with Smokey. Callie turned, stepped up to the bottom of the arch, and slammed the golden scepter in her hands down at the base of the pulsing, red line in the living darkness that throbbed in the center of the looming stone columns.

An unholy sound split the air, as if a thousand demons had screamed at once. The crimson line wavered and dimmed. It flashed out of existence a second later.

The scepter shrank until it was an ivory cane once more, the runes on its pale shaft glowing gold before they vanished. Callie's Chimera shape receded.

Drake found his gaze drawn to a crimson rift at the rear of the cave. It was the last one still shimmering in the air. He headed toward it, his dark wings beating the air powerfully.

Something was watching him from the other side of the crack in space. A pair of outraged red eyes. Eyes that Drake sensed he knew, deep in the marrow of his soul. He placed the tip of his flaming black sword at the bottom of the rift and moved it up, the end of the metal sealing the flickering edges of the gap shut.

"Not today, asshole," he growled at the demon gazing at him in fury.

A howl of rage escaped the creature a second before the rift closed. Drake's lips twisted in a grim smile. He turned and moved toward the stage. His wings and armor disappeared as he landed lightly on the stone floor. His sword and shield assumed their normal, benign appearances in the next moment.

Tom sat up with a choked cry where he'd lain buried under a thick layer of ash next to the stone pedestal to Drake's right.

"Whaza-huh?" the super soldier said in gargled voice.

"What happened?" He twisted around wildly, his gaze sweeping the cave. He paused. "What the hell is in my mouth?" He grimaced and spat out a mouthful of cold cinders. "And where is that demon, the one with the wings?"

Lou sighed and limped over to him. "He is here, there, and, well, everywhere."

He pointed out the mounds of black ash filling the cave as he pulled the fallen super soldier to his feet.

Artemus, Callie, and Smokey closed the distance to Drake. Artemus's wings and armor had also disappeared and his sword was back to being a switchblade. His skin, Drake was relieved to see, was no longer silver. The four of them exchanged silent looks, the knowledge of what had been revealed to them all resonating strongly between them.

Serena and Nate joined their side a moment later.

"Hey," Serena said awkwardly. "That was—"

"Awesome," Nate said with deep-seated reverence.

"Yeah," another super soldier murmured, eyes blazing with admiration. "The wings, the flaming swords, the glowing skin and eyes. That was *sick*, man!"

Tom turned to Lou. "What wings and flaming swords?"

"I'll tell you later," Lou replied, his expression wary as he glanced at Drake and Artemus.

Callie's face fell. "Oh."

Drake followed her gaze. Artemus moved past him and headed swiftly for the group standing over the motionless body some twenty feet away.

"Isabelle," Elton murmured. "I'm so sorry."

Shamus laid a heavy hand on Isabelle's shoulder as they stared at Mark. There was an ugly hole in the dead man's chest where a demon had torn into him.

Isabelle dropped down on her haunches, a muscle working in her cheek. She closed her eyes and rubbed a hand tiredly down her face.

"Ten years," she muttered with a sigh. "Ten bloody years we've managed to keep this a secret and you have to go and die in plain sight of everyone."

She prodded Mark's body irritably with the barrel of her gun.

"Hey," Artemus mumbled. "There's no need to—"

Mark gasped and opened his eyes. "Shit!" He sat up, clutched the wound on his chest, and looked around wildly. "What happened?!"

Isabelle grimaced. "What happened is that you just blew our cover, dumbass."

What little color had returned to Mark's face drained away when he registered the sea of shocked stares leveled at him.

"Oh," he mumbled in a somewhat embarrassed tone.

Lou looked at Serena accusingly. "Did you know?"

Serena hesitated before dipping her chin. "I found out this morning."

Disgruntled murmurs broke out among some of the super soldiers.

Tom stared at Isabelle and Mark as if they had grown horns and talons.

"Goddamned Immortals!" he stated in a tone filled with disgust.

# CHAPTER FORTY-SIX

JEREMIAH CHASE STARED AT ARTEMUS AND ELTON where they sat across the desk from him in an interrogation room in a Chicago PD precinct.

"Those are your final words on this matter?" he said in a tone full of skepticism.

Artemus stayed silent.

Chase's gaze drilled into Elton. "You honestly expect me to believe that you have no idea why those people turned on you and your staff, and committed the violent acts they did a week ago?"

"The world is full of strange things these days, detective," Elton said, unperturbed. "Just put this down as one of them."

Artemus kept his expression neutral, conscious that Elton's reply did not even begin to touch on the incredible things they had both witnessed in the past few days.

"What of the cane that was stolen? Have you come across any rumors of its possible whereabouts from your contacts in the antique world?" Chase said gruffly.

"I'm afraid that item is probably in the vault of some collector by now," Elton muttered.

They left the precinct a short while later and stood on the steps of the building's entrance for a moment. It was a beautiful winter's day and the air was cool and crisp; for once, gales were not blowing through the windy city.

"I don't know how long he's going to buy that bullshit you just sold him," Artemus said, looking up at the crystal-blue sky.

"I think we have bigger fish to fry than Detective Chase right now," Elton said darkly.

Artemus sighed. He knew the discovery they had made about Isabelle and Mark during the battle that had taken place in Manhattan still rankled his old friend. The two Vatican agents had remained resolutely tight-lipped about their real identities since their return to Chicago.

"If you want to find out more, you'll have to talk to Rome," Isabelle had finally conceded that morning before Artemus and Elton left the auction house.

Elton had stared at her and Mark. "You mean Rome knows? That you two are—Immortals?"

Mark had grimaced at the evident distaste in Elton's voice when he said the word. "Only the highest ranking members of the Vatican hierarchy have been told about our existence."

Elton had stiffened. "You mean the Cardinals?"

"And some of the Archbishops," Isabelle had admitted reluctantly.

Elton had paled. "Archbishop Holmes knows?"

Holmes was the one Elton had approached all those years ago, when he'd arranged to go to Vatican City as a result of the investigations he had made following Karl's death. From what Elton had revealed to Artemus, Holmes had been heavily involved in the original task force that had eventually led to the formation of their organization.

"He does."

Elton had grabbed the back of a chair with a white-knuckled hand.

"And the Pope?" Artemus had asked curiously.

Isabelle had shared a guarded glance with Mark. "She knows." She had looked straight into Artemus's eyes. "And she has already been informed about the events that took place in Manhattan."

A haunted expression had washed across Elton's face. "Wait. She—she isn't one of you, is she?"

"No," Mark had replied. "She isn't."

Artemus couldn't help but feel that the man had just told them a half-truth.

"Are there—" Elton had swallowed convulsively, "are there many of you?"

Isabelle had shrugged. "Yes. There were more of us in the past." A grimace had twisted her lips. "We are a race that was at war for quite a significant portion of our history. And a plague wiped out half our numbers during the fourteenth century."

"How old are you?" Artemus had said.

Isabelle had sighed. "You really want to know?"

"I wouldn't have asked if I didn't," Artemus had said with a faint frown.

Isabelle had rubbed her chin lightly before reluctantly admitting her age. "Three hundred and ten years."

Artemus had blinked at that. A low whistle had left his lips. "You look great for someone who technically should be very, er, dry."

Isabelle had flipped him the middle finger.

They got in Elton's car presently and drove to Artemus's mansion.

Callie, Drake, and Serena were examining the ivory cane in the kitchen. Nate was cooking something divine-smelling on the cast-iron range. Smokey was sitting on the dining table, the chocolate fur around his muzzle coated in blood as he munched on a piece of raw prime rib.

"Was that tonight's dinner?" Artemus said with a scowl.

"He was hungry," Callie said defensively.

"Yeah, well, he's always hungry," Artemus muttered. Smokey's eyes flashed red for a moment. "He's gonna eat a hole into my savings."

"Maybe you should invest in a ranch," Drake said, deadpan.

"Ha-ha, asshole," Artemus said. "So, we any closer to figuring out what that thing really is?"

He indicated the cane and went to grab a glass of water.

Serena frowned. "No. I tried putting some nanorobots in it to find out what it's made of but that didn't work."

"But I can now do this," Callie said.

She took hold of the cane, closed her eyes, and concentrated.

Sigils flashed into existence on the ivory shaft. It morphed into the golden scepter a second later.

Artemus choked on his drink.

"I'm telling you, we should send that thing to Rome and have them analyze it," Elton said while Artemus coughed and spluttered.

Callie narrowed her eyes at Elton. "The scepter stays with me."

Artemus wiped his chin, placed his empty glass inside

the sink, and cast a cool stare at Callie, Serena, and Drake. "By the way, why is everyone still here? In my house?"

They looked at him as if he were an idiot.

"Because this is now our base of operations," Serena said bluntly.

"Like the Batcave," Callie added brightly.

"Oh, Batcave," Nate muttered as he stirred the contents of a pan. "I like that."

"Besides, you don't really think this is over, do you?" Drake asked.

Artemus met his dark gaze.

"No, I don't," he admitted reluctantly.

Despite the best efforts of the Vatican and the super soldiers, no one was any closer to finding out the name of the organization Park had been a member of. That the law firm in New York had just been a local branch was evidenced by the fact that demon sightings had taken place in other major cities. This had long since told Rome that this group was an international one.

The stone arch they had seized from the cave was now in the possession of the Vatican and being pored over by their experts.

"I call dibs on the tower room," Callie declared.

Serena frowned. "I wanted that room."

"It's the only one big enough for me and Smokey," Callie said stubbornly.

"You have a mansion in Philadelphia," Serena retorted.

"And London. And Paris. And Baja," Drake muttered under his breath while the two women argued.

"The tower room is haunted," Artemus said.

Callie paled.

"You can have it," she told Serena.

"You're a deadly, ancient, mythological creature," the super soldier said dully.

"Spirits give me the heebie jeebies," Callie said with a shiver.

The front doorbell rang. Artemus sighed and wandered down the corridor to the foyer. There was only one other person who had the code to the gates of the property and could wander into the grounds at will.

Otis stood on the porch, a box in his hands. "I brought this month's receipts."

"Thanks," Artemus murmured, taking the box.

"You should really think about going digital with that stuff," Otis said.

He paused and sniffed the air as a mouthwatering aroma wafted through the vestibule from the kitchen.

Artemus hesitated. "Wanna stay for lunch?"

Otis's jaw dropped open. "You—you *cooked?*"

Artemus scowled and started closing the door.

"Alright, I'm sorry!" Otis yelled.

His assistant followed him to the kitchen.

"Food's ready," Nate said as they walked into the room.

The super soldier was untying the apron around his waist.

"Oh." Otis stopped dead in his tracks. "I'm sorry. I didn't know you had guests."

"Hey, Otis," Elton murmured.

"Hi, Elton," Otis mumbled, ears reddening when he found himself the subject of the others' curious stares. His eyes widened behind his glasses. "Cool! The Scepter of Gabriel." He crossed the kitchen and lifted the golden artifact lying on the table, an enthusiastic expression dawning on his face as he peered at it closely. "This is a really good replica."

Artemus froze, his heart starting a heavy drumming as he stared at his assistant.

Otis turned and twisted the relic in his hands, examining it from every angle. He went still when he registered everyone's shocked expressions.

Callie rose to her feet and gazed wide-eyed from the scepter to Artemus's assistant.

"What did you say?" she whispered hoarsely.

Otis swallowed, his face turning pale as he sensed the tension thrumming the air. "I, hmm, said this was a really good replica?"

"Before that," Elton said stiffly.

"The Scepter of Gabriel?" Otis looked at the item he was holding. "That's what it looks like to me."

"By Gabriel," Artemus asked, his mouth dry, "do you mean *the* Gabriel? As in the Archangel?"

He shared a stunned glance with Drake and Serena.

Otis blinked. "Who else would I mean?"

A loud clap echoed around the kitchen. Artemus startled.

Drake was holding his fully transformed sword in his right hand. On his left arm, the watch had assumed the shape of the dark shield with the runes once more. He grunted as he struggled to hold the weight of the weapons. The tip of the black blade thudded heavily onto the marble floor seconds later, the yellow flames on the serrated edges dancing harmlessly across the white tile.

"Shit," he grumbled. "Looks like we can only lift these things when we are in our—" he grimaced, "full forms." He looked at an ashen Otis. "Do you know what these are?"

He indicated the broadsword and the shield.

Otis shook his head jerkily. "No, I don't."

Artemus hesitated before removing the switchblade

from his boot, his pulse racing. He clenched his jaw and concentrated.

The knife changed, lengthening and thickening with a flash and a boom. He gasped when the full weight of the pale broadsword dragged his arm down, the pointed end thumping onto the floor.

"The Sword of Michael," Otis said in an awed voice. He stared from the flaming blade to Artemus. "How did you do that?"

# CHAPTER FORTY-SEVEN

THE FARM WAS LOCATED IN LOW HILLS, SOME TWENTY miles southwest of Pittsburgh. The sun was starting to dip below the horizon when their SUVs pulled through a pair of rundown gates and started up an icy, pothole-ridden drive.

Bullets peppered the ground in front of them when they rounded a bend in the land and came in sight of a dilapidated farmhouse sitting atop a low rise.

"Shit!" Serena barked, slamming on the brakes.

Drake swore as their SUV lurched to an abrupt halt, the seatbelt digging sharply into his gut. In the rear seat, Nate removed his gun from inside his jacket.

Otis jumped out of the vehicle ahead of them and dashed toward the farmhouse, arms waving frantically above his head and feet skidding in the slush.

"Dad! It's me, Otis!" he yelled. A bullet smashed into the ground several inches from his left leg. "*For Christ's sake, old man, will you stop shooting?!*"

The firing stopped.

Drake carefully exited the vehicle with Serena and

Nate, his senses on high alert. Artemus, Elton, and Callie stepped out of the other SUV, their breath pluming in the cold air. Smokey jumped out of the footwell where he'd been sitting and landed in a puddle. An irritated growl rumbled out of him.

Metal groaned and creaked some twenty feet to the right of the driveway. A trapdoor opened and thudded onto the ground next to a barn, raising a splatter of mud. Someone climbed out of the hole and peered at them.

"Otis?" the apparition mumbled.

Drake stared at the middle-aged man with disheveled hair and clothes holding a sawed-off shotgun in his grimy hands.

Otis gazed from the figure to the farmhouse. "Did you rig guns in the main house?" he asked, shocked.

"Yeah." His father eyed the rest of them suspiciously. "Who are these people?"

$\sim$

IT TOOK A WHILE TO FIGURE OUT WHY WILLIAM BOONE was living in a bunker under his barn.

Artemus glanced around at the narrow, bare stone passage they were negotiating before studying the two figures ahead of him. Otis bore only a passing resemblance to his father. They were talking agitatedly, the younger Boone berating the older man in low whispers for the state of the farm and his unkempt appearance.

"So, how long have you known him?" Drake muttered.

Artemus caught Smokey's glance from where rabbit hopped by their feet.

"Two years," he replied. "I advertised for an assistant to

help me run the shop. He was the only one who applied for the position."

Serena frowned. "And you didn't know that he was—?"

She paused and waved a hand vaguely in the air.

Artemus narrowed his eyes. "What, a holder of cryptic knowledge? That question wasn't part of the interview, no."

Elton sighed. "I think she means the farmhouse and his father."

"Oh." Artemus grimaced. "No. We don't talk about that stuff."

His gaze found Otis's back once more. *Although I get the feeling that that's about to change.*

He still couldn't detect anything out of the ordinary from his assistant. No latent energy that told him the younger man was something other than a normal human. From the way Drake and Callie had been studying Otis with faint frowns, neither could they.

The passage opened into a room that appeared to serve as Boone's living and sleeping quarters. It was sparsely furnished and bore the mark of someone who did not really care for anything beyond the most basic of human comforts. Boone led them through the chamber and into a narrow corridor on the other side.

A thick, metal door appeared at the end of the passageway. It was secured by a dozen locks. They waited patiently while Boone entered codes into six digital devices before lifting a large, jangling ring of keys from inside his ragged housecoat and working through the mechanical locks. He finally pulled the door open and ushered them across the threshold into the room beyond.

Artemus slowed and stopped.

The chamber they'd entered was over twice the size of

the one they had just passed. It was also pristine, with not a speck of dust in sight.

Otis froze, the color draining from his face. He ignored the towering bookcases, the boxes on the floor, and the piles of notebooks heaped upon the immense table in the center of the room, his feet leading him almost half-consciously toward the boards that took up most of the study's south-facing wall.

Shock reverberated through Artemus as he stared at the charcoal sketches pinned and taped to the wall amidst hundreds of newspaper clippings and dozens of maps. He exchanged dazed looks with Drake and Callie and saw his own incredulity reflected in their eyes.

"Mom's drawings," Otis mumbled in a low voice filled with pain.

He raised trembling fingers to the yellow, aged papers that bore figures, objects, and symbols that Artemus partly recognized.

One was a representation of Smokey in full, three-headed beast form. Another was a drawing of the Chimera. The next two were of a pair of winged beings that bore an uncanny resemblance to Artemus and Drake in their angelic manifestations. The scepter was also there, as were the symbols that had appeared on the cane and Artemus's flaming sword.

"I thought you'd destroyed them." Otis turned an accusing glare upon his father. "You said they were gone!"

"They *were* gone," Boone muttered. "I brought them down here after your mother's death."

A muscle jumped in Otis's cheek and his hands fisted at his sides.

Artemus blinked. He had never seen his assistant so worked up.

"What *is* this place?" Otis asked in a hard voice. "Why are you living down here, like an animal?"

A tortured expression flashed across Boone's face at his son's harsh words.

"Because this is a safe place," he admitted hesitantly. "They can't seem to find me down here. I think it's the iron in the ground."

Otis scowled. "Who can't find you? What the hell are you talking about, Dad?"

"I think he means demons," Drake murmured, his gaze fixed on Otis's father.

Boone stiffened. He took a step toward Drake, his expression tense. "What do you know of them?"

# CHAPTER FORTY-EIGHT

"At first, I thought they were figments of my imagination."

Drake studied Boone where the man sat nursing a glass of Scotch at the table.

Otis's father seemed relieved to finally be able to tell his story to people who did not think he was mad. Drake glanced at Otis.

*Although, judging by the expression on his son's face, the jury's still out on that one.*

"The first time I saw them was on the day of Catherine's—" Boone paused and took a huge gulp of whiskey before wiping his mouth with the back of his hand. "The day of my wife's funeral."

"Why did you never tell me any of this?" Otis asked stiffly.

Boone looked at his son with tired eyes. "Because I thought I was losing my mind."

Silence descended on the room.

"You mean like Mom?" Otis said bitterly.

Boone closed his eyes briefly, a spasm of agony distorting his features.

"Since this is going to take a while to tell, why don't I summarize the sordid details of the story for them?" Otis continued grimly. He turned to the other occupants of the room. "Twenty-three years ago, a woman fell pregnant. This woman was a school teacher, incredibly well read, and sharp-witted as a pin. She was married to an older man, a professor of literature and linguistics who suddenly decided to buy a farm out in the middle of nowhere one day and quit his tenured college job to grow sorghum. One night, during the third trimester of her pregnancy, the woman started suffering from delusions. At first, they were mild. But as she drew closer to her due date, they got worse. She stopped eating and was plagued with insomnia. She also began to write and draw things."

He indicated the boards on the wall and the notebooks on the table. "Things that were fanciful and grotesque. Things that her psychiatrist said came from her primitive mind. Most of the stuff she wrote down was in a language she had made up. A language nobody recognized." He swallowed, his gaze growing hooded. "The day after I was born, they committed her to a psychiatric hospital. And there she remained, until her death six years ago."

"How did she die?" Artemus said quietly.

"Septicemia," Boone replied in a low voice. "She was frail and thin and she refused to eat most days."

"And the demons?" Serena asked. "How did you know what they were?"

"Because I realized shortly after Catherine's death that she wasn't crazy at all," Boone said. "She had sensed them. Foreseen them, maybe. Whatever happened to her the night it all started seemed to have given her the ability to

—foretell things." He sighed and ran a hand through his bedraggled hair. "I started seeing these demons everywhere. Then I started to see things in the papers. Things that I remembered Catherine mumbling about during my visits to the hospital. After that, I began to discern a pattern in the notebooks she'd filled. A code she had hidden among her mysterious words. It took me some time to decipher what her writings and drawings meant. To translate some of the ancient language. I—"

"I thought the stuff you told me about before I left for Chicago was what our pastor had related to you," Otis said. He indicated the sketches on the board. "Like the Scepter of Gabriel and the Sword of Michael? I thought Pastor Robinson said Mom had been sketching out stuff she'd seen in the Bibles she kept at the hospital and embellishing them in her delusions."

"I lied," Boone admitted with a guilty expression.

"May I?" Artemus interrupted.

Drake looked at the blond man, surprised by the sudden urgency in his voice.

Artemus indicated the stack of notebooks next to Boone. Boone hesitated before dipping his chin.

Artemus lifted one of the notebooks and carefully leafed through the faded pages. "Elton, you need to see this."

The two men examined Catherine Boone's writing for a couple of minutes.

"It's the same one," Elton said with a jerky nod.

Otis and his father stared at them, nonplussed.

Artemus removed his gun from his jacket and laid it on the table. Understanding dawned inside Drake as he looked at the inscriptions on the ebony grips of the weapon.

"This gun was made for me by a man who was killed by demons," Artemus said quietly.

Boone's hands trembled slightly as he lifted the gun and examined the runes.

"We believe it's Enochian," Elton said.

Boone swallowed. "It is. This is a powerful rune."

He laid the gun down, rose to his feet, and headed for one of the bookcases. He grabbed a handful of tattered books and returned to the table.

Drake stared at what he dumped on the wooden surface. They were all Bibles.

Boone reached for a notebook at the bottom of a pile and started cross-referencing the content with the scriptures. "There! Found it! It's a prayer and a curse attributed to Zaqiel, the fifteenth leader of the Grigori. It says here..." He ran his index finger along the faded writing in the notebook. "It says here that it contains the power to send demons back to Hell."

"Whoa," Nate mumbled.

Artemus picked up his gun and gazed at the engravings on the grips for a silent moment. He looked up at Boone. "Who's Zaqiel? And what's a—Grigori?"

Boone blinked. "Oh. I guess not many people know the story these days."

"The story of what?" Serena said.

"The story of the War in Heaven and the Fallen Angels."

"IN THE BEGINNING WERE SEVEN. SEVEN ARCHANGELS, or the Highest Seraphims, as they were also called. These Seven have been known by many names throughout the various forms the Bible and other sacred religious texts have taken over the millennia since this tale was first told." Boone paused. "The names they are most commonly recognized by now are Uriel, Michael, Raphael, Jegudiel, Sariel, Gabriel, and Ramiel."

Artemus's pulse thrummed rapidly as he listened to Boone talk. He could feel the power that dwelled inside him resonating with the words the man was speaking.

"There were many other kinds of angel. Cherubims. Elders. Heavenly Governors and Guides. Even the ones humans call Guardian Angels," Boone continued. "The other names for angels were Watchers or Grigori. Many of the Watchers were tasked with looking after the Dominion of Earth and the offspring of Adam and Eve. But, over time, some of them came to lust after human women."

Artemus startled when Elton spoke.

"*And the Grigori, who, with their Prince Satanail, rejected the Lord of Light and went down to Earth from the Lord's Throne, laid down with women and befouled the Earth with their deeds, resulting in confinement under the Earth.*" He made a face at Artemus's shocked stare. "I work for the Vatican. I have to know some of this stuff."

Boone nodded. "It is as you said. The War in Heaven was a holy battle between the army of angels led by Archangel Michael against the two hundred Grigori who took human wives and taught mankind forbidden knowledge which corrupted them. These two hundred Fallen Angels were, in turn, led by Satanail or Satan, and nineteen other Watchers. They were described as the twenty leaders."

"*And Michael and his Angels fought against the Dragon,*" Elton quoted quietly. "*The Dragon and his Angels fought back*

*but were defeated. They fell, like Lightning from Heaven, to be
punished in everlasting fire. Bound in the valleys of the Earth
until Judgment Day and their consummation. To be led to the
Abyss of Fire, to the torments and prison in which they will be
confined forever.'"*

Callie shivered. "That's horrible."

"The first Book of Enoch tells the tale of the Fall of
the Watchers in the Fifth Heaven, which Satan ruled,"
Boone said. "Satan was known by many names. Satanail.
Lucifer. Samael. He was the Angel of Death and the
commander of two million of his brethren. After his fall,
he became known as the Dragon and the Ancient Serpent.
He was described in some religious texts as a great red
beast with seven heads, ten horns, seven crowns and a
massive tail, similar to the four beasts from the sea and the
Leviathan in the Hebrew Bible. It is said that he wanted to
be equal in power to God himself and rebelled at the
divine order to bow down to man on the occasion of the
creation of mankind. He hated mankind with a passion
and he abhorred God's declaration that all in Heaven and
on Earth would be subject to his son, the Messiah, who
would take the form of a man."

"What does any of this have to do with your wife's
writings?" Drake asked.

Artemus observed Drake's tense expression with a
frown.

"It's all linked," Boone explained. He indicated the
Bibles, the notebooks, and the boards on the wall. "All of
it. I believe what Catherine was trying to do was warn us.
She was—possessed by something that night it all started.
Something that wanted to warn us all of what is to come."

"And what is that?" Serena said coolly.

Boone blinked. "Why, Judgment Day, of course."

# CHAPTER FORTY-NINE

"Judgement Day?" Drake repeated stiffly.

He could feel the demon stirring inside him. It seemed weaker than usual though. He glanced around the chamber and recalled what Boone had said about iron in the ground.

"So you're saying Mom was possessed?" Otis said. He jumped to his feet, his face red with anger. "All of this is *bullshit*! Bullshit you made up to cover up the fact that you abandoned her in that hospital!"

Boone's face crumpled.

Artemus rose and laid a hand on the trembling young man. "Hey, calm down."

"No!" Otis yanked his arm free and glared at his father. "I'm not having this. I'm not having you sully Mom's name like that!"

The hairs rose on Drake's arm. He stared at the boards behind Otis.

They were trembling slightly, as if caught in an earthquake. Except the rest of the room was still as stone.

"Otis," Artemus said quietly, his gaze riveted to the boards.

"What?" Otis barked.

He finally registered where everyone was looking and followed their gazes. He paled.

Boone was also on his feet, his expression as shocked as his son's.

The boards stopped shaking.

"What the——?" Otis mumbled.

"It's you," Callie said in a stunned voice, eyes wide as she stared at Otis.

ARTEMUS'S HEART POUNDED IN HIS CHEST WHEN HE grasped Callie's meaning. He dragged his gaze from Otis to Boone.

"The night you're talking about," he said shakily. "The night it all started and your wife began——" he indicated the sketches and the notebooks, "doing these things. Do you remember the date?"

Boone blinked. "Yes. It was the early hours of August 14th 2017."

Artemus's legs nearly collapsed under him. He sat down heavily and exchanged a dazed stare with Drake. They had already discovered from Callie that her marks had appeared the same night.

"It was an awakening," Callie murmured in a low voice. "What your wife experienced wasn't a possession. It was an awakening." She looked at Otis, her expression growing confident. "An awakening of the one she carried inside her."

"What do you mean?" Boone asked.

Callie glanced at Artemus and Drake. Artemus hesitated before nodding. Drake dipped his chin stiffly. Callie started talking. About everything that had happened since the night she brought the cane to Elton's auction house in Chicago. About the first battle with the demons and the ones that had followed. About Park and his organization. About Manhattan and their final clash with the enemy. About the marks she, Artemus, and Drake bore. Marks that had appeared on them all the same night, twenty-two years ago. Marks that defined what they were.

She did not mention the forms she, Smokey, Artemus, and Drake had taken in Manhattan.

"We believe their aim was to open a gate to Hell," she concluded.

Boone listened to all this with a waxen expression.

"Do you have them?" Artemus asked Otis.

Otis stared at him, his face as dumbfounded as his father's.

"Do you have marks too?" Artemus said insistently.

Otis hesitated before shaking his head.

Artemus turned to Boone. "The name of the scepter and my sword. You said you translated them from your wife's writings. What else did she say in those notebooks?"

Boone was quiet for some time, his hands trembling where he'd laid them on the table. "She spoke of dark days to come. Of things that mankind will soon witness. Things born of our worst nightmares." He paused. "Of Judgment Day. But not the Judgment Day as we know it from the Bible. This will be a different kind of reckoning. One brought to Earth by Hell itself."

A heavy silence fell across the study.

Artemus pointed out the drawings that resembled the forms he and Drake had taken when their powers had been fully unleashed in the cave in Manhattan. "Do you know who they are?"

Boone hesitated. "I'm not completely confident of my translations, but I believe these two are brothers."

A buzzing started in Artemus's ears. Smokey stirred at his feet.

DRAKE FROZE. HIS MOUTH WENT DRY. "WHAT?"

"I have barely begun to translate my wife's writings and I haven't done the best job of it," Boone explained in an awkward voice. "But those sketches were the first she drew. And the story that accompanied them was among the first things she wrote. The tale was of two brothers prophesized to play a major role in the advent of the Judgment Day she spoke of. Twins. One born of light and the other of darkness. Brothers by virtue of sharing the same womb but not the same father."

"How is that possible?" Serena asked, glancing at Drake.

He registered the incredulous expression on her face absentmindedly and finally met the gaze of the man who had been staring unblinkingly at him for the last thirty seconds.

Artemus's eyes blazed with soul-jarring shock. The same shock echoing through Drake's very bones.

"There were stories of others too." Boone indicated the drawing of the Chimera and the three-headed hellhound. "Like these two beasts. They too will play a part in the dark times to come."

"You mean there are more?" Elton said. He kept glancing between Artemus and Drake, the bombshell

Boone had just dropped evidently rattling him to the core as much as it had all of them. "More of these creatures?"

"Yes," Boone replied. "But, alas, I reached the limits of my abilities a while back."

"What do you mean?" Callie asked.

"I mean that I haven't been able to translate the rest of her writings."

Silence echoed across the chamber.

"The gate," Drake mumbled. "Did you read anything about a gate or the name of the organization these demons belong to?"

Boone blinked. "I haven't translated anything about a gate. But there was one word Catherine wrote over and over again. She'd scribble it in the margins of her notebooks, as if in a trance. Her notes were often completely illegible, so frenzied was her writing. It was one of the last things I managed to translate." He paused.

"The word was—Ba'al."

# CHAPTER FIFTY

THEY SPENT THE NIGHT AT THE FARMHOUSE AND LEFT late the next morning. Boone accompanied them when they walked out to the SUVs under a clear, crisp blue sky.

"Come to Chicago with me," Otis told his father quietly.

They had passed most of the night talking quietly with one another. Artemus knew his assistant regretted the harsh words he had spoken the day before. A change seemed to have come over the younger man when he'd awoken that morning. He seemed more focused. More *there*. As if his father's confessions had finally soothed the wounds he had carried in his heart since childhood and freed him to be what he was meant to be.

They still didn't know what that was or how his fate was linked to theirs.

A wry grimace crossed Artemus's lips.

*And what a twisted fate it is indeed. Was it coincidence that made our paths cross two years ago when I put out that ad? Or was it always meant to be?*

He looked over at Drake and met the other man's

hooded gaze. They hadn't talked about what Boone had said to them last night. Somehow, Artemus sensed Drake was as unprepared to broach the subject as he was.

*Brothers, huh?*

He sensed someone's stare and glanced at Smokey. The rabbit's nose twitched and he looked away.

*And he hasn't said a word since yesterday.* Artemus's gaze shifted briefly to Callie. *Neither has she.*

He understood why everyone was preoccupied with their own thoughts. It wasn't every day you discovered that you were to play a paramount role in the upcoming Apocalypse. And there were many questions still left unanswered. About the identity of Ba'al. About the gate. About the woman he had seen in the cave before his full angelic transformation. About the Immortals.

*And about who sent Smokey to me the day this all started.*

"We can move you to one of our safehouses if you wish," Elton told Boone.

Boone shook his head. "No. I would rather stay put." He gazed out over the farm, a nostalgic look washing across his face. "She was happy here."

They bade him goodbye and drove down the hill, the boxes containing Catherine Boone's writings and drawings rattling around in the trunks of their vehicles. Elton had received Boone's permission to let the Vatican take a look at them, with the solemn promise that they would be returned to the farm intact.

As a wintry, hilly landscape unfolded across the skyline and the sun melted the snow and ice in the fields they passed, Artemus sensed dark clouds gathering on the horizon. Whoever Ba'al was, they were still out there. And there was a good chance they would come to discover the details of what Artemus, Drake, Callie, and Smokey had done in Manhattan.

"I know everyone is shell-shocked about what happened yesterday but, still, it's pretty mind-blowing when you think about it," Elton muttered beside him.

Artemus looked at him. "What is?"

"You possess the sword of the Archangel Michael and Callie the scepter of the Archangel Gabriel," Elton said.

"I guess that's true," Artemus mumbled.

"And your wings manifested themselves again," Elton added.

"Yeah."

Drake stirred behind Artemus. He was riding in the back of their SUV since the other one was mostly filled with boxes. Artemus also suspected he was avoiding Serena for some reason.

"Not that he knew what to do with them at first," Drake muttered.

Artemus frowned and looked in the rearview mirror. Drake had his head tilted back on the headrest and his eyes closed.

"Well, excuse me for being shocked at suddenly acquiring the ability to fly!" Artemus snapped.

"If I hadn't grabbed you, we'd still be scraping pieces of your skull off that cave ceiling," Drake said.

Artemus scowled and twisted in his seat. "Look, just because you—"

"Oh God," Otis said leadenly.

Artemus followed his assistant's gaze. "Oh shit."

Callie awoke with a startle where she sat between Otis and Drake.

"What?" she mumbled blearily, wiping a sliver of drool from the corner of her mouth.

"Elton, we need to make a pitstop," Artemus said urgently.

"Why?" Elton said. "You need the little boy's room? Can't you hold it in? We're almost at the air—"

"Oh crap," Callie said.

"What?" Elton barked.

"Stop the car, Elton," Drake said grimly.

"Why?" He looked over his shoulder, drew a sharp breath, and slammed on the brakes. "Son of a—"

Serena's SUV screeched to a halt inches from their tailgate. The super soldier scowled and gestured at them through the windshield. No one paid any attention to her.

"I think I saw a Taco Bell next to that gas station a couple of miles back," Artemus said.

"Okay." Elton glanced at Callie. "Can't you do anything about him?"

They all stared at Smokey where he sat chomping on something metallic in the footwell at Callie's feet.

"He looks a bit wild, right now," Callie said. "Like he's in a hunger-induced stupor."

"He's your brother," Elton said sharply.

"I just had a flashback from when we were kids. He may have bitten me in the past," Callie said. She drew her legs carefully up onto the seat. "Under these exact circumstances. He goes crazy when he's ravenous."

The back door opened. Serena stuck her head inside the vehicle and glowered at them. "What the hell are you guys—?"

"Smokey got hungry and ate a hole in the car." Artemus pointed at exhibits A and B.

Exhibit A's lips peeled back to expose deadly fangs.

The super soldier stared at the rabid rabbit. "Are you kidding me right now?" she muttered dully.

"Callie says he's gone feral." Drake's expression barely concealed his disgust. "We're heading back to that Taco Bell we just passed."

Serena sighed. "Didn't he have breakfast with us, like, two hours ago?"

"Waffles and a banana doth not a hellhound fill," Artemus said.

Callie nodded in agreement.

Nate wandered over to the SUV. "What's up?"

"The hellhound is hungry," Serena said coldly. "We need to make a pitstop at a Taco Bell."

"Oh." Nate blinked and patted his washboard stomach. "I could do with some Tex-Mex."

## THE END

∾

# AFTERWORD

Thank you for reading BLOOD AND BONES! I hope you've had a blast with this first book in the SEVEN-TEEN spin-off series. The next book in LEGION is FIRE AND EARTH.

If you enjoyed BLOOD AND BONES, please consider leaving a review on your favorite book site. Reviews help readers find books! Join my VIP Facebook Group for exclusive sneak peeks at my upcoming books and sign up to my newsletter for new release alerts, exclusive bonus content, and giveaways.

Turn the page to read an extract from FIRE AND EARTH now!

# FIRE AND EARTH EXTRACT

Yashiro Kuroda stepped out of the black sedan and paused to look at the sky to the west. The setting sun was an orange fireball dipping below the dark line of the Pacific Ocean, way out beyond the surf crashing onto Long Beach. Above it, the heavens were scored with a dizzying kaleidoscope of ever-changing reds and purples.

A trace of disquiet danced at the edge of his consciousness as he gazed upon the crimson hues tainting the horizon.

"Is everything okay, sir?" one of his bodyguards murmured.

Yashiro hesitated before dipping his chin at the hard-faced man beside him. "Yes, thank you, Riuji. I was thinking of a silly superstition. One Haruki and I learned of when we were still living in Kyushu." He grimaced. "Among the many other garish stories told to us by our nannies."

Riuji Ogawa studied the blood-red sky. "It is a rather ominous color."

Kaito Sasaki climbed out of the vehicle behind them

and stood nervously watching the dark building they had pulled up in front of, his briefcase clasped to his chest. For once, Yashiro couldn't blame the skittish man. Tian Gao Lee, the Triad gang leader they had come to discuss business with, had chosen a rather unsavory spot for their meeting.

Yashiro headed for the main door of the run-down warehouse with Riuji, Sasaki, and Masato, his second bodyguard.

"Master Haruki will be back the day after tomorrow, won't he?" Riuji murmured as they crossed the blacktop.

"Yes." Yashiro sighed. "Though why he had to go all the way to Stanford to get his MBA is beyond me. At least he'll be home for his birthday."

Riuji maintained a diplomatic silence.

They both knew the reason why Yashiro's younger brother had chosen a university so far away to get his business degree.

They slowed when they entered the shadow of the building. Yashiro scanned the empty parking lot at the side with a faint frown.

"Their cars must be out back," Riuji said, his tone cautious.

Yashiro smiled faintly, grateful once more for the man's presence. Riuji had been in the employ of the Kuroda Group for twenty-five years and his personal bodyguard for almost as long. The man had always been able to read him, even when Yashiro was still a snot-nosed, little brat.

Darkness and silence greeted them when they stepped inside the warehouse. Yashiro's eyes slowly adapted to the gloom. Shapes materialized out of the shadows.

A sudden wave of tension emanated from Riuji and Masato. Yashiro stiffened, his senses on high alert.

Fifty feet away, beyond the carcasses of abandoned machinery and piles of rusting drums, a group of people stood silently watching them from the other end of the abandoned depot.

"Is that you, Tian Gao?" Yashiro called out in a steady voice. He could hear Sasaki breathing fast next to him.

For a moment, there was no reply. A cigarette lighter suddenly flicked into life, the click so loud it echoed around the vast space.

Sasaki gasped and startled in the shadows to his right. Yashiro ignored the man and watched the dancing, yellow flame illuminate a scarred and ghoulish face across the way.

"Who else were you expecting, Kuroda?" Tian Gao Lee said gruffly.

A spotlight came on and washed across the interior of the building.

Yashiro relaxed as he gazed upon the familiar, pock-marked features of the Triad gang leader. He ignored the inner voice warning him that something was off and closed the distance to Tian Gao and his entourage.

There was no way the man would jeopardize the alliance between the Triad and the Kuroda Group. Not after the years of gang warfare and bloodshed that had preceded their current truce.

Riuji's expression remained guarded, he and the other bodyguard sticking close to Yashiro.

Yashiro stopped a few feet from Tian Gao and examined the other man with a neutral smile. "Of all the places you could have chosen for our meeting, this does not exactly suit your flamboyant style."

The corner of Tian Gao's mouth hitched in a lopsided smirk. "You mean it doesn't suit yours, don't you?"

Yashiro sighed. "There is nothing wrong with liking the finer things in life, Tian Gao." He scanned the faces of the silent men behind the Triad gang leader. "I see you've had a change of personnel. Did you get bored with your old guard?"

Something flashed across Tian Gao's face for a second.

He shrugged. "I decided to make some new friends."

Yashiro stared. It was a strange term for the Triad gang leader to use in relation to the men in his employ. His gaze moved to the watchful figures behind Tian Gao once more. Though he couldn't quite put a finger on the why, there was something about them that was putting his nerves on edge.

"How's your old man keeping?" Tian Gao said.

"My father is fine, thank you," Yashiro murmured. "And how's your boss?"

Tian Gao grimaced. "As tight-assed as ever."

Yashiro started to smile. That was when it came to him. The reason why the men with Tian Gao were making him uneasy.

*They're not blinking.*

Fear washed over Yashiro then. An irrational, gut-wrenching fear that stemmed from the most primitive part of his brain. With it came a sudden premonition.

*We'll be lucky if we get out of here alive.*

Riuji glanced at him, the stiff set of his shoulders telling Yashiro he had also picked up on the strange vibe coming from the men with Tian Gao. Yashiro avoided the bodyguard's gaze and kept his eyes firmly on the Triad gang leader.

"Now that we've exchanged pleasantries, let's talk business, shall we?" he said in a light voice.

Tian Gao's expression grew sober. "Yes, let's."

He walked up to Yashiro and punched his right fist straight through his chest.

Yashiro gasped and rocked back on his heels, fingers rising instinctively to grip the other man's wrist. Shock reverberated through him as he looked down to where Tian Gao's hand had disappeared inside his body.

*Impossible! That's impossi—*

The pain came with a fury that robbed him of his breath. Yashiro grunted and sagged to his knees. Screams reached him, the sounds echoing dimly above the loud roar of blood in his ears. He turned his head stiffly and saw the men with Tian Gao tear Riuji and Masato from limb to limb.

Except they weren't men. Not anymore.

As the horror of what was unfolding before him finally registered in his mind and coldness swamped his body, Yashiro realized that the gruesome folk tales of his childhood were not made-up stories after all. That monsters did exist and that they walked this world inside the bodies of ordinary-looking men.

"Why?" Yashiro whispered.

Something hot bubbled up his throat and filled his mouth with a coppery taste. Blood burst from his lips. It splattered onto the clothes of the man who had his fingers wrapped around his heart.

Yashiro stared up at Tian Gao. The thing that looked back at him smiled savagely, features distorted by the beast within.

"Don't take this personally, Kuroda," Tian Gao said, his words underscored by a faint animal growl. "This is just business."

Yashiro's gaze found the remains of his bodyguards. The creatures who had killed the two men were crouched over them, hands and mouths filled with gore as they feasted upon the flesh of their victims.

Rage erupted inside Yashiro. He gritted his teeth, his racing pulse throbbing through his body with every beat of his dying heart as he called upon the last reserves of his strength and courage.

*This is unbecoming of me. I am the heir to the Kuroda Group, goddammit!*

He lowered his right hand from Tian Gao's arm, flicked his wrist, and sliced through the Triad gang leader's forearm with the spring-loaded blade that appeared from beneath the cuff of his suit.

Tian Gao roared and staggered back a couple of steps, his severed limb spraying out a black liquid that splashed onto the ground and stained his clothes.

Yashiro reached for the stump still embedded inside his body and ripped it out of his chest with a guttural cry.

Sound faded. The world shrank to a rapidly diminishing circle of darkness.

Yashiro thudded onto his side. The last thing he saw before death claimed him in an icy embrace was his bloody, battered heart shuddering to a stop inside Tian Gao's hand on the ground before him.

Get Fire and Earth now!

## ABOUT A.D. STARRLING

Want to know about AD Starrling's upcoming releases?
Sign up to her newsletter for new release alerts, sneak
peeks, giveaways, and get a free boxset and exclusive
freebies.

Join AD's reader group on Facebook:
The Seventeen Club

Like AD's Author Page

Check out AD's website for extras and more:
www.adstarrling.com

# BOOKS BY A.D. STARRLING

## SEVENTEEN NOVELS

Hunted - 1

Warrior - 2

Empire - 3

Legacy - 4

Origins - 5

Destiny - 6

## SEVENTEEN NOVEL BOXSETS

The Seventeen Collection 1 - Books 1-3

The Seventeen Collection 2 - Books 4-6

## SEVENTEEN SHORT STORIES

First Death - 1

Dancing Blades - 2

The Meeting - 3

The Warrior Monk - 4

The Hunger - 5

The Bank Job - 6

The Seventeen Series Short Story Collection 1 (#1-3)

The Seventeen Series Short Story Collection 2 (#4-6)

The Seventeen Series Ultimate Short Story Collection (#1-6)

## LEGION

Blood and Bones - 1

Fire and Earth - 2

Awakening - 3

Forsaken - 4

Hallowed Ground - 5

Heir - 6

Legion - 7

## DIVISION EIGHT

Mission:Black - 1

Mission: Armor - 2

Mission:Anaconda - 3

## MISCELLANEOUS

Void - A Sci-fi Horror Short Story

The Other Side of the Wall - A Horror Short Story

## AUDIOBOOKS

Go to Authors Direct for a range of options where you can get AD's audiobooks.

CPSIA information can be obtained
at www.ICGtesting.com
Printed in the USA
BVHW040410151222
654214BV00003B/156